The Billionaire's Heart

Bec Linder

CHAPTER 1

Sadie

The baby had gotten fat.

Not in a bad way. Babies were supposed to be fat. But this one had been a skinny little thing when it was born, long and lanky, and it had stayed skinny for the first two months. The last time I saw it, only a week ago, Regan had been convinced that it had failure to thrive and that she was a horrible mother. That was no longer a concern, it looked like. Kid had ballooned up overnight. It had two separate fat rolls between its wrists and its elbows.

Surprise: I wasn't much of a baby person.

I held it carefully, hands beneath its armpits, and stared at it. It stared back, a thin trail of drool running down its chin. It looked about as unimpressed as I felt.

Babies were fine. They were cute, mostly, when they weren't funny-looking. After they learned how to smile and sit up, they could even be fun to play with, for about ten minutes. But this one was still in the newborn slug phase, what Regan called the "fourth trimester." It was like a little grub: eat, poop, sleep, repeat, sometimes in a slightly different order.

"He's adorable," I told Regan. Part of friendship was knowing when to lie.

She beamed. "Isn't he? I'm so happy he's finally gaining weight. I thought maybe I wasn't producing enough milk, but I guess he just wasn't ready to start growing."

The baby squirmed in my grasp and let out a tiny mewl, and I hastily returned it to Regan, who draped it over one shoulder and made some cooing noises, kissing its slimy face.

My personal feelings about babies notwithstanding, it was nice to see how much Regan adored her tiny slug creature.

"No, you're not hungry yet," she said to the baby. "Oh, what a fussy little dumpling!" She patted his back, and looked at me and smiled. "Sorry. I feel like having a baby has killed off at least half of my brain cells. Let's have some grownup talk."

"Do they teach you how to make that voice before you leave the hospital, or is it innate?" I asked.

Regan groaned and scrunched her face up. "I know, okay? It's so embarrassing. It just *happens*! I can't help myself."

"Does Carter do it, too?" I asked, genuinely curious.

Regan laughed, moving her hand back to support the baby's diapered butt. "He's worse than me," she said. "I'll have to record him and send it to you."

"Oh my Lord, please do," I said. "I could sell it to the tabloids for eight million dollars, and never have to work again."

"That bad?" Regan asked, frowning at me, and I cursed myself and my big mouth. I shouldn't have mentioned anything that Regan could construe as a complaint. "I thought your boss—"

"I don't want to talk about it," I said. "Whatever. I'm working on it. It's fine."

Regan gave me a skeptical look. "If you say so. It's just that you've been unhappy for so long, Sadie. You won't look for a better job, you won't leave that awful apartment, you won't date..."

This again. I gritted my teeth. Regan was my best friend, and I loved her like a sister, but she really needed to stop harping on my love life. "I'm not ready to date," I said.

"It's been a year," she said. "He wouldn't want you to mourn forever."

"I don't think," I said, really annoyed now, "that any of us are really in a position to say what Ben would or would not have wanted."

Regan leaned away from me slightly, eyes widening.

I sighed, and closed my eyes. That had come out sharper than I intended. She was so sensitive "Sorry," I said. "I'm just... I'm not ready."

"Not ready for what?" a voice said behind me.

I turned to see Carter, Regan's husband, coming into the room, briefcase in hand and suit jacket slung over one arm. He must have been at the

5

office. It was Sunday afternoon—did the man never take a day off? He smiled at me as he crossed to where Regan was sitting, and bent to kiss her on the top of her head. He brushed one hand over the baby's downy skull. "How's that fussy baby?"

"Fussy," Regan said, smiling up at him. "Sorry I didn't tell you that Sadie was coming over. I didn't think you'd be home so early."

"Mi casa, et cetera," he said. He looked at me, one eyebrow cocked. "What's she hassling you about now?"

"Dating," Regan said, before I could open my mouth. "Don't you think it's time?"

"Hmm," Carter said. "Maybe you should let Sadie decide that for herself."

At last, a voice of reason. I hoped Regan would listen to him, and stop giving me the business.

Or maybe the baby would start crying, and that would be the end of it.

But instead, Regan frowned and said, "I just want her to think about it."

"Leave her alone, darling," Carter said. "Let's hassle her about something else. Sadie, have you quit that terrible job yet?"

"Oh, God, you're ganging up on me," I said, groaning dramatically and flopping to one side on the sofa. "Lord take me now. I can't deal with the stress."

Carter laughed. "Just think about it. That's all I ask. Are you staying for dinner?"

"Oh, you should!" Regan said to me. "Caleb

goes to bed early, and then we can drink wine and talk about grownup things."

I grinned. Again with the grownup talk. Regan was spending a year at home with the baby before she started law school, and it seemed like she was going a little bit stir-crazy. I didn't blame her. Being stuck at home with a newborn sounded like an absolute nightmare.

Regan's home wasn't anything like my tiny apartment, though. She and Carter had recently left his penthouse in the Meatpacking District and moved to a brownstone in Chelsea. It was a shockingly unpretentious dwelling for one of the richest men in the country, but still pretty damn swanky. I didn't think I would mind being at home all day if I got to drink coffee in my private garden every morning.

Regan's life was basically ridiculous, like something from a movie. She and Carter met when she was working as a cocktail waitress at a high-class, trumped-up strip club. Regan had always been sort of cagey about the exact circumstances, and Carter didn't really seem like the sort of guy who frequented nudie bars, but somehow they had made it work. They'd been married for almost three years now, and seemed happier than ever.

And of course I was thrilled for her—overjoyed for her, so happy that she had found someone who treasured her the way she deserved—but it hurt, still, even after a year, to see how much they loved each other.

I'd had that, once. That kind of love.

And then I lost it.

I didn't want to think about it. "If you're offering to feed me and give me free wine, I am definitely down to stay for dinner," I said.

Regan beamed at me. "I'm so glad," she said. "Let me go change this dumpling and I'll see what I can throw together. Carter, do you want something to drink? Marta got that Scotch you wanted to try."

"Lifesaver," Carter said. He took the baby from Regan and kissed it on each fat cheek. "This is a smelly baby."

"He has to poop to make room for more food," Regan said, standing and moving behind the sofa to join Carter. "Maybe I'll feed him, too. How was your day? We never talk about anything except the baby, anymore."

"Much better, now that I'm home with you," Carter said, bending to kiss her.

I sat and watched them talk to each other, the fond, familiar sort of conversation that flowed between lovers. Maybe Regan was right. Maybe I needed to start dating again.

It was so daunting, though, the thought of putting myself out there, going on first dates, making awkward conversation, trying to find someone whose eccentricities meshed with my own. Relationships were *work*, finding them and building them, and I was tired. I just plain didn't want to. I didn't know if I had the strength to go through all of that again.

Regan went upstairs with the baby, and Carter poured himself a drink and joined me on the sofa, loosening his tie and rolling up his shirt sleeves. "You want a drink?" he asked me.

I shook my head. "Not that nasty Scotch you drink. I'm holding out for the wine crypt."

That was an old joke between us—Carter's apocryphal medieval wine cellar. Carter and I weren't friends, exactly, but we got along well, and I enjoyed talking to him. It didn't hurt that I was basically the reason that he and Regan were still together, and he would be in my debt until the end of time.

"Regan's been hoarding a few bottles of that horrible Riesling you both like so much," Carter said. "I imagine you'll have a good evening." He sipped his drink and frowned at me. "Look, I know you're tired of hearing about this, so if you really aren't interested, I'll never bring it up again. You should go freelance. Your job is a waste of your talent. I know so many people who are desperate for a good designer that I can guarantee you would never be out of work." I opened my mouth to protest, and he held up one hand and said, "Just think about it. We won't talk about this any longer. I'm going to get you some wine."

"Well," I said, mollified by this blatant peace offering, "I guess I won't yell at you, then."

"Think about freelancing," he said. "That's my only condition."

"Okay," I said. "I'll think about it."

I wasn't willing to promise him anything more than that.

CHAPTER 2

Sadie

I dragged myself into work the next day feeling like I'd been trampled by horses in the middle of the night. I couldn't even blame the wine—Regan and Carter kept early hours, now, and I'd been home and sober by 9:00. It was just Monday, and the prospect of facing yet another week at my horrible, soul-sucking job.

Maybe I *should* think about going freelance. It was such a precarious existence, though. I kept in touch with some former co-workers who had jumped ship, and they were always just barely scraping by, living paycheck to paycheck. No thanks. I liked my retirement account.

It was hard to stay motivated when I worked for the Evil Empire, though. Even the building depressed me: a Brutalist monolith in Midtown. The office was on the twenty-seventh floor, but there was no view except for more skyscrapers, and my cubicle was roughly three miles from the nearest window anyway. The closest I came to "nature" or "daylight" was the artificial potted plant on my desk.

Cubicles were probably invented to crush the spirits of office workers and keep the proletariat from rising up in revolt.

I slung my bag onto my desk and sighed loudly.

Tom, my favorite co-worker, rolled his chair out from his own cubicle and gave me an amused look. "Long weekend?"

"Not long enough," I said, the standard response. "Yours?"

"Same," he said. "Another day, another dollar. You want coffee? I'm about to go perform obeisance at the altar of shitty drip coffee."

"God, please," I said. "That sounds incredible." How sad was it that the bright spot in my morning was free office coffee?

He laughed and stood up. "Maybe I'll even make a fresh pot," he said. "Kerry's been here since 8, and you know she always fucks it up."

"Pour it down the drain," I said. "All of it. The entire pot."

"I heard that," Kerry yelled from her cubicle.

Tom laughed again and headed in the direction of the break room.

I sat down and turned on my computer, opening up my calendar to see what I had scheduled for the day. Useless department meeting in the afternoon, team lunch about the new client, and of course, the appointment I'd been dreading for the past week: a mid-morning chat with my boss to review the latest concepts I'd put together.

It wasn't that I wasn't ready. I was; I'd had everything completed for days, now, and I *knew* my work was top-notch.

It was just that, well, my boss was an asshole.

Tom returned with coffee and handed me a cracked mug that read "World's Best Mom!"

"You're hilarious," I told him.

"Mom to tiny, adorable design concepts, ready to go make their way in the world," he said. "You're meeting with Mr. Potato Head today, huh?"

"Don't remind me," I said. Our boss's name was Steve, but we always called him Mr. Potato Head due to an unfortunate resemblance, and also the fact that he was roughly as intelligent as a potato. Not even a Yukon Gold: more like one of those really sad, lumpy baked potatoes you got at a third-rate steakhouse.

"Hey, your stuff looks great," Tom said. "It's what you showed me last week, right? Yeah, it looks great. Don't let the man get you down."

"If only the man didn't control my paychecks," I said dryly.

Tom shrugged. "You know how to manage him. It looks great, though, seriously. He won't be able to find anything to complain about."

I wasn't convinced, but I just thanked him and turned back to my computer. I had time to make a few changes before my meeting. I wanted everything to be exactly right.

At precisely five minutes to 10, I gathered my

things and went up one flight to Potato Head's office. If I was early, he would complain that I was rudely interrupting his important business; if I was late, he would accuse me of wasting his time. I timed it so that I was waiting outside his office right on the dot of 10, when he opened his door and gestured me inside.

"Sadie, right on time," he said. "Good thing, too; don't want to keep me waiting."

What did you even say in response to that? I gave him a tight smile and sat in the chair placed in front of his desk.

He ponderously lowered himself into his massive leather executive chair and folded his hands on top of his desk. "So, what do you have for me?"

"I finished the mock-up that you asked me to do," I said, handing him a manila folder. "I included a few variations on the concept, so that you'll have a number of options to choose from. I can also easily incorporate elements of one version into any of the others, if you'd like a combination I haven't specifically presented here."

"Hmm," he said. "Well, let's take a look." He opened the folder and began working his way through.

I sat at the edge of my chair, heart pounding.

The concepts I'd mocked up were great. They were *awesome.* There was no way that Mr. Potato Head would be anything less than thrilled with my work.

That was what I kept telling myself, at any rate.

"Hmm," he said again, and flipped to the next page.

Was that an encouraging noise or not? I couldn't read the man to save my life, even after working for him for years. Maybe it had something to do with how he was an unpredictable, power-hungry sociopath.

Not that I disliked him or anything.

He went through the folder I'd given him one sheet of paper at a time, lingering so long over each page that I was practically vibrating with impatience by the time he closed the folder and looked up at me. "Well, Sadie," he said, "this is certainly… interesting."

Interesting was good, right? I sat up a little straighter.

"You had very specific instructions for this project, though, and only one of these concepts meets the requirements." He frowned at me, and my heart sank. "The rest of this is useless, and a waste of company time."

I felt my face flush hot with anger, and I was glad my skin was dark enough that he wouldn't be able to tell. I fought to keep my voice steady. "Actually, I did most of that on my own time, in the evenings. I understood the guidelines, but I thought that maybe it would be useful to explore a broader range of possibilities, in case—"

He shook his head. "I'm afraid not. I've spoken to you about this before, Sadie. You're a gifted designer, but you don't seem to understand that we have a corporate image to project. Consistent branding is the key to success. The way you keep going off-message—well, it makes me think that this just isn't the right fit."

Cut through the manager-speak, and it sounded like he was firing me. My pulse thumped loudly in my ears. "I'll do better," I said, ignoring the pleading, desperate note in my voice. I could *not* afford to lose this job. "I won't make extra versions anymore. I'll just do exactly what you tell me to, and—"

"It's too late for that," he said. "You just aren't a team player. You don't have the right mindset for this job. I'll contact HR about your final paycheck. Please have your things out of your cubicle by the end of the day." He closed the folder and handed it to me.

I took it with numb fingers. Had he really just fired me? *Me?* After all of the unpaid overtime I'd put in, the pet projects I'd worked on for him at the expense of my *actual* job, the three major clients I'd convinced to stay with the company after they were ready to walk—all of that, and he was *firing* me?

"I'll be happy to give you a good reference, of course," he said.

That was the final straw. I stood up, blood boiling in my veins, and said, "You know what? *Screw* you. I don't need one. Have fun with your pathetic little life."

Maybe that was petty, but I didn't care. I was so angry I could hardly see straight, and I tripped on the stairs as I made my way back to my cubicle.

God. What was I going to *do*?

I had bills to pay, and absolutely zero leads on a new job.

My computer was still turned on at my desk, with my most recent revisions pulled up on the screen, glowing brightly, mocking me. I sat in my chair and stared at the screen without seeing anything.

It looked like it was time to go freelance.

"How'd it go?" Tom asked, breaking my reverie.

"I got fired," I said. The words felt strange in my mouth. I tried again. "Potato Head fired me."

There was a long pause. "What?"

I looked up and saw my own shock reflected in Tom's face. "He told me I'm not a team player," I said.

"He's delusional," Tom said. "He can't have— did he really *fire* you?"

"I'm supposed to remove all my things by the end of the day," I said. "So yes."

"That's not—he can't *do* that," Tom said.

"I'm afraid he can," I said. "He's the boss."

Tom blew out a slow lungful of air. "Shit. What are you going to do?"

Well. That was the question.

* * *

First, I decided, I was going to get drunk.

That was pretty easy to accomplish. I left the building, hauling the cardboard box with all of my things in it—my stapler, my granola bars, the pictures of the Bahamas I'd tacked to my cubicle wall—and headed for the bar down the block where we always went for happy hour. Well: where I used to go with my former co-workers. There would be no more happy hours for me.

The bar was almost empty at that time of day, which was a small mercy. I didn't want to interact with anyone. I ordered a beer and sat at one end of the bar, my box on the stool beside me, and planned my next move.

I needed a job, but more than that, I needed a *plan*. I had spent the last year just going through the motions, some twilight creature who ate and worked and exercised but didn't really *live*.

I thought maybe I was ready, now, to be alive again.

The problem was how best to go about resurrecting myself.

I ordered a second beer, and dug a notebook and pen from my box. I turned to a blank page and wrote SADIE'S LIFE PLAN at the top, and underlined it with a thick, dark line. I was a big fan of lists. There was usually so much stuff bouncing around in my head that the only way to keep track of it all was to write it down.

My top priority, of course, was getting a job. *Find interesting work*, I wrote, and underlined *interesting*. God, I'd turned into such a princess.

There were more important things in life than having a rewarding, interesting job. Like not getting evicted. But this was my LIFE PLAN. I might as well go all out.

Go on a date. At least that would get Regan off my back.

Adopt a pet.

Stay out all night dancing. I hadn't done that in ages.

I hesitated, and then wrote, *Clean out the apartment.*

And, *Maybe move.*

I crossed that one out. Not yet.

My life plan was turning out to be surprisingly boring. When had I become a boring person? I used to be fun. *Be more fun*, I wrote.

Too vague. What did *fun* even entail? Getting really drunk and sleeping with people I barely knew? That was what I had done during college, at least. I was probably too old for that now. Or not too old, really. Just too sad.

Don't mourn. Be happy.

Disgusted with myself, I tossed everything back in the box and put on my coat. If I was going to be a maudlin sad sack, I might as well do it at home.

I started looking for jobs that evening. There were a lot of positions available—I did, after all, live in New York—but none of them seemed very appealing. It was mostly the sort of boring corporate work that I'd been doing for the last five years, and I was sick of it. I wanted room to be creative, not just

19

march in lockstep with the company paradigm.

Interesting work, my ass. Who was I kidding? I needed to put on my big girl panties and find something that would pay my bills.

Grimly, I opened my resume and started tailoring it for the least distasteful job.

I thought about what Carter had said, about all the people he knew who were desperate for a good designer. I hated accepting handouts, but I really didn't think my spirit could survive another five years of some horrible office job.

Anyway, it wasn't really a *handout*, I told myself. It was just *networking*. I was appropriately utilizing my social connections.

I would apply for five jobs, I decided. Just to make sure I was covering all my bases. And I would talk to Carter, and see what he had in mind.

I put it off for two days. I stayed in my apartment like some sort of cave-dwelling gnome and fooled around with my portfolio until I got sick of my own procrastination and buckled down. I applied for three jobs, made another pot of coffee, painted my toenails, watched some online videos of baby goats, and then admitted to myself that I was avoiding making the phone call out of sheer, stubborn pride, and dialed Carter's number.

He picked up on the third ring. "Sadie, what a pleasant surprise," he said.

I grinned. "I can't tell if you're being sarcastic, so I'll just assume that you're delighted to hear from me," I said. "Are you busy? I don't really care, you shouldn't have answered if you are. So you remember what we talked about the other night, about freelancing?"

He huffed out a soft breath of air. Amused, I decided. "I'm never too busy to talk to you," he said. "So you've decided to go rogue?"

"Well, sort of," I said. "The thing is, I got fired."

He was quiet for a moment. "You haven't spoken to Regan yet, I take it."

"No," I admitted. "And don't you tell her, either. I'll call her."

"You have two days, and then I'm spilling the beans," he said. "I know she fusses, but she deserves to hear it from you. Lecture over. So, you need a job."

I nodded, and then remembered that he couldn't see me and said, "Yeah. I've sent out a few applications, but…"

"But," he prompted.

"But none of the jobs sound all that interesting," I said, and sighed. "I'm so spoiled, right? I feel ridiculous, acting like I deserve *interesting* employment. But, you know. I'm tired of working for the man."

"How do you feel about working for *a* man?" he asked. "I told you I know people who need good designers. I've got a friend who's running a clean water start-up, and I'd be happy to put you in touch with him, if you're interested."

"Clean water, huh?" I asked. "I'm intrigued. Tell me more."

"His name's Elliott," Carter said. "He's terrific.

We grew up together. He's one of my closest friends. I think you'll like him. He's a little... what's the term? Crunchy."

"Crunchy," I repeated. "Like—wait a minute, are you telling me this guy's a *hippie*?"

Carter laughed. "That's what I'm telling you."

A rich hippie. Oh God, what if he had white boy dreads? I wouldn't be able to take him seriously at all. "What kind of work would he need me to do?"

"General branding, I imagine. Web design, that sort of thing," Carter said. "I'm not entirely sure. We haven't discussed it in depth. He's only been back in New York for a few months. He was in Uganda for almost a year, and he came back in October to launch his company."

Well, working for a clean water hippie would be immeasurably better than working for some amoral corporate behemoth. "Sure," I said. "I'm game. Give me his number and I'll call him tomorrow."

"Great," Carter said. "I'll text you his number as soon as we're done. He'll be thrilled. The company's very new, so he's looking for good people to help him grow it. I'm not sure he'll have a full-time position to offer you, but it will be steady contract work, at the very least."

"That's fine with me," I said. "I'm sure I can rustle up some more freelance work."

"I'll be sure to let you know if I hear about anything else," Carter said. "And don't make that face. This is how the world operates, Sadie. It's not a

22

meritocracy. It's about who you know. I know you hate it. I hate it, too, but there it is."

"If you can't beat them, join them, I guess," I said.

"You and Elliott are going to get along great," he said. "I should probably be worried. Put the two of you in a room together, and you'll be overthrowing the capitalist bourgeois within six months."

"That means you'll be out of work and probably laboring away in a gulag somewhere," I told him.

"That's a risk I'm willing to take," he said. "And now I have a meeting to attend, and you have a couple of phone calls to make."

"Yeah, yeah, I'll call Regan right away," I said. "This afternoon. Definitely."

"I know where you live, Bayliss," he said, and hung up.

I rolled my eyes.

Shit. He hadn't told me Elliott's last name.

CHAPTER 3

Elliott

I looked up from my laptop, eyes dry and aching, and glanced at my phone. No wonder my head was pounding: it was almost 9:00 in the morning, and I'd been at the office since the previous afternoon.

And had accomplished essentially nothing. Nice going, Sloane. What a productive all-nighter this had been.

I had what was colloquially referred to as "a problem."

Or, as my father would call it, "an opportunity."

Well. My father and I had somewhat different ideas about certain fundamental aspects of life.

Part of the reason he wasn't currently speaking to me.

On cue, our last conversation re-played itself in full Technicolor glory, complete with visuals of the disappointment writ large on my father's face. *You're a dilettante, Elliott. A dabbler. I funded all of those trips abroad because I hoped they would help you realize how important it is to make something of yourself.*

The implication, of course, being that I had not and never would serve as a useful cog in the industrial machine. That was what mattered to my father: money, and then more money, and pay no mind to anyone you stepped on during your climb to the top.

Anyone who couldn't rise to the top of the heap didn't belong there. Social Darwinism at its finest.

His words stung so much because they were, in part, true. I *had* dropped out of Harvard and spent most of my twenties backpacking around the world. I *had* abdicated from my expected position as heir to my father's empire. And I *had* failed, at the advanced age of thirty-four, to settle down with an acceptable woman and start producing the next generation of Sloanes. My father had even picked out the perfect woman for me—well-mannered, biddable—and still I insisted on, as he put it, maintaining my foolish charade of independence.

But I hadn't just been backpacking. I spent those years working with NGOs, first as a volunteer and then in various official capacities. I had been in Uganda for most of the last year, working on sanitation outreach with Médecins Sans Frontières. I hadn't simply been gazing at my own navel.

Annoyed with myself, I shoved my laptop away and stood up, moving to stare out the window onto the street below. Even my silent excuses sounded weak to me. Whiny. *You're trying to expunge your white guilt,* my father had said, sneering, and he was right. All of my motives were, at heart, selfish.

My father knew me too well. He knew precisely what to say, what barb to launch that would strike home and fill me with doubt.

I realized that I had clenched both hands into fists, and forced them to relax. I was a man, now, not a cowering boy, afraid of my own shadow. My father had no power over me.

Other than monetarily.

And there was the rub: he had cut me off. My personal accounts held enough money for a year of expenses, but after that—well. I would *make something* of myself, grow a profitable business, and finally be truly independent; or I would go crawling back to the paternal fold, dutifully accept my corporate role, and abandon every dream of creating a meaningful change in the world.

Either way, my father would win.

No son of his would be allowed to languish in obscurity.

Hence, my problem: I had an idea, but no product, and no capital with which to hire the people I needed to turn said idea into a reality. I knew venture capitalists aplenty, but they all wanted something more concrete than what I had. They wanted diagrams, research, bar charts.

I needed money to get the things that I needed to have in order to get money.

The universe had a sick sense of humor.

To get funding without a solid product spec, I

would have to sell myself. I needed to convince potential investors that both I and my business were worth the risk. I would have to be charming and persuasive without coming off as too slick: a charismatic, upstanding guy with a worthwhile product.

And that was my problem: I was neither charming nor persuasive, and any attempt to sell myself would be roughly as successful as an eight-year-old trying to pick up a supermodel.

He's reserved, my mother always said. *The strong and silent type. Still waters run deep, you know.*

The boy's shy, my father declared, and packed me off for elocution lessons.

Shyness was an unacceptable trait in a Sloane. I was no longer the awkward, tongue-tied adolescent I had once been, and practice and maturity had eased the worst of my social anxiety, but I would never have the easy manner that came so naturally to some people. Like Carter.

I sighed, and leaned my head against the window. My father had spent my entire life wishing that I were more like Carter Sutton. And, to be honest, I often wished for the same thing. Carter was everything I could never be: charismatic, successful, content with his lot in life. He had a lovely wife, an adorable child, a beautiful home, and a seemingly charmed existence.

I had—what? An empty office, a dwindling bank account, a hollow shell of a life.

All because I was determined to prove my

father wrong.

I had a job waiting for me with MSF. I could already be back in East Africa, doing the work I loved. But some part of me—some weak, terrified part of me—was still the young boy desperate for his father's approval.

I would never get it, of course. That ship had long since sailed.

And yet. Here I was.

My office phone rang, interrupting my reverie. I turned around and stared at it. As far as I knew, there were only three people who had that number, and they would have called my cell instead.

I took the few steps to the desk and snatched up the receiver. "Hello?"

"I'm calling for Elliott Sloane," a voice said.

I raised my eyebrows. "This is he."

"Mr. Sloane, great," the man said. "Do you have a few minutes? Let me ask you a question: have you thought about life insurance recently?"

"Life insurance," I repeated, incredulous.

"That's right," the man said. "Estate planning is a vital part of your full financial package. It's important to provide for your heirs if, God forbid, something were to happen for you. You wouldn't want to leave your loved ones alone and afraid, would you?"

"Don't call this number again," I said, and slammed the received back into its cradle.

Telemarketers. Unbelievable. You could move to the Empty Quarter, cancel your phone service, and reject every aspect of modern life, and they would still find you.

The phone rang again, and I cursed a blue streak before I realized that it was my cell phone and not the office line. Someone who actually knew me, then.

I picked up. "This is Elliott."

"Answering your own phone? Surely a businessman of your caliber can afford to hire a secretary."

I sighed. "Hello, Carter."

"Long night? I thought we talked about the all-nighters." He sounded amused, and well-rested. I despised him. "I have good news for you."

I sat down in my chair and slouched down, head tipped back against the seat, staring up at the ceiling. "Don't keep me in suspense."

"I found a graphic designer for you," he said. "Assuming you're still looking for one."

"I'm still looking," I said. "Tell me more." I had grappled for some time with the necessity of hiring a graphic designer. Part of me thought it was an unnecessary expense, but I knew that I needed to present the company well in order to attract investors. At this point, I didn't even have a website.

"She's Regan's friend," he said. "And I know what you're about to say, but you're wrong. I've seen her work. She's good."

"Then I can't afford her," I said.

Carter sighed. "She just lost her job, so I'm sure you can. I wish you would let me give you some seed money. I believe in what you're doing, and you know the money is nothing to me. A drop in the bucket."

"Exactly," I said. "That's why I won't accept." I had no desire to be Carter's charity project. If I started accepting handouts, my father would never believe that I had been successful on my own merits.

"You're incredibly pig-headed," Carter said. "That's not a compliment."

"Glad to know you care," I said. My office line started ringing again, and I said, "I have to swear at another telemarketer. I'll talk to you later."

"Come over for dinner this weekend," he said. "Regan wants to fuss at you a little."

"Roger that," I said, and hung up.

I picked up the land-line receiver with my other hand and said, "Sloane."

"Mr. Sloane, I'd like to talk to you about life insurance!" a voice said.

"You must be fucking kidding me," I said, and hung up.

It was shaping up to be a truly *excellent* day.

CHAPTER 4

Sadie

I called Elliott the morning after my conversation with Carter, who—thank God—had included Elliott's last name in his text message, so maybe I wouldn't sound like a complete idiot.

The phone rang and rang until I was about to hang up and try again later, when someone finally picked up.

"If you're trying to sell me something, I'm not interested," a deep voice said.

I raised my eyebrows. Elliott needed a better receptionist. "I'm not selling anything," I said. "My name is Sadie Bayliss. I'm calling to speak with Elliott Sloane about—"

"He isn't in," the man said, and then he *hung up on me.*

I listened to the dial tone for about fifteen seconds before I realized what had happened. I pulled the phone away from my ear and stared at it in shock. What kind of company was this guy running?

I called back. Nobody answered, and the call went over to voice mail. Well, fine: at least that way I could finish my sentence. "This is Sadie Bayliss," I said. "I'm friends with Carter Sutton. He told me that you're looking for a graphic designer. You really need to hire a receptionist who doesn't hang up on people." I gave my phone number, and then said, with a touch of sarcasm, "I'm looking forward to hearing from you soon." Hopefully Elliott would be a little more polite than his receptionist was.

I shook off my annoyance and headed to the hair salon. I had an appointment to get my hair braided. I'd been twisting it myself for the last few months, but I figured a freshly braided head of hair would make me feel awesome, and it probably wouldn't hurt my job search.

The salon was almost empty when I got there. Unexpected bonus to unemployment: running errands in the middle of the day when most people were at work. I usually liked the camaraderie and gossip at the hair salon, but today, I didn't feel much like talking to anybody.

My regular hairdresser, Tanya, came over to greet me and said, "Goodness, you look pissed."

"I am," I said. "I got fired. Job searching sucks."

"Sorry to hear that," she said. "Sounds like you need some job-searching hair and a little peace and quiet."

"You read my mind," I said, and she smiled and led me over to a chair.

True to her word, she didn't talk to me much,

just worked on my hair and let me sit and flip through a stack of trashy gossip magazines. I was in the middle of an article about some starlet's latest stint in rehab when my phone rang.

I pulled it out and glanced at the screen. I didn't recognize the number; maybe it was someone calling about an interview. I answered, trying to sound upbeat yet professional.

"This is Elliott Sloane," a voice said. "I'm returning your message."

I recognized that voice: it was the rude asshole I'd talked to earlier, the one who hung up on me. And who was apparently the guy I was trying to work for. Terrific. "Sounds like you decided I wasn't trying to sell you something," I said.

A pause. "I'd like you to come in for an interview," he said.

We weren't going to talk about the hanging up incident, then. Okay. He seemed like a jerk, and not necessarily the kind of person I wanted as an employer, but I might as well get some interview practice in. "Okay, sure," I said. "When? I just got fired, so my schedule's pretty open."

Another pause. I fervently hoped that my bluntness was making him uncomfortable. "Tomorrow at 3:00, if that works for you."

"Absolutely," I said, fumbling around in my purse for a pen and paper. "What's the address?"

He gave me an address in Midtown. We confirmed the time and hung up, and I put my phone away.

I just got a job interview," I told Tanya.

She laughed. "That's how you talk to your future boss? You've got balls, Sadie, I'll give you that."

I sighed. She was right; I probably shouldn't have been quite so confrontational with Elliott. I was short-tempered and impatient: my worst qualities. My mother always got after me about my inability to tolerate bullshit. She said that putting up with people's crap was the mark of a grownup. Well, maybe I hadn't made it to adulthood yet, but at least I let people know when they sucked. It was a public service.

On my walk home, I finally called Regan. Carter was right: she was my best friend, and she deserved to hear it from me, not second-hand from Carter. She took it better than I thought she would, and seemed relieved that I was already looking for jobs.

"What did you think I was going to do," I asked her, "sit around in despair and gaze at my navel?"

"That's probably what I would do," she said. "So it's not really that far-fetched."

"Well, you know me," I said. "I've never taken anything lying down."

Regan made a skeptical noise.

I didn't want to go down that road with her, so before she could start giving me any grief about my year-long pity party, I said, "Why don't you get me a job at that club you worked at? I know how to shake my moneymaker."

"You can't call it that," Regan said. "That's awful. And no."

"Why not?" I asked. "You did it. Easy money. I could use the cash."

"You would hate it," she said. "You would lecture all of the clients about how they shouldn't objectify women. You would convince all of the dancers to unionize and then the club would shut down because all of the clients would leave. I think you can find a real job."

"You're no fun," I said. "Anyway, I'm home now, so I need to spend the rest of the day working on my portfolio. You want to get coffee this weekend?"

"Of course. I want to hear all about the job search," Regan said. "You'll have something within a week. I've got a feeling."

"I hope you're right," I said. She could be right. Stranger things had happened.

* * *

Two hours before my interview with Elliott, I stood in front of my closet, trying to figure out what to wear.

Carter had told me that Elliott was a hippie, which would suggest a floor-length skirt and an embroidered peasant blouse. But he sounded like a corporate asshole on the phone, which meant black pantsuit and silk blouse. But I was applying for a design job, and everyone expected creative types to wear something quirky and off-beat, like ordinary business casual dress would suck all of the artsy inventiveness straight out of our DNA.

I was at an impasse.

The perfect outfit eluded me. I wanted to look confident and capable, like I made grown men cry every day of the week, but I also wanted to look like good ideas were dripping out of every pore.

It didn't really matter. It wasn't like I cared about getting this job. Elliott was a jerk. I didn't want to work for his stupid company.

But he would probably pay me a lot of money.

But I didn't want to sell my soul to some Wall Street douchebag.

But... *money.*

I sighed and shook my head. I needed to make a decision. Fine: I would go all-out. I pulled clothes out of my closet. High-waisted black pants, sky-high hot pink heels, long-sleeved black leotard. Jade drop earrings. I pinned my braids into a knot on the top of my head, slicked on my favorite crimson lipstick, and looked at myself in the mirror, one hand on my hip.

I looked creative as shit. *I* would hire me. The woman in the mirror wasn't really me, though. She was the person I'd been a year ago, and that Sadie was long since buried.

It would have to do. There wasn't time to change again.

I took the subway to Midtown and walked the few blocks to the address Elliott had given me, enjoying the decisive sound of my heels clicking along the sidewalk. My father liked to tell me that 75% of success was faking it until you made it. I was never sure how he arrived at that exact number, but right then, I wanted to believe he was right. I would blow into Elliott's office like a hurricane, and he would fall all over himself to give me a lucrative contract plus benefits.

And then… what? I would tell him to get lost, that I didn't want to work for someone like him?

Get real, Sadie. If he offered me a job, I would probably take it. My parents didn't raise a fool.

I watched the elevator numbers slowly tick up to the sixteenth floor.

The doors slid open and I stepped out.

Directly in front of me was a vacant reception area with a large paper banner tacked to the wall that read, "ZAWADI YA MAJI LLC." A single light fixture above the receptionist's desk served as the only illumination. Beyond the desk, a huge, almost entirely empty space stretched the full length and breadth of the building, with huge windows along the far walls casting rectangles of light onto the bare concrete floors.

Okay, creepy abandoned office, not exactly what I was expecting. I took a deep breath and took a few steps into the gloomy interior of the room. "Hello?" I called.

A scraping noise caught my attention, and I whirled around to see a person standing up from a desk shoved against one of the windows. The figure was back-lit by the windows, and too far away for me to make out any details, but from the height I guessed that it was a man. Elliott, no doubt, hanging out alone in this fright factory.

Bracing myself, I walked toward the mystery man, plastering a cheery smile on my face. If I was going to get murdered and dumped in an alleyway, at least I would look good doing it.

"Elliott Sloane?" I asked, as I approached.

"You must be Miss Bayliss," he said, and I recognized that voice: deep like a distant clap of thunder. He came forward, away from the window, and as my eyes adjusted to the dim light, I was able to make out his features.

He was, quite frankly, the best-looking man I had ever seen. And I lived in New York, and saw models on the street on a somewhat regular basis, so that was saying a lot. He was tall—certainly over six feet—and had a surprisingly full mouth that was offset by the strong line of his jaw. His hair, so blond that it was almost white, was combed back from his forehead and buzzed fashionably short on the sides. He wore a suit and tie, and I wondered why he was so dressed up when he was the only person in the office. Not that I was complaining. There wasn't much better in life than a good-looking man wearing a well-tailored suit.

Really, though, what on earth had Carter been talking about? This man was no hippie.

He extended a large, freckled hand, and I shook it automatically, feeling a little shell-shocked. Our palms touched. His felt rough and callused in sharp contrast with his perfect hair and nice suit. It was the palm of a man who worked for a living, and I couldn't imagine this man doing a day's labor in his entire life. I watched his hand completely enfold mine. It made me feel small in a way that sent a delicious shiver down my spine.

My libido, neglected for so long, sat up and took notice.

Oh no. Down, girl. No inappropriate lusting after rich weirdos. Especially rich weirdos who happened to be white. I had promised myself that I was done fooling around with white boys.

I licked my dry lips and said, "It's a pleasure to meet you." With any luck, he wouldn't notice that my voice sounded a little more squeaky than usual.

"Likewise," he said. "Carter told me you're very talented."

He didn't mean it as innuendo, but my filthy brain was happy to interpret it that way. I would have loved to spend a few hours showing him *exactly* how talented I was… in bed.

Shut up, brain. "You'd probably like to take a look at my portfolio," I said, and felt myself blush. *Portfolio* wasn't supposed to be a euphemism. "If there's somewhere we could sit…" I glanced around the barren office space.

Elliott cleared his throat. "Yes. Well." He looked at me, unblinking, and I waited, not sure where this was going. God, he was gorgeous. "If you'll excuse me for a moment," he said. "I'll need to locate a second chair."

I started laughing. I couldn't help it. The whole situation was just so absurd. "Why on earth," I said, "are you renting this huge space if you don't even have an extra chair?"

"The company needs room to grow," he said, very stiffly, like I had offended him.

Oops. So much for this job. Well, interview practice. I decided to roll with it and see how far I could push him. I took an exaggerated look around the room and said, "Yeah, I can see that you and your fifty employees are really in danger of outgrowing the available space."

He smiled. It was a small smile, reluctant, but it was there, and it made him even *more* attractive. I was truly screwed. "Carter should have warned me about you," he said.

"Yeah, well, he's used to me," I said. "Don't worry about the chair. We can stand at your desk."

The smile disappeared. "I'll find a chair. Please wait for one moment." He strode off into the shaded depths of the room.

I shook my head. What a strange man. I moved toward his desk, just a few feet away, and slid my coat off my shoulders. Then I took my laptop out of my bag. The wonders of the digital age: my portfolio was 100% portable.

I had everything booted up and ready to go by the time he returned, carting a plastic chair that looked like it had seen better days. He set it down beside me and crossed around to the other side of the desk, where he took a seat in an enormous, over-designed leather chair, one of those things with mesh and titanium and adjustable lumbar support, all the bells and whistles. That must have been where his entire furniture budget went.

I took a seat in the sad plastic chair. It wobbled beneath me on uneven legs.

"So, do you want to see my portfolio?" I asked.

I sat and watched him click through my portfolio, feeling oddly nervous. A job offer would be nice, but more than that, I wanted him to be impressed with me. It was so stupid. I didn't know anything about him, but the focused way he stared at my computer made me want him to turn that intensity on *me*, to gaze at me like he wanted to understand everything about me.

I'd always been a sucker for a pretty face.

I had expected Elliott to give my portfolio a cursory once-over, the way people who didn't know much about design usually did. But instead, he spent a long time going through it, frowning slightly, a small vertical line wrinkled between his eyebrows.

The minutes dragged on. Finally I couldn't take it any longer. I cleared my throat and said, "I'll be happy to answer any questions."

"I don't have any questions," he said, without looking away from my computer.

Well, okay then. I crossed my legs and looked out the window, dangling one shoe from my toes. The view was completely uninspiring: an office building across the street, and beyond it, another

41

office building. I wondered why Elliott had chosen this space as his office. Maybe he was a masochist, and enjoyed working in bleak, creepy environs. He needed to invest in a rug, or at least some decent overhead lighting. A few throw pillows. Maybe a comfy sofa for naps.

Shit, maybe I should just try to get a job with Google.

Elliott's voice interrupted my interior design fantasies. "You can do web design, is that correct?"

I turned my head away from the window and said, "That's right. If you look—I think it's number 29, with the—"

"The red background," he said, clicking. "Yes, I see. And can you code it as well?"

I shrugged. "I did that one from scratch, but it's just the CSS and HTML to make it look nice. I can't do any of the back-end stuff."

"I wouldn't expect you to have any experience with software engineering," he said. "That's fine." He clicked a few more times, that line between his eyebrows making a reappearance, and then looked up at me and said, "I'd like to offer you some work."

I sat back in my chair, trying to decide how I felt about that. Excited? Terrified? "What do you have in mind?" I asked.

"It would just be a contract position," he said. "Frankly, I can't afford to hire a full-time employee at this point."

"Benefits and whatnot," I said. "I understand."

He nodded. "There's a major international

development conference in four weeks, and I'd like to have a full branding package by then. Business cards, website, informational packets. I'll pay you $100 an hour."

That was a good rate: on the high end for freelancing, but not so high that it felt like pity or a personal favor. Elliott was a strange bird, but he fascinated me, and he couldn't possibly be a worse boss than my last one. And it would get Carter and Regan off my back. I took a deep breath and said, "When do you want me to start?"

He smiled at me, wide and genuine, and it hit me like a punch to the gut. I wanted this man: fast, hard, and as often as he liked.

And now he was my boss, which meant he was totally off limits. I had really put myself in a bad situation. It was going to be a long, frustrating four weeks.

Suck it up, Sadie. Sexual frustration was better than eviction or starvation.

"You can start on Monday," he said. "If that isn't too soon."

"Monday is fine," I said.

"Good," he said. He stood up and extended his hand. I scrambled to my feet and shook hands with him, feeling that same staticky charge as our skin met.

Lord help me.

"I'll see you Monday morning at 9, then," he said.

"I'm looking forward to it," I squeaked, and got

myself out of there before I did something dumb.

CHAPTER 5

Elliott

Every night, I returned to Africa in my dreams.

I dreamed of the town in northern Uganda where I lived for a year, and my house there, and the amarula tree outside where the neighborhood children waited each morning, first for a glimpse of the strange white man, and then, after they grew to know me, to say good morning and show me whatever treasures they had accumulated in the past day: an empty Coke bottle, a new puppy. I dreamed of the dirt road out of town, and the thorny cattle kraals where the herds spent their nights, and the women walking to the market in their brightly-colored skirts.

I dreamed of the mountains, green and silent, clouded in thick fog, where I went to see the gorillas at Bwindi while I still had the chance. They would be gone in another generation, wiped clean off the face of the earth. I dreamed of the small clearing where I crouched among the foliage and watched a female gorilla placidly strip leaves from a branch and eat them one by one, while her infant—only four months old, the guide told me—clung to her furred belly and gazed at me with dark, solemn eyes. Rain dripped from the trees overhead. Somewhere a bird called and then fell silent.

And then I woke to the sound of a taxi honking on the street outside my apartment, and knew I was back in New York.

I sat up and swung my feet onto the floor, and rubbed my hands over my face. I should have stayed in Uganda. I was a stranger there, permanently marked by the color of my skin, but I was a stranger here, too. I hadn't spent more than six months in New York in almost a decade, and for most of the last five years I was in East Africa, in one country or another. The US was foreign to me now. Everything was too clean and bright. The first time I went into a supermarket after returning from Uganda, twelve hours after landing at JFK, I had to turn around and leave, overwhelmed by the fluorescent lights and the sheer selection of food. I was fluent in four languages and knew enough of a handful of others to hire a taxi or ask for directions. I had lived through the crisis in Kenya after Kibaki was elected. I had fallen in love with a Kenyan woman and lived with her for almost two years. And now here I was, in the shitty apartment I had rented, rootless and adrift in the city of my birth.

I never should have come back.

My phone chirped at me from the nightstand. It was my calendar reminding me that I needed to get to the office earlier than usual so that I could set up Sadie's workspace.

Seeing her name brought forth a vivid, unexpected memory of the other dream I'd had that night: a woman beneath me, her warm curves pressed against my bare chest, her arms wrapped around my neck…

I pressed my fists against my eye sockets, hard enough to see bright spirals behind my closed lids, and then I stood up and headed for the shower.

The woman I had dreamed about was Sadie, of course. When she walked into my office, slim waist accentuated by the same pants that highlighted the shape of her ass, I knew I was in deep, sexual-harassment-lawsuit trouble. She was my employee, now. My attraction to her was irrelevant. Dreams were the brain's sad mulling over of the day's events, like a cow chewing its cud. It meant nothing.

She was a talented designer. That was the extent of my interest in her. We would have a productive working relationship, and once she had completed the branding work I needed, I would send her on her way with a glowing reference.

Heaven help me.

I had never been particularly good at lying to myself.

Fine: she was gorgeous, intelligent, sharply funny—a deadly combination. And I was just fool enough to lose my way and do something regrettable.

Four weeks wasn't such a long time. I could

hold out for that long.

I walked to the office, my hands shoved in my coat pockets, head bent against the January chill. I didn't remember New York being so *cold*. I thought that my bones might freeze and shatter, too brittle to withstand the icy winds that whipped through the Midtown streets.

Always complaining, Sloane. Uganda was too hot; New York was too cold. *Delicate as a woman*, my father would say, sneering. As if women were somehow fragile and worthy of his contempt. As if he had never noticed the steel rod my mother had in place of a spine.

I would never know why she had agreed to marry him. It was too late to ask.

The building was quiet still, this early. The lobby was empty aside from the security guard, who nodded at me in a weary, companionable sort of way. This was hardly the first morning he'd seen me in before 8. I knew I should stop and chat with him, ask him about his family—surely he had a family— but I had never developed a knack for initiating a conversation with a stranger. Three months in, and I still didn't even know his name.

A shameful trait in a businessman, of course. I should be greasing palms and charming women out of their panties. But my allegedly inborn charm had failed to develop. I was tongue-tied, awkward. A disgrace.

I stepped out of the elevator on the sixteenth floor and hit the switch on the wall. The light above the receptionist's desk flickered on. Belatedly, I realized that I should have turned the rest of the lights on yesterday before Sadie arrived, to lessen the office's undeniable air of "serial killer horror house," but I was so accustomed to working beside the windows that it hadn't occurred to me at the time. Keeping the lights off saved energy. I was conserving the environment, and my bank account.

The office building was aging, well past its prime, but it was half-empty and rent was cheap. I liked the deserted air: no one to bother me, and free rein to spend as many nights as I pleased sleeping on the floor beneath my desk. And, as an added bonus, I could poach furniture from the empty offices above and below me.

That was what I did now. I had a desk for Sadie, but I needed a decent chair—ergonomic, lumbar support—and a lamp. Maybe two lamps. Maybe a poster of a tropical island, to remind her that there was more to life than bleak midwinter New York. "YOU COULD BE HERE."

Maybe that would be cruel.

One floor down, I found a chair that looked suitable. It was leather, in relatively good condition, and—when I sat in it to test it out—comfortable enough to pass muster. I took it upstairs in the elevator, and wheeled it to the desk I'd chosen for Sadie, close enough to mine for easy communication, but not so close that she'd feel I was constantly looking over her shoulder. I plugged in the table lamp I'd found and turned it on, pleased when the bulb lit up.

I wanted her to—well. Not *be happy*. Office work had never made anyone happy. But I wanted her to at least be content, to enjoy her workspace and not dread coming to work each morning. I wanted us to get along well, and for her to do good work for me, and for everything to go smoothly.

We were both professionals. I was a professional. I could control myself.

Everything would be fine.

She arrived promptly at 9:00, blowing into the office in a whirlwind of coat and scarf and enormous totebag and boots that clicked across the floor as if to say: I'm Sadie, here I am, look at how lovely I am and how unexpected.

You are, I told her silently. You're both of those things.

"Hi, Mr. Sloane," she said. "I guess you don't have a coffee maker, huh? I should have stopped somewhere on my way in, but I didn't think of it until just now."

I drew in a steadying breath. "There's a place just around the corner where I usually get coffee," I said. "You're welcome to step out whenever you'd like."

"Yeah, I probably will," she said. She unwound her scarf and shoved it in her totebag. She scanned the office, head swiveling, and I saw her gaze light on the new desk. "That's for me, I guess."

"That's right," I said. "If the chair isn't suitable—"

"It'll be fine, I'm not picky," she said. "Although I've noticed lately that my back hurts if I sit at the computer too long. Getting old, I guess."

"You aren't old," I said automatically, well-trained by my mother and sisters.

She grinned. "Turning thirty this year. That's a big birthday, you know. Over the hill."

"You aren't over the hill until you're forty," I said.

She waved one hand, dismissive. "Whatever. Is there any paperwork I need to sign?"

The sudden change of subject made my head spin. "Uh, yes. I drew up a contract that outlines the terms of employment—"

"I'm sure it's fine," she said. "I'll sign it. I won't understand it anyway, and Carter wouldn't let you screw me over."

She had an optimistic view of Carter's influence over my actions, but I handed over the paperwork without comment.

She scribbled her signature, head bent over the papers, and then she glanced up and said, "Look, I'm going to go get both of us some coffee, because you sure look like you could use it, and then let's sit down and you can explain what I should be working on. I still don't even really know what the company *does*. Carter told me you're doing stuff with clean water, but that could cover a lot of ground. Okay?"

"Sure," I said, amused by how neatly she had taken charge.

"How do you take your coffee?" she asked.

"Let me guess: black."

"Cream and two sugars," I said. "I'm not nearly man enough to drink my coffee black."

She laughed. "If you're lying to me, you're going to be sorry," she said, "because I'll make it plenty light and sweet. Okay, I'll be back in like five minutes, and then we'll get started."

She left again, shoes clicking back toward the elevator, and I watched her go with the distinct sensation of having been hit over the back of the head with a blunt object.

It was going to be an interesting four weeks.

CHAPTER 6

Sadie

I gave myself a stern mental dressing-down as I waited in line at the coffee shop. Elliott wasn't my *buddy*. We weren't *pals*. He was my boss, and I needed to remember that and not fall into bantering with him like he was a co-worker. It didn't matter how ridiculously drop-dead sexy he was. I worked for him now, and I wasn't going to cross that line. At least not for the next four weeks.

When I wasn't working for him anymore, well—all bets were off.

Not that I would date him or anything. But maybe I could screw him just once, to get it out of my system.

"Hello? Do you want coffee?" the girl at the counter asked, squinting at me, and I realized that I'd been standing there thinking about Elliott's broad shoulders like some sort of fool.

"Yeah, sorry, uh, coffee," I said, fumbling with my wallet, and the girl rolled her eyes.

When I got back to the office, Elliott was sitting

at his desk, suit jacket slung carefully over the back of his chair, sleeves rolled up to bare his freckled, ropily muscled forearms. It was amazing that he was so pale after spending—what had Carter said?—the last *year*, at least, in Africa. He must have used some high-octane sunblock. Or maybe he carried around a parasol like the Japanese tourists did.

"Coffee delivery," I said brightly, walking toward him with the cups in my hands.

He looked up from his computer and blinked, brow furrowed like he wasn't quite sure why I had interrupted him. Then his expression cleared, and he reached for the coffee. "Full of sugar, I hope," he said.

"You'll be bouncing off the walls like a toddler before naptime," I said, and then wished I could stuff the words back in my mouth. Lord, couldn't I ever shut up? "Uh, so can you tell me a little bit about the company?"

He nodded. "Pull up a chair," he said. "I realize I didn't give you many specifics when we spoke yesterday."

No specifics at all, really, but I wasn't going to quibble. I set my things down on my own desk and then wheeled my chair over and sat down. Elliott had pulled up some type of presentation on his computer screen. *Importance of Providing Clean Water to Sub-Saharan African Communities*, it read.

Oh boy. This was going to be dry.

I scooted my chair a little closer. He was wearing some sort of rich cologne, and I had a powerful urge to lean in and press my face against his neck and breathe. Who cared about a boring presentation when you had gorgeous eye candy to distract you?

"I want to build a better water filter," Elliott said.

That wasn't the opening I had expected. Maybe the presentation wouldn't be so dry after all. "So you're worried about water-borne diseases, right?" I asked. I had done some research over the weekend, and wanted to show off what I'd learned. I wanted to impress him. "I mean, I know that clean drinking water is a huge problem in many parts of the world, but what's wrong with the water filters we already have? I've got one of those pitchers in my fridge and it works pretty well."

"Right," he said. He clicked forward a few slides, past pictures of sad African children and microbes. I'd passed that test, then. "You're talking about commercial carbon filters. Those are excellent for removing bad tastes from water, but the one in your kitchen won't filter out any microorganisms. Chlorine doesn't kill protozoa, and boiling doesn't remove chemical impurities, and it's not very environmentally friendly. There are more options in urban areas, but in rural areas there are basically two solutions: dig a well, which is of course very time- and labor-intensive, or use a BioSand filter." He clicked forward to a picture of a tall concrete cylinder. "These are very effective, but they have to be constructed and maintained, and it takes time for the water to filter through."

He seemed like a different person when he was talking about his work: less inhibited, more animated. Even his hand gestures were more expansive. "Okay, that all makes sense," I said. "So what are you planning to do?"

Mistake. His lips compressed. It was like watching a computer shut down. All of his eager openness disappeared. "I'm still working on the details."

"You mean you don't have a plan," I said. Great. I'd be lucky if he could even afford to pay me for the four full weeks.

"That's not entirely true," he said, and rubbed one hand over his face. "I have some ideas. But I'm not an engineer, and I can't afford to hire one right now. I need investors."

"You need a marketing plan," I said, realizing now why he had hired me. "So you want me to do a slick branding package, make you seem important, and then—that's the conference you mentioned on Friday. You're going to try to find investors."

He nodded. "I need money before I can move forward."

"Can't Carter give you money?" I asked. "And aren't you rich, too? Carter doesn't know anyone who isn't rich."

"You aren't rich," he pointed out.

"That's different," I said. "He only knows me because of Regan. Hit him up for some cash, he's got more than he knows what to do with."

"He offered," Elliott said. "But…" He trailed off, and shrugged.

"You're too proud, huh?" I asked. I knew how it was. I was the same way. "Okay, let's do it. I'll get you some investors. What else do I need to know?"

"I'll direct you to some existing clean water charities so you can see how they're presenting themselves," he said. "For now, I'd like you to focus on developing a logo and a general scheme for visual branding. We'll go from there."

"Sure," I said. "I'll send you some color palettes by the end of the day." I tipped my head to one side and considered him. "How come you're doing this, anyway? There can't be a lot of money in clean water."

"I don't imagine there will be," he said.

I waited for him to continue, but after a few seconds, it was obvious that was all he was going to say. He hadn't answered my question, but I wasn't going to push it. "Well, I'll get to work then," I said.

He grunted and turned back to his computer. Okay. Conversation over.

I wheeled my chair back to my desk and opened my laptop. I didn't understand Elliott at all. I had spent the weekend reading about clean water and international development, and it wasn't *interesting*, necessarily, but it was *important*. It might even count as meaningful. The sheer number of people who died each year from dirty drinking water had stunned me. Maybe Elliott's business plan wouldn't work and his plans would fizzle out, but at least he was actively trying to make the world a better place. It wasn't what I expected from a rich boy. Carter was kind, well-meaning, and philanthropic, but I couldn't imagine him devoting himself to something so unglamorous as water filters.

But Elliott had a fire in him. I barely knew him, but it wasn't hard to spot. He was on a mission. I wondered what had happened in his life that made him the way he was: odd, focused, intense. He had a dry, subtle humor that I liked, but he also seemed like he was so involved in his work that it was hard for him to remember other people existed.

I glanced over at him. He was frowning at his computer, hands poised over the keyboard.

Well, he wouldn't be annoying company, at least. I would get *a lot* done, as long as I could keep myself from wasting all my time gazing at him longingly.

We definitely needed a coffee pot, though. Caffeine fostered creativity. Everybody knew that.

* * *

My first week working for Elliott was one of the busiest and most productive times of my life.

When I showed up on Tuesday morning, brand new coffee pot in my arms, Elliott was already at his desk, and his rumpled shirt and the three cardboard coffee cups beside him told me he'd been there for quite a while. I glanced at my watch. I wasn't late. I was actually a few minutes early.

"Burning the midnight oil, Mr. Sloane?" I asked.

He looked up at me, brow furrowing. "Sadie." He stared at me for a moment. "Is that—"

"Yeah, I bought a coffee pot," I said. "It was cheap, don't worry. Consider it my investment in the company."

"Hmm," he said. He opened his mouth, and then seemed to reconsider whatever it was he had been about to say. "Please call me Elliott. *Mr. Sloane* makes me feel ancient."

"You're my boss, though," I said. "I have to call you by your last name. It's tradition."

He raised his eyebrows. "Fuck tradition."

The profanity was so unexpected that I burst out laughing. I'd thought Elliott was too buttoned-up to swear like that, but obviously I was wrong. I liked it. Strait-laced men were boring. "Okay, *Elliott*," I said. "Whatever you want."

His dedication to his work was infectious. I would have been inclined to slack off a little, maybe take fifteen minutes in the afternoon to look at cat pictures and text my brother, but Elliott spent all day sitting at his computer, barely moving, usually skipping lunch, and faced with that example, I couldn't justify any wasted time. I had a set of preliminary logos drafted by the time I went home on Tuesday, and after a brief meeting with Elliott on Wednesday morning to select the best one and make some changes, I went to work on the full branding package.

Elliott was easy to work for. He didn't have any irritating habits, like clearing his throat constantly or leaving used tissues crumpled on his desk to ooze pathogens. He was quiet. He didn't try to talk to me when I was in the middle of something. But he wasn't cold or aloof, either. We made polite chit-chat when I arrived each day and again before I left. And on Thursday, he actually ate lunch with me.

There was no lunch room, of course, so I had gotten into the habit of eating at my desk. On that particular day, Elliott had put on his coat and headed out a couple of hours earlier, for some mysterious errand he hadn't bothered to explain to me, but just as I took out my lunchbox I heard the elevator doors open.

I watched him as he came in. The collar of his coat was turned up against the cold, and his face was flushed red, like he had been running laps. He looked cozy. I wanted to unbutton his coat and slide my hands inside. He would be warm and muscular —

I derailed that train of thought. "How's the weather?" I asked.

He smiled at me, more with his eyes than with his mouth. His cheeks lifted and his eyes crinkled at the corners. It was a soft, intimate look, and I felt it straight down to the soles of my feet. "Frigid," he said.

I was blushing. Just from him smiling at me. Oh, I didn't stand a chance. I fumbled to remember

60

what we were talking about. "It's going to snow tomorrow," I said.

"I heard," he said. He was carrying a paper bag, and he set it down on his desk and shucked his coat. I looked away, refusing to let myself stare. Lunch. I was eating lunch. I unzipped my lunchbox, and he turned at the sound and watched me take out my leftovers and navel orange. "You're eating lunch?" he asked.

"Yeah," I said, trying to keep the *no shit* out of my voice. I got the impression that Elliott sometimes stated the obvious just because he wasn't sure what else to say. It was sort of sweet.

"Do you mind if I," he said, trailing off and gesturing to my desk.

Did I mind if he *what*? But I knew what he was asking, and I said, "Of course. Pull up a chair."

He joined me at my desk, and took a sandwich out of his bag. It was wrapped in wax paper and was leaking mayonnaise at one corner. It looked pretty gross.

My face must have reflected some of what I was thinking, because he said, "What do you have for lunch, then, that's so much better than my sad deli sandwich?"

"Leftovers," I said primly. "Chickpea salad with walnuts and balsamic dressing."

"Sounds healthy," he said, and smiled again. "But I'll bet mine tastes better."

I gaped at him, too surprised that he was teasing me to think of a snappy comeback. "Well," I

61

said.

Still smiling, he unwrapped his sandwich.

I decided it was time to change the subject, and grasped at the first thing that came to mind. "So what does the name of the company mean?" I asked. "Zawadi Ya Maji."

I was sure I was mispronouncing it, but he didn't correct me. "Hmm," he said. "Gift of water, in Swahili."

"That's what they speak in Uganda?"

"Yes," he said.

I rolled my eyes. Getting information out of this man was like squeezing blood from a stone. "I thought it was more of a lingua franca," I said, showing off a little. "Don't they speak it all through East Africa?"

He sighed deeply, like I was causing him indescribable amounts of pain with my questions. "That's true. There are a number of languages spoken in Uganda. Each ethnic group has its own language, and they can be highly politicized. I picked Swahili because of its relative neutrality, although it's less neutral in Uganda than it is in other East African countries. I thought of using Luganda, but that could be interpreted as aligning myself with a particular group."

"I took an African history course in college, and the professor said that's why the colonial languages are still used in so many countries," I said. "Because every country has so many ethnic groups, and they all speak different languages, so if the president gives a speech in French, or whatever, it's less likely to piss people off."

"That's exactly right," he said. "That's also why many countries have multiple official languages."

"My international relations lesson for the day," I said dryly.

To my surprise, he looked chagrined, and said, "I'm sorry. I don't mean to lecture."

"You're not lecturing," I said. "I asked you a question, and you answered it. You happen to know more about this topic than I do. If you asked me a question about graphic design, you wouldn't be able to get me to shut up before dinnertime."

He chuckled. "I suppose that's fair."

So all in all, it was a pretty good week.

By Friday afternoon, I had enough of the branding work done to show him.

He looked through all of it without speaking, while I hovered nervously at his shoulder. I already cared so much about his good opinion that I probably would have melted into the floor if he didn't like my work. Finally he turned his chair to face me and said, "Sadie, I can't believe you did all of this in less than a week."

"I can make changes," I said, inordinately pleased. "It's all still very preliminary, and—"

"It's great," he said. "It looks great. We still have three weeks to work on it. It doesn't need to be perfect yet. It's very good."

"Thanks," I said, gazing down at him. His praise made me feel warm and melting inside. His eyes were a ridiculous pale green color, like sea glass. Nobody's eyes should look like that. Fine stubble sprouted along his jaw and glinted gold in the sunlight streaming through the window by his desk. He was gorgeous, and there was no way I would survive an entire month of working for him without embarrassing myself in one way or another.

"You're welcome," he said, looking straight at me, close enough to touch.

Bad Sadie. No touching. "Three weeks isn't a lot of time," I said. "I haven't even started on the website yet."

"That's what we'll work on next week, then," he said. "Why don't you take the rest of the afternoon off?"

"It's only 3:00," I said.

"I know," he said. "You've worked hard this week. I'll pay you for the full eight hours, of course."

"Well, okay," I said. "Thanks. I'll see you on Monday." I hesitated for a moment, actually thinking before I opened my mouth for once, but then I went ahead and said it anyway. To hell with caution. "You should take some time off. The security guard told me you're usually here all weekend."

He made a wry expression. "I knew I should have made friends with him. Now he's informing on me to the enemy."

"I'm not the enemy," I protested. "I just think that people need, you know, sleep and relaxation."

"I'll take that under advisement," he said. "Thank you, Sadie. I'll see you on Monday."

I sighed, but that didn't exactly leave any room for disagreement, so I turned away to gather my things and pull on my coat. If Elliott wanted to work himself to the bone, it wasn't my problem.

It *was* my problem, though. A tired boss was a grumpy boss.

And, okay, I had started to care about him, maybe. Just a little bit. I didn't want him to run himself ragged for no reason.

I was so stupid. There was no way this was going to end well.

CHAPTER 7

Elliott

I was too hot: sweating, burning.

I was in Africa again, in Uganda, digging a well under the midday sun.

I turned over. I wasn't in Uganda. I was in my bed in New York, and Sadie was lying beside me, eyes closed, fast asleep.

The covers were pulled up to her chin, white sheets against dark skin. I wasn't surprised to see her there. Of course she was in my bed: it was where she belonged. She lay on her back, and the thin top sheet clung to the curves of her body. The fabric, slightly sheer, revealed the shape and color of her nipples.

My cock took an immediate interest in the proceedings.

I moved closer and set my hand on her hip. Her skin felt warm even through the sheet. I slid my hand toward her waist, dragging the sheet upward, and she turned her head toward me and opened her eyes.

My breath caught. I knew there was a reason I shouldn't be in bed with her, although I couldn't quite remember what it was, and I hoped she wouldn't be angry with me, or—worse—scream and jump out of bed, taking her warmth and her glorious breasts with her.

But she didn't scream or run away from me. She raised her arms above her head and stretched, languid and sultry, and smiled at me. "Hello there, Mr. Sloane."

I had told her to use my first name—I was *sure* I had told her that at some point—but hearing her call me *Mr. Sloane* in that voice, soft and sleep-rough, turned me on so quickly that it was like hitting a switch. My cock went from "mildly intrigued" to "diamond-hard and throbbing" within about two seconds. Even high-performance sports cars didn't have that sort of zero-to-sixty acceleration.

"Sadie," I said. "Or should I call you Ms. Bayliss?"

"I think we're past the formalities, don't you?" she asked, and drew the sheet down to her waist.

I didn't reply. I couldn't: I was too mesmerized by the sight of her breasts, round and soft and a warm, deep brown color that glowed in the sunlight. I wanted to put my mouth on her nipples and suck on them until she moaned.

There was no reason why I couldn't. And so I did, licking first and then using my teeth a bit, just enough to add an edge to her pleasure, and she squirmed and gasped and cupped my head in her hands, holding me against her chest like she was worried I would escape from her.

It was, in short, heavenly.

I didn't stop until her nipples were hard nubs beneath my lips and tongue. Then I lifted my head and gazed down at her. She was breathing in shallow pants. Her mouth was open slightly, and her eyes were glassy.

Victory.

She opened her eyes and squinted at me. "Why did you stop?"

"I'm just getting started," I promised her.

The sheet still covered her below the waist. I supported myself on one elbow and used my free hand to draw the sheet away from her body.

Merciful Zeus.

She looked incredible, and I couldn't wait to put my mouth on every inch of her bare skin.

She smiled at me, not at all bashful—I couldn't imagine Sadie ever being shy—and slid one hand down her body, down between her legs.

"You filthy girl," I breathed, impressed and incredibly turned on. None of my furtive daydreaming about Sadie had prepared me for this. She gave me a sly look and moved her fingers. Her eyes slid shut, and I stared, struck dumb, as she began stroking herself.

There was nothing more arousing than the sight of a woman touching herself. Every man would agree. No pornography in the universe could compare to the contented sigh that escaped her lips. My cock throbbed between my legs, hard and ready.

But looking wasn't enough. I wanted to *touch*. I

wanted to be the cause of those noises.

I moved closer, pressing myself against the side of her body. My cock bumped against her hip, and I rocked against her, enjoying the friction. She laughed, and I rolled my hips again and said, "What's funny?"

"Nothing," she said. Her breath caught. "I would never laugh at your masculine prowess."

"I'm glad to hear it," I said, and moved my hand between her legs, my fingers tangling with her own. She bit her lip and spread her thighs a little wider, inviting me in. I dragged my fingers against her slick, soft flesh, and she tossed her head back and moaned. Delicious. I liked a woman who knew what she wanted, and wasn't embarrassed about enjoying it.

Time dilated. I spent a slow eternity touching her while she tossed her head and rolled her hips against my hand. I listened to her breathing, fast and shallow, and watched her breasts jiggle slightly with each inhale.

"You're not going to keep me waiting, are you?" she asked, after three centuries had passed.

"Keep you waiting for what?" I asked, not really listening, and bent to kiss the salty hollow of her throat, damp with a fine sheen of sweat.

"I think you know," she said, suddenly coy, and tugged my head up to draw me into a kiss.

Our mouths met, and I wondered why I hadn't kissed her already. The folly of youth. She yanked at my hair, a sharp bite of pleasure, and nibbled at my lower lip until I couldn't stand it and plunged my tongue into her mouth, taking control of the kiss. I didn't want Sadie to get the idea that she was in charge here.

I drew back and kissed her neck again, her breasts. She moaned my name, and it was music to my goddamn ears. My cock throbbed urgently between my legs.

"Come on," Sadie said, wrapping one small hand around me and shifting her hips, and then I was inside her, buried in her soft, wet heat.

I moved against her, and that one motion was almost enough to undo me.

"Sadie," I said, through gritted teeth. "It's not fair that you feel *so fucking good*."

She laughed, bright and happy, and said, "Are you going to come already? I thought you would have more stamina than that."

"Oh, I'll show you stamina," I growled, and thrust into her until she quit laughing and instead let out a moan with each roll of my hips.

It was glorious to lie there on top of her and feel the way our bodies worked together. We *fit*. And I was going to take my sweet time and enjoy every second of it. First I would make her come, and then I would put her on her stomach and—

"You have to touch the purple eggplant," Sadie said.

I frowned. What eggplant? "I don't know what you're talking about."

"The purple one," she insisted. "You have to

touch it, or the spelunkers are going to get lost in the cavern!"

"I don't see an eggplant," I said, and Sadie rolled her eyes at me, pushed me away from her, and disappeared.

I woke up.

I was in my bed in New York, and Sadie wasn't beside me.

My dreams had always been vivid, ever since I was a child, but they weren't usually so detailed and realistic. I rubbed my hands over my face, trying to shake off the weird haze of the dream and bring myself back to reality. It had seemed so *real*. Touching Sadie, kissing her—

It wasn't real. And a good thing, too. I couldn't afford the distraction of a real live Sadie in my bed.

I had a company to run. Worlds to conquer.

With a groan, I rolled over and looked at my phone. It was Wednesday. I had an hour to get to the office and shake off the last sticky remnants of the dream, so that I could look Sadie in the eye without blushing.

"Hump Day" had never been more painfully accurate.

CHAPTER 8

Sadie

I had dinner at my parents' house every Friday night, even on the days my mother had a late shift at the hospital and couldn't make it. It was a family tradition. They lived in Astoria, which was a real pain in the butt to get to from my place in Carroll Gardens. I had to take the subway into Manhattan and then back across the East River. It was only ten miles, but it usually took me about an hour. That was part of the reason we'd switched from Sunday to Friday dinners: it was easier for me to head to their house directly from work. Elliott letting me out of work early screwed up my timeline a little, but I just ran some errands in Midtown until it was time to take the train to Queens.

My parents lived in the same place they'd lived my entire life, a rowhouse just north of Broadway that my father had gut-renovated back in the '80s. The house was his pride and joy, and each summer the small flower garden in front of the house was a little more elaborate than the summer before. It was all dormant now, though, or lying quietly underground to wait for winter to pass. I walked up the sidewalk and climbed the front steps, but before I could raise my hand to knock, the door opened.

"Sadie! You're late," my brother said.

I rolled my eyes. Devin was two years older than me, and he acted like it was his life's work to boss me around. "Dinner's at 6:30, and it's not even 6:00 right now," I said. "If you think that's late, you need to learn how to tell time."

He smirked. "6:00 means it's past time to start drinking. I brought wine. Ma isn't home yet, but she called and said she was getting on the subway. Come on in and let's get smashed."

"A man after my own heart," I said, and went inside.

The house smelled familiar. I was never quite sure what it was—some combination of laundry detergent, floor cleaner, food, and the terrible scented candles my mother loved—but it smelled like *home*. Devin disappeared into the back of the house, and I took off my coat and hung it in the hall closet, taking my time, enjoying being in a familiar place with familiar furnishings, warm and sound. The house was always untidy and a little cluttered, because neither of my parents was much of a housekeeper, and it was perfect just as it was.

My dad was in the kitchen, cooking up a storm. He was an insurance agent, and his more reasonable work hours meant that he was usually the one who ended up making dinner. He claimed he had learned to like it over the years, and as time went by, Saturday dinners became increasingly elaborate. I went in to say hello, and he accepted a kiss on the cheek, but then said, "I want you and that brother of yours out of my kitchen. The two of you never do anything but get underfoot."

"I could chop things," I said, feeling guilty.

"The time for chopping was half an hour ago," he said. "Now it's the time for you to leave me be. Get out of here."

"Sadie, I'm opening the bottle," Devin called from the dining room, and I was no fool. I went to where the booze was.

I sat at the table, resting my elbows on the rumpled white tablecloth, while Devin mucked around with the wine. He filled my glass almost to the top, and I raised my eyebrows.

"You look like you need it," he said.

"I guess so," I said. "I also need a job."

He sat across from me with his own overflowing glass. "I thought you were working for that start-up, though."

"I am," I said. "But it's just a contract position. I'll be out of work again in less than a month. I need to find something else. I've put in some applications."

"So why do you look so depressed?" he asked.

I sighed and took a big sip of wine. "Because I sort of like the contract work. The guy's a real do-gooder, saving starving babies in Africa and all that—"

"Oh Lord, spare me the white guilt," Devin said.

"—and I like working for him. Shut up, Devin. He's not like that."

"Okay, sure," Devin said. "Whatever you say. You're still gonna keep looking for other work, right?"

"Yeah," I said. "I'm going to call some places on Monday to follow up on my applications. If anyone offers me a job, I'll take it. I'm not an idiot."

"I don't know if I'd go *that* far," Devin said.

I rolled my eyes. "What about you? How's *Freedom Writers* going?"

He sipped his wine and scowled at me.

"Oh, I'm sorry," I said. "Wrong movie. I mean *To Sir, With Love*."

"Why can't I be Hilary Swank?" he asked. "Is it my skin color? Are you racially profiling me?"

"Children," my dad called from the kitchen.

"Okay, I'm done," I said. "Sorry. For real, though. How's the new semester?"

Devin sighed. "Tiring. It's like they forgot everything over Christmas break. Logarithms, subtraction, basic hygiene..."

"One day you'll give in and get a cushy job at a private school in Forest Hills," I said.

I heard a noise at the front door, and then my mother's voice calling, "Where are my little babies?"

"Quick, finish the wine," Devin said, and I chugged my glass, trying not to laugh or choke, while he called out, "We're in the dining room, Ma."

She came in, still wearing her scrubs and looking worn out. I set my glass on the table—only half-empty, despite my best efforts—and stood up to give her a hug. "Hi, Mom. How was your day? Do you want some wine?"

"That's the Devil's drink," she said sternly, and then, "Pour me a glass."

Devin laughed and emptied the bottle.

Dinner was pork roast, greens, and fluffy yeast rolls. I set to work stuffing my face while my mother told a story about one of her patients who had gotten fed up with the hospital food. When we all finally stopped laughing, she turned to Devin and said, "Have you met a nice girl yet?"

Devin and I exchanged a meaningful look. She asked this question every week. Devin was gay, and had been out to my parents for a solid decade now, but my mother was still in denial about it. "No, Ma," Devin said gently. "I'm still with Mohammed. You met him at the barbeque, remember?"

"He's a very nice young man," my father said. He wasn't totally on board with the gay thing either, but he'd accepted that it wasn't going to change, and I thought his awkward attempts to show support were very sweet. Parents were adorable.

My mother sniffed. I wasn't sure if she disapproved of Mohammed more because he was a man or because he was Muslim.

Then Devin got a wicked look on his face and said, "You should ask Sadie about her new boss. Sounds like she's crushing hard."

I kicked him under the table, and he yelped, but it was too late. My mom turned to me with a gleam in her eyes that said, *GRANDCHILDREN!*

"*No,*" I said. "He's my boss. I like him, but *not like that*. Nothing is going to happen. Stop looking at me like that, Ma."

"I just think it's time for you to start dating again," she said. "It's been a year, sugar."

"Cheryl, leave her alone," my father said.

"We've *been* leaving her alone," my mother said. "I know you agree with me, Kevin. It's not good for a person to be sad for so long. I know you loved him, Sadie, but that boy told me he wanted you to move on with your life. And you aren't moving at all, sugar. You're going nowhere."

I sat there, stunned, feeling a tight, achy heat gather behind my eyes. This was not at all what I had expected from the evening.

I was *not* going to start crying at the dinner table.

"Excuse me," I said tightly, and stood up and headed for the door.

"Let her go," I heard my father say.

I should have just gone home.

CHAPTER 9

Elliott

I didn't take the weekend off, but I went home before midnight on Friday, and on Saturday morning I slept in and didn't make it to the office until after lunch.

I hoped Sadie would approve.

She was infuriating, and she amused the hell out of me. I still wasn't sure that hiring her had been a good idea—she was a deadly distraction, and I couldn't afford to be distracted—but fantasizing about taking her to bed made a nice change from worrying about my finances and my father's inevitable meddling.

He knew I was back in New York, and probably knew what I was up to, but I hadn't spoken to him since our brief conversation in August, when I called him from the embassy in Kampala and learned that he was cutting me off. That was what had sparked my return to the States: fury, and a foolish desire to prove him wrong. My job with MSF paid more than enough to live comfortably in-country, and my head of mission told me she would see about getting me a raise—but it wasn't about the money, at that point. It was about showing my father that I had become a man.

Now, months later, I felt less like a man and more like a misguidedly rebellious boy. Such was life.

As if thinking about my father had somehow drawn his evil, unblinking attention, like the Eye of Sauron pulsating wickedly on the horizon, I received a call on Sunday morning from the oldest of my three younger sisters, the one who had taken over as heir apparent when my father reluctantly conceded that a woman was better than a non-Sloane.

"Cassie," I said when I answered, having recognized the number. "What a pleasant surprise."

"Elliott," she said grimly. Cassie and I had never gotten along well, and in the last few years she had turned into a younger, more feminine version of our father, full of disapproval and boring statistics about international markets.

"What have I done to deserve your attention?" I asked. I was already enjoying myself. Cassie had no sense of humor to speak of, and pissing her off had long been a favorite pastime.

"Father told me to check up on you," she said. "He gave me your number. So. I'm checking. What are you doing?"

"Well, right now, I'm doing laundry," I said. That was a lie; I was sitting on my bed watching the Duke vs. North Carolina basketball game.

Cassie sighed. "Don't be difficult, Elliott."

"All right," I said. "I'm working on my start-up. Which is exactly what I told our father I would be doing. I haven't starved to death yet, and I'm not out on the streets. You can check up on me again in three months."

"Fine," she said. There was a long pause. I waited. Finally she said, "Kristin would like to hear from you."

Kris was my middle and favorite sister. I hadn't contacted her because I didn't want to create any problems. I told Cassie as much, and she sighed and said, "You act like Father is the Devil incarnate. I know you've had your problems, but he isn't actually the Gestapo. He isn't having us followed. He isn't tapping our phones. You're allowed to meet Kristin for coffee."

I thought he probably *was* having all of us followed, but I held my peace. "Maybe I'll call her, in that case. Please keep me abreast of any developments in our father's attempts to sabotage me."

"Good grief," Cassie said, and hung up.

I smirked at my phone. Every time I managed to make Cassie hang up on me, I mentally added ten imaginary points to my score.

Family intrigue was such a delight.

I called Kris.

She didn't answer. I knew she wouldn't—she screened all of her calls, and she wouldn't recognize my new number—but I left a message telling her I

80

wanted to see her, and she called back ten minutes later.

"If you're not Elliott, you aren't funny," she said, when I picked up.

I broke into a helpless grin at the sound of her voice. I hadn't seen her in two years, not since the last time I was in New York, and I had missed her every day since then. "It's really me," I said.

"You're a real jerk, you know," she said. "You've been in New York for *months* and you didn't call me."

"I know," I said. "I'm sorry, Kris. I just thought—with our father—"

"Yeah, I get it," she said. "Apology accepted. What are you doing right now? Can we get dinner? You know I hate talking on the phone."

I glanced at the clock. "Of course. We can go anywhere you want. I'll even go to that terrible beer garden in Times Square."

"You're watching the Duke game, aren't you?" she asked.

"Busted," I said. "They're probably going to lose."

"You'll have to drown your sorrows in delicious food, then," she said. "I know just the place. I'll text you the address. 7:00, okay? Don't be late, or else."

"That's a pitiful threat," I said.

She laughed at me, and hung up.

We met at a Thai place in the East Village. Kris was waiting for me outside on the sidewalk. Despite her bravado on the phone, she raised her hand to her mouth when she spotted me, and as I drew closer I realized she was crying.

"Oh, Kris," I said, my stomach knotting with a combination of guilt and terror. I never knew what to do with a crying woman. I took her in my arms and patted her back while she clung to my coat and wept. "Kristin. Please don't cry." We were making a scene. A passing hipster scowled at me, like I had done something horrible. Maybe I had. I knew Kris felt that I had abandoned her.

Public weeping didn't match Kris' image of herself, and she pulled herself together after just a few minutes and carefully wiped her fingers beneath her eyes. "Did my mascara smear?"

I dabbed one black fleck from her face and said, "You look beautiful."

"What a charmer," she said. "God. Fuck you, Elliott. Don't ever go away for two years and then not call me the instant you get back. That sucks. That was a shitty thing to do."

"You're right," I said. Looking at her tear-stained face made me feel like a pathetic worm. "I'm sorry. I wish I could go back in time and call you from the airport. I suck."

"You have too many daddy issues," she said. "We all need therapy. Every single one of us. Especially Cassie. Dad has totally brainwashed her."

"Don't pathologize," I said. "She's always been like that. Are you ready to go in now? Let's eat. We'll get a bottle of wine."

"Two bottles," she said.

The restaurant was one I hadn't been to before, but the food was spicy and authentic, and the waiter kept our water glasses filled and otherwise left us alone, so all of my requirements for an acceptable dining experience were filled. Kris talked a little about her job—she was a junior editor at a major fashion magazine—and got me up to speed on the latest family gossip. Julie, my youngest sister, had never even attempted to do anything with her life and was still living at home and buying expensive crap with our father's credit card, and Kris told me a delightful story about Julie's new cockapoo puppy, whatever that was, pissing all over our father's favorite oriental rug.

"I wish I could have been there to see his face," I said.

"Me too," Kris said, "but Cassie did a pretty good job of describing it. She's gotten a little better lately, you know. I think maybe she's finally realized that Dad is an asshole."

"Wonders will never cease," I said.

"Yeah," she said. "Oh, by the way, let me tell you this before I forget. Mom's attorney has called me a few times, trying to get in touch with you. He says it's something about her estate. Probably some paperwork or something, I don't know the details. But you should call him."

"Sure," I said, and sighed. My mother had been dead for more than a decade, but it seemed like there was always more paperwork to sign. "Is it still that old guy, what was his name—"

"Harrison," Kris said, and grinned. "No. It's a new one. Young. He's pretty cute."

"Kris," I said.

"I'm just saying," she said. "It doesn't hurt to look. Anyway, please call him so he stops calling me."

"I'll do it tomorrow morning," I said. "First thing."

"Good," she said. "Now I want you to tell me all about this company you're starting. Don't spare any details. I want every last boring tidbit."

"If you insist," I said. "But we're going to need another bottle of wine."

CHAPTER 10

Sadie

It happened like this.

Ben rolled over in bed one morning and said, "I don't feel right."

One week, five blood tests, and two doctors later, he was diagnosed with acute myeloid leukemia.

I was at work during the appointment, but he called me after, his voice cracking slightly, and said, "The doctor told me to check into the hospital."

I spun in my chair to face my cubicle wall, not wanting any of my co-workers to see my face. I asked, "When?"

"As soon as possible," he said. "Like, today."

That was the moment I knew it was serious.

Ben hadn't felt well for weeks. Mysterious bruises bloomed underneath his skin and disappeared, and he started going to bed earlier and earlier, until he was asleep half an hour after dinner. I told him to go to the doctor and he wouldn't, insisted he was fine, until the morning he finally admitted that he wasn't.

He wasn't fine.

We took the subway to the hospital, at his insistence. A cab would be wasteful, he said. There was no need, he said, and I gave in. I didn't want to upset him.

The hospital was noisy, crowded, and aseptic, all white corridors and bustling nurses, but Ben's room was quiet, just him and an older man who was rapidly dying of brain cancer. It was a small oasis, there on the ninth floor, with a view over the East River and Queens beyond it, and a small artificial plant on the windowsill. I wondered who had left it there. I didn't think the hospital would waste money on something so frivolous.

"It's nice," Ben said, perched on his bed with an IV already dripping a clear fluid into his veins. "I guess."

"For a hospital," I said.

His oncologist came by that first evening to introduce himself. He was a tall, extraordinarily skinny man. Dr. Mukherjee. I hated a lot of people at that hospital, but Dr. Mukherjee wasn't one of them.

"It's most known in children, of course," he said, in the calm, straightforward manner I came to appreciate so much over the course of the next several months. "Leukemia, I mean. But not uncommon in adults. We'll need to do a biopsy to be certain, but I have little doubt that's what we're dealing with here. We'll start you on the standard chemotherapeutic treatment."

"What are my chances?" Ben asked, squeezing my hand tightly.

The doctor looked down at his clipboard. "Your blood counts aren't great," he said. "I won't lie to you: it concerns me. Five-year survival rates for adults with this type of cancer are between thirty and forty percent."

"That's less than half," Ben said, and I looked at him and saw that his face had gone white.

"Try to remain optimistic," the doctor said. "There's no better treatment you can give yourself. I won't give up on you, as long as you promise that you won't give up either."

After he left, I leaned into Ben's side, just for a moment, letting him bear up my weight, and then I said, "Do you want me to call my mom?"

"Yeah," Ben said, "I'm—I want to know what she thinks."

I nodded, and kissed him on the cheek.

My mother was a pediatric oncologist at Mt. Sinai. She'd seen plenty of leukemia before, and when I told her Ben's blood count, she sighed and said, "That's not great. It's not *terrible*, but it's not great. Let me come by and talk to his doctors."

"They seem pretty competent," I said, because I didn't necessarily want her showing up and *meddling*, the way she was so good at doing; but on the other hand, this was probably the sort of situation that called for a little meddling.

"Don't you sass me," my mother said. "I'll come by tomorrow. Tell that Ben to drink a lot of

87

fluids and stay positive."

I passed along the message, and Ben grinned and said, "Is your mom going to come boss me around? I can't wait."

"The fact that you enjoy her fussing is the sign of a sick mind," I told him, and then bit my lip and looked down at the floor, because he *was* sick. I couldn't joke about things like that anymore.

My life changed between one day and the next. I woke up that morning, the day Ben was admitted to the hospital, as a care-free twenty-something hipster, and the next day I felt thirty years older. I had more to worry about, now, than paying rent and getting a spot in my favorite spinning class.

I read everything I could find, whenever I had a quiet moment at work, looking for anything, any hint of a miracle cure, any experimental treatment that might help. I learned the names of all of Ben's nurses, and did my best to get on their good sides. And I worried. I tried to hide it from him, but I felt it sitting in my belly, a dark lump, a cold stone, slowly dragging me down to earth.

I was afraid.

A few days after he was admitted, I showed up at the hospital after work and found a strange woman sitting beside Ben's bed. She turned when I came in the room and gave me a look of distaste I recognized all too well: *Who's this black girl?*

"Mom," Ben said to the woman, "this is Sadie, my fiancée."

"Your *what*?" his mother said, the pitch of her

voice rising sharply, and I knew then that Ben hadn't told her anything about me.

He tried to explain, later, when we were alone. "They're really racist," he said, "my entire family, and I just didn't want to deal with it. I didn't want any trouble."

"Okay," I said, still numb. Three years. We had been together for three years, engaged for one, and he never even *mentioned* me. They lived in New Jersey, and he'd never bothered to introduce us. And I, stupidly, had never questioned it, had assumed they were estranged, or lived too far away, or—well, whatever it was that I had thought.

"I didn't think you would care," he said. "I guess I should have."

"It doesn't matter," I said, even though it did, it *did* matter, like a knife through my heart—that he had loved me, promised to spend the rest of his life with me, and never spoke one word to the people who raised him.

He didn't want the *trouble*?

If I'd found out six months earlier, we would have had a raging fight. He would have yelled, I would have thrown dishes, we would have slept in different rooms—and then we would have made up, and put it behind us. But I couldn't throw a wine glass at his head, as sick as he was. There was no room for anger anymore. No outlet for it. Any capacity for rage had left me, drained away and replaced by sorrow. I needed it, that anger, to lance the wound and drain out the poison. It festered instead.

I would have forgiven him, if he asked for my forgiveness, but he didn't ask.

His mother hated me. It was obvious from our first meeting, and it only got worse as the weeks went by. She refused to make eye contact with me, and responded in monosyllables to all of my attempts to make conversation. I quickly gave up on being friendly and tried to avoid her, but she never called ahead, just showed up at the hospital whenever she felt like it, and it was hard to make excuses to leave that didn't sound like obvious excuses to leave.

It sucked, but I could have handled it. So what if she hated me? I wasn't going to cry about it. But what really chapped my ass was that she got herself listed as next of kin, and excluded me from every important decision about Ben's care. It wasn't so bad early on, when he was still able to make decisions for himself, but toward the end, when he was totally out of it, she was calling all of the shots.

There was nothing I could do. We weren't married. We had been waiting, saving up for a nice honeymoon in the Bahamas, and I came to regret that decision so hard I thought I would never be able to put it behind me. The medical decisions were the big thing, the major regret, but there was also little stuff, things I never would have thought about in my former life, the one I inhabited before Ben got sick. For instance: Ben had insurance, but it was a bare-bones, high-deductible plan, and mine had every bell and whistle. For instance: I used up all of my vacation days and sick leave, and after that I had to go back to work, struggling through every miserable eight-hour day before I could make the trek to the hospital, because I didn't qualify for FMLA. If we had been married, if I hadn't insisted on the fancy trip, if, if—

Hindsight, and all that.

By the time he got sick, it was too late.

I tried to get him to marry me, just get a marriage license and have it done quick and dirty, but he wouldn't agree to it. "I don't want you to be stuck with my bills," he said. "Let my mom pay off my student loans. She deserves it."

"You aren't going to die," I said.

"Just in case," he said, and that was that.

We originally expected Ben to be in the hospital for a month, for his first round of chemotherapy, and then to be discharged and spend a month at home before the second round. That didn't happen. Dr. Mukherjee came to speak with us toward the beginning of the fourth week and said, "I'm afraid that your cancer isn't responding the way we hoped."

"What does that mean?" Ben croaked out, and I scooted closer to him on the bed, wanting to offer whatever comfort I could.

"We'll have to take a more aggressive approach," the doctor said. "I won't be discharging you at the end of the week. It's best if you stay here so that we can monitor your progress on a daily basis."

"Do I need a bone marrow transplant?" Ben asked.

The doctor shrugged. "It may come to that," he said. "But not yet. A few other things we can try, first."

He said a few more platitudes and then left us alone to cope with the bombshell he had just dropped.

I started crying. I didn't mean to. Ben had enough on his plate, without worrying about me having an emotional breakdown, but I just couldn't cope with it anymore. He was my best friend, my partner in crime, my safe harbor, and I didn't know how I would go on with my life if he died and left me.

"Sadie, what's wrong?" he asked, sliding one arm around my shoulders and hugging me close.

"I don't want you to die," I sobbed, tears streaming down my face, my words almost incoherent.

"I'm not going to die," he said firmly. "We have plans. We're getting married. We're going to have kids and grow old together. I'm not going to leave you alone."

"Promise me," I told him. "Promise me that you won't die."

"I won't die," he said, and I believed him, for that one moment.

The moment passed.

Dr. Mukherjee's backup plan seemed to work at

first: Ben's white count improved, and he seemed to have more energy, to be more like the man I fell in love with and less like the hollow-eyed wraith he'd become. But then he regressed, and regressed further, and the nurses started frowning at his chart in a way that told me there wasn't much hope to be had.

I broke down and called Regan, finally. She knew that Ben was in the hospital, but I hadn't told her how bad it was, had kept reassuring her that he was fine, getting better, home any day now, nothing to worry about. Regan was a grown woman, but in some ways she was still a child, with a child's innocent view of the world, and I wanted to protect her as long as I could. But it wasn't fair to keep lying to her. She cared about Ben. She deserved to be able to say goodbye.

"Sadie, I haven't heard from you in ages!" she said, when she picked up. "Is Ben okay? Are *you* okay?"

I leaned against the wall and slowly sunk to the floor, sandwiched between an empty laundry cart and a stray chair. A passing nurse gave me a sympathetic look. They were all accustomed, here, to relatives in various stages of grief. I rubbed my free hand over my face and said, "Ben's dying."

It was the first time I had admitted it to myself, but it was true: he was dying, and everyone knew it, the doctors, the nurses, him, me.

Regan was quiet for long moments, processing, and then she said, "What do you need? How can I help you?"

I wasn't sure what I had expected her to say, but it wasn't that. I closed my eyes, overcome with gratitude, and swallowed past the hard lump in my throat. "Come visit," I said. "He'd like to see you. We could both use some cheering up."

"I will be *so* cheerful," she said. "Oh, Sadie. I'm so sorry. You don't deserve this."

"I don't think it's about deserving," I said. "It's just how the chips fell."

I had to believe that: that it was random chance, that nothing I had done, or that Ben had done, had caused this. That we couldn't have prevented it by drinking bottled water or eating more organic vegetables or whatever.

My parents were deeply religious, and I was too, as a kid, but somehow I fell out of the habit during college. God started seeming trite, or old-fashioned, or something. Uncool. I hung out with cynical, post-modern hipsters who liked to smoke weed and argue about nihilism. There wasn't much room for belief there: only logic, and Nietzsche.

Anyway, I started praying again, after I talked to Regan that night. I didn't think it would work, really, but it gave me some comfort.

Three months after Ben was first admitted, Dr. Mukherjee told us there was nothing more he could do.

"Well," Ben said, by then too sick to muster much enthusiasm for anything, even the news of his own impending death. "Thanks for trying."

94

We fought about that, after the doctor left. I wanted Ben to rage against the proverbial dying of the light, and he just wanted it to be over: the suffering, the chemo, his life. "I hurt," he told me. "Everywhere. All the time. It never gets better. I want it to end."

"You can't just give up and *die*," I told him, so angry I was shaking. "You *promised* me."

He sighed, weary, and closed his eyes, his head falling back against the pillow. "I know. I shouldn't have done that."

My anger vanished, like someone had cut the strings holding me up. I sank to the floor, kneeling there on the cold linoleum, and rested my forehead against the metal frame of his hospital bed. A maelstrom churned inside me: grief, self-pity, love.

He was everything to me. My entire world.

"Ben, you can't leave me," I said.

He didn't respond. When I looked up, I saw that he had fallen asleep.

By the end, I slept in his hospital room every night after work, curled on the vinyl-covered recliner in the corner, going back to our apartment every so often to shower and pick up clean clothes. It took two grim, horrible weeks after the doctors said there was nothing else they could do. I wanted hospice; I wanted to take him home with me so that he could die in peace, in his own bed, but his mother refused. No hospice. She wasn't going to give up on him, unlike *some people*, said with a dark glare in my direction.

What was I supposed to do?

We weren't married. There was nothing I could do.

He slept, most of the time, but sometimes he woke and had brief moments of lucidity. I was there for one of them, a few days before he died: shoving greasy takeout in my face, trying to catch up on work, and he turned his head toward me and said, "Sadie."

I went to his side, crouched down on the floor and stroked his face, gently, not wanting to cause him any further pain. "I'm here," I said.

"I'll miss you," he said. "Do you think there's an afterlife?"

"Yeah, baby," I said, throat closing up. "I do."

"I don't want to go if you're not there," he said. He frowned at me. "Sadie, will you be happy?"

"I don't know, baby," I said. "I guess I'll have to try."

"Promise me," he said. "Don't mourn. I love you. Be happy."

I would have wept, if I could, if I had any tears left in me. Instead I squeezed his hand and said, "Try to sleep."

Those were the last words he spoke to me. He died while I was at work, on a Thursday afternoon, and I didn't find out until I went to the hospital that evening and found his room already empty, his things waiting in a cardboard box.

I took the subway home that night and stayed awake until dawn, sitting on our sofa with one of his flannel shirts wrapped around my shoulders, gazing out the window and feeling a great emptiness opening inside me, my chest like a cage with no bird in it.

At dawn, I got in the shower and went to work.

His mother didn't invite me to the funeral.

I only found out because I went by the hospital to tie up some loose ends and one of the nurses commented on the touching obituary. I looked it up when I went home: beloved son, brother, nephew, cousin, laid to rest, private ceremony—two days prior.

I cried, then, for the first time in weeks. Cried until my eyes hurt and my face felt swollen and bruised. He was gone from me, dug deep into the earth, and that was all. That was the end of it, the end of our story.

Life after love was a pallid country, seasonless. Weeks passed without my notice. I worked and went home to an empty apartment, fed myself, showered, slept alone, woke in the morning and did it all over again, mechanically, unthinking. Friends came by at first, with casseroles and wine, but they were uncomfortable with my grief. They didn't know what to say, or how to comfort me.

Nothing could have comforted me, probably.

I hated him. I was so unbearably angry with him for dying, for leaving me, for lying about me to his mother, for breaking every promise he ever made, for giving up. And I hated myself for my anger. I thought about moving, during those first terrible months, when everything in the apartment served as a constant reminder of Ben's absence: the pots and pans he'd used to cook so many meals, the furnishings we'd picked out when he moved in and we decided to get an actual grown-up coffee table that wasn't stuffed with newspaper.

But as time went on, I came to treasure those reminders. Seeing a book he had loved, a mug he had shattered and glued back together, made me feel that he wasn't fully gone from my life. If he was a ghost, I welcomed the haunting. It reminded me that I hadn't always been alone.

A year passed.

CHAPTER 11

Sadie

I went out dancing with friends that weekend. Some of them I hadn't seen in months; they gave up on me when I kept turning down invitations after Ben died. But when I sent out a group text asking if anyone wanted to hang out, my friend Edith immediately replied, *SHE'S BACK!!!!*

We went to a club in Williamsburg and I stayed on the dance floor until the lights came on and my feet were so blistered I could barely walk. Then we went to an all-night diner and crammed into a booth, eating cheese fries and laughing as the sun came up. I felt a little like my old self, the Sadie who drank and swore and stayed out all night and lived without limits.

I wasn't that person anymore, of course. But it was nice to pretend.

I rolled into work on Monday feeling tired but happy. The little aloe plant I had bought for my desk hadn't died over the weekend. Elliott had made a big pot of coffee and there was still enough in the carafe to get me going. I had some good ideas for the website. Things were looking up.

Elliott wandered over, holding his coffee mug. For all of his silent disapproval about my office upgrades, he sure was happy to use my coffee pot. I forced myself not to smirk at him. Smugness wasn't attractive. "How was your weekend?" I asked.

"One Drop," he said.

I frowned at him, but he just kept looking at me with that brand expression on his face. He was baiting me, I knew, but curiosity had killed me along with many cats. I bit. "Okay, I'll bite," I said. "Elucidate."

He raised one eyebrow, an elegant arch. "I'm instituting a ten-dollar fine for every word over three syllables before 10:00."

I made a show of counting on my fingers. "You owe me ten bucks, then, because *instituting* is definitely too long."

"One Drop," he said again, pretending he hadn't heard me, "is the new name for the company. You mentioned last week that you thought Zawadi Ya Maji was too obscure and difficult to pronounce. I thought about it and decided you were right."

Huh. I leaned back in my chair, considering. It was kind of boring, but also kind of perfect: accessible without being too obvious. "I like it," I said.

"You do?" he asked.

I smiled at him. "I really do. I'll make a new logo that's a little—like, a little anthropomorphized raindrop, holding a tiny water filter—"

"That's *five* syllables," he said.

"I'm not give you ten dollars," I said. "Sorry. But I'll buy you lunch if you're really that hard up for cash."

He gave me a look like he was annoyed but also amused despite himself. "No smiling water droplets. Nothing with a face."

"Okay," I said. "I'll keep that in mind."

Conversation over, but he kept standing there like he had something else he wanted to say. I waited. I'd learned that Elliott would spit it out when he was good and ready, and not a moment before. He took a sip of his coffee, scratched his forehead, and then said, "I'm going up to Boston later this week."

"Work or fun?" I asked.

His mouth twitched. "Work. I've been corresponding with a grad student at MIT who's doing some interesting work with ceramics. I'd like to talk to him about hiring him on as a product engineer once I've managed to acquire some funding. I'm also going to meet with a few potential investors." He took another sip of his coffee. "I'd like you to come with me."

Oh boy. That was a recipe for disaster. What if he expected us to share a hotel room? I would probably sleep-walk for the first time in my life and come to my senses buck-naked and straddling him in bed. Delightful, but mortifying. Just thinking about it made me want to stay in my house for the rest of time. "I don't think that's really necessary," I said. "It's not like investors want to meet the graphic designer."

"No, I wouldn't subject you to that," he said. "But I'd like you to meet the MIT kid. If I hire him, it's important that we're all able to get along."

Was it? Okay. Elliott had some pretty strange ideas about running a company. So what if the engineer was a weird mouth-breathing neck-bearded cave-dweller? He could just sit at his own desk in the corner and be as nerdy as he wanted. We could get a lot of work done without being best friends. "I'm sure we'll be pals," I said. "It's not necessary. I'll just stay here and work on the website."

"I insist," he said. "We're getting close to the conference, and I don't want to lose any work days."

I shrugged. As long as the company was paying for it, I wasn't going to complain about a free vacation. Boston was a neat city. I could keep it in my pants for a couple of days. Probably. "Okay, you win. When are we leaving?"

"Wednesday," he said. He looked pleased that I had given in so easily. I was tempted to tell him not to get used to it. "Just an overnight trip. We'll take the train up on Wednesday. I'll meet with the investors that evening. We'll go to MIT on Thursday morning, and come back to New York that afternoon."

"I'll make sure someone waters my houseplants," I said. It would be fine. Elliott and I were both professionals. I wasn't going to suddenly lose my mind and try to make out with him in public.

Probably.

Boston was freezing.

There was half a foot of snow on the ground, and as we exited South Station, I turned up the collar of my coat against the chill. It was mid-afternoon, and already growing dark.

I hated winter.

Elliott glanced at me and said, "We're staying at the Ritz-Carlton. It's about half a mile from here. Do you mind walking? I'll hail a cab if you're too cold."

"I think I can handle a mile," I said, because I was determined to be cheerful and a good sport, even though I would have really, really liked to take a cab. As we set off, I asked, "The Ritz-Carlton?"

He grimaced. "I know. Money begets money. I'm having dinner with the investors in the hotel restaurant, and the Best Western wouldn't have the same effect. It's all about keeping up appearances."

"That's stupid," I said. "You're asking them for money. If you already have Ritz-Carlton money, why do you need *their* money?"

He shrugged. "We're talking about potentially millions of dollars, Sadie. They need to have confidence in me, and part of that comes from signaling that I'm their equal. If they think I'm just like them, they'll feel safer investing their money with me."

"It's just a good old boys club," I said, a little disgusted.

"In a way," he said. "I won't claim it's fair. But this is how the world works."

"The world sucks," I said.

He smiled at me. "I agree," he said. "That's why I'm trying to change it."

I mulled that over as we walked through the narrow streets. Boston, with its dense tangle of haphazard streets, was so different from New York's orderly grid. I liked it. It felt old, like how I imagined Europe must be. It had history.

Maybe Elliott would rustle up some investors in Brussels, and I would get a free trip to Europe.

My nose was a frozen chunk of cartilage by the time Elliott came to a stop in front of a large building and said, "We're here." He looked down at me and tucked his hands in his coat pockets. His nose was red, and he was wearing a slouchy blue beanie that clashed with his Important Businessman overcoat and dress shoes. "I want you to know. I reserved separate rooms."

God, how awkward. I had been a little worried, of course, but I didn't expect him to actually *say* anything. "Good," I said, "because I snore."

He pursed his lips. "I'm afraid I can't employ anyone who snores. We'll have to put you on the next train back to New York."

I stared at him, feeling my eyes widen. It took me a second longer than it should have to realize that he was teasing me. "You're a monster," I said.

He grinned. "Shall we?"

The lobby was—well. I was too conscious of my own dignity to ever gawk like an awestruck tourist, but I definitely felt the impulse. Everything was so *shiny*. The walls were paneled in wood the same warm golden color as the floor, and it all glowed like a lantern. Elliott checked in while I loitered off to one side, trying to look inconspicuous. I wished I had worn a nicer coat. I wished I *owned* a nicer coat.

Elliott came over after a few minutes and handed me a key card. "We're on the third floor," he said. He headed for the elevators, and I followed him, clutching my overnight bag. As we waited for the elevator, he said, "I'm meeting the investors for dinner at 6:00. You can do whatever you'd like this evening. There are some good restaurants nearby, or—do you shop?"

What a strange question. Shop for what? He probably had a vague idea that women enjoyed shopping and had never stopped to think what we might be shopping *for*. "I think I'm just going to do some work and go to bed early," I said.

The elevator doors slid open, and we stepped inside. "We're meeting the MIT kid tomorrow morning at 9," he said. "We'll take a cab. It isn't far. We can have breakfast first."

"Are you going to refer to him as *the MIT kid* to his face?" I asked. "He might object."

"I'll try to behave myself," Elliott said, and the doors opened again on the third floor.

As we left the elevator, I felt his hand settle,

briefly and lightly, at the small of my back. It was the sort of polite touch that well-mannered men allowed themselves, a sort of old-fashioned chivalry: careful, helpful, guiding me on my way. I was sure he didn't mean anything by it. He had been raised in the upper echelons of New York society. Good manners had been hammered into him since birth.

But the weight and warmth of his hand set me on fire nonetheless.

God, I was so screwed.

I was in room 306. He walked me to the door and said, "Let's meet in the lobby tomorrow morning at 8." He glanced down at the key card envelope he was holding, and said, "Apparently I'm right next door if you need anything."

"I don't think I will," I said. "Good luck with dinner."

He made a wry face. "Thanks," he said. "I'll need it."

If the lobby had been over-the-top luxurious, my room was more along the lines of your run-of-the-mill hotel room: bed, table, armchair, television. Not that I was complaining. The bed was enormous, and looked comfortable as shit. I was going to sleep like a—well, not like a baby. Babies cried a lot and woke up every two hours.

I checked the time. It was only 4:00: too early to eat. I settled down with my laptop and got to work. We only two and a half weeks left until the conference, and I was starting to feel the pressure. I worked until my stomach growled so loudly that I decided I couldn't ignore it anymore, and then I ordered room service, took a hot bath, and climbed into bed to watch trashy television until I was ready to go to sleep.

The bed was even more comfortable than it looked.

After flipping channels for a while, I settled on a reality show about women with more money than sense. As far as I could tell, the point of the show was to film the women being catty about each other. One of them was shopping at Saks and pitched a fit when the salesgirl brought her the wrong size dress. It was horrible and amazing at the same time. America: where people got famous for being idiots.

I was completely engrossed.

A little after 10, I heard a knock at the door.

I got up and went to answer, retying the belt of my complimentary bathrobe more firmly around my waist. My mother didn't raise any fools, and I checked the peephole before I let some serial killer into my room.

It was Elliott, of course.

I drew in a deep breath and exhaled through my nose. I didn't want to let him in. There I was, naked beneath my bathrobe, face washed clean, braids hanging loose around my shoulders. I hadn't been expecting to see him again tonight, and I felt far too stripped bare and exposed to have a conversation with him.

But there was also a small, greedy part of me that wanted him to see me like this. It would be a forced intimacy, but intimacy nonetheless, the two of us in my hotel room, with my bed right there, and my skin prickling already with the thought of him touching me. The reasonable Sadie said this was a terrible idea, but the hot, burning heart of me wanted nothing more than to let Elliott in.

And so I did it. I opened the door and pulled it open and looked at him without saying anything.

He *flushed*. His cheeks turned bright red, and I was sure he had spent most of his life, and certainly all of his adolescence, cursing his fair skin. I loved it. He was so inscrutable that it was a rare gift to have any insight into what he was thinking.

I wondered if he was thinking about tugging open the knot in my belt and sliding the robe from my shoulders.

I thought he probably was. I hoped he was.

"Uh, sorry," he said. "I thought you would still be up. We'll talk tomorrow."

"It's fine," I said. Well, not *me*, but the naughty Sadie, the one who wanted to untie her robe and let him look his fill. "I was just watching TV. Come on in." I stepped back, making room, and I hoped he was too polite and well-trained to refuse an obvious invitation.

And he *was*. He came in, still red-faced, and stood just a few inches too close to me as he looked around my hotel room. I saw his gaze linger on the rumpled bed, and it scared me—I wasn't ready—and delighted me all the same.

"Here, sit down," I said, motioning to the table.

I wanted that space between us like a shield. "You can enjoy my executive workstation."

He laughed and took a seat. "Is that what they call it?"

"I read the information binder," I said, sitting across from him. This was familiar ground, our easy back-and-forth, and far easier on my nerves than him standing too close and looking down at me with that bright heat in his eyes. "How was the meeting?"

He sighed and ran one hand through his hair, ruining his carefully arranged hairstyle. Blond strands fell to either side of his face, softening his appearance. He looked younger, and a little bewildered. I wanted to kiss him until he smiled again. "I think it went okay. They seemed interested. No firm commitments, of course, but they said I would hear from them within the next week."

"Were they just being polite, or do you think they meant it?" I asked.

"It's impossible to say," he said. "I hope the latter."

I looked at him, the lines bracketing his mouth, the fine lattice of lines beside his eyes. He looked tired. "You're running out of money, aren't you?" I asked. "You don't have enough to keep the company going for much longer."

He rubbed one palm against his chin. I imagined the fine hairs scraping against the ridged skin of his hand. "Yes."

I had already suspected, but hearing him admit it made my stomach drop like a stone in a well. "You shouldn't have hired me," I said.

"Hmm," he said. "Shouldn't I have? I don't regret it. The branding work you're doing for me isn't exactly optional. We'll get funding or we won't, and if we don't I'll just go back to Uganda. And you, my dear, will land on your feet either way."

My dear. The words sent a slow wave of pleasure curling its way up my spine. I wanted him to say it to me again, but this time whispered into my ear while we lay together in bed, nothing between us but air.

Lord. That glass of wine I'd had with dinner was really messing me up.

"Someone will give you money," I said firmly. "I'm sure of it."

"Your faith warms my black heart, but I'm afraid there are no guarantees," he said. "We'll have to wait and see." He sighed and picked up the paperweight resting on the table, turning it in his long fingers. "Tell me something, Sadie."

My heartbeat kicked into high gear. "What?"

"I don't know. Anything. I'm tired of worrying about money. Tell me a ridiculous story from your childhood."

"I don't have any," I said, which was a lie, of course. I chewed on my lip for a second, and then said, "I've been watching—if you want, I'm watching this ridiculous show about rich housewives, or something, and they keep talking trash about each other on camera. It's really lowbrow, but—"

"It sounds like exactly what I need right now,"

he said.

And so that was how I ended up watching trashy reality television with my boss, sitting on my bed with him a safe two feet away on the other side of the mattress, leaning forward and laughing as two of the women got into a screaming match on a street corner. It sort of weirded me out that he was so into it, but I also found it charming. I didn't get the feeling that Elliott watched a whole lot of reality TV.

Sitting there, I had one of those out-of-body experiences where you consider your situation from an outside perspective and decide that what you're doing is incredibly fucking stupid. It wasn't like I was *surprised* that I was attracted to Elliott. He was an incredibly good-looking man, and he was also smart and interesting and unexpectedly charming. But I wasn't ready for a relationship—I wasn't even ready to *date*, and as much as my body wanted sex, I wasn't sure I was ready for that, either—and he was also my *boss*, and totally out of my league in more ways than one.

And yet there I was, in bed with him—well, *on* bed, which was almost as bad—and so tempted to turn to him and kiss his whiskered cheek and his mouth that it was a physical urge.

I fought it. I dug my fingernails into my palms and told myself that he was my boss and that I would only end up hurting both of us.

Finally, the show ended, and he stretched his arms over his head, something in his back making a loud cracking noise, and said, "I'd better get some sleep. We've got a full day tomorrow."

"Right," I said. I climbed off the bed after him and walked with him to the door. "You said 8 in the lobby, right?"

"That's right," he said. "I'll buy you breakfast." He smiled at me, warm and open, like he had never had a dirty thought in his entire life. "Sleep well, Sadie."

"You too," I said, and watched him walk down the hallway, and that was the moment I knew I was well and truly fucked.

CHAPTER 12

Sadie

In the morning, we took a cab across the river to Cambridge. It was a bright morning, and bitterly cold, and Elliott had wrapped a scarf around his neck in a way that I found disarmingly adorable.

Should I have been thinking that he was adorable? I wanted to fuck him.

But I wasn't supposed to want to fuck him. Maybe it was safer to think he was adorable.

The cab dropped us off in front of a nondescript brick-and-glass building, and then we walked for a few minutes across an open quad. It was Thursday, and students were out walking to classes, toting coffee cups and backpacks. A small group of boys shouted cheerfully and tossed snowballs at each other. Okay, not boys: they were men, technically, but they looked like babies to me. I had graduated from college less than a decade ago, but it felt like a thousand years.

I wasn't young anymore. I was an adult.

It was weird to think about.

"I think that's him," Elliott said, and I looked where he was pointing, to a man standing on the steps of a nearby building. He wore a huge down coat unzipped to reveal a plaid shirt, and his dark hair radiated from his head in a wiry halo—what my mom would admiringly call a *Jewfro*, and then look around to make sure nobody had heard her and was offended. She was always impressed when a white person could grow that much hair.

As we drew closer, the man came down the steps, hand extended, and said, "Are you Elliott Sloane?"

"That's me," Elliott said, shaking the proffered hand, and then turned to me and said, "This is Sadie Bayliss, my graphic designer."

If the man was surprised that Elliott had brought his designer on a business trip, he didn't show it. He shook my hand with a firm grip and said, "I'm Jim. It's a pleasure to meet you."

"Likewise," I said, smiling at him. I'd always thought geeks were supposed to be socially awkward weirdos, but Jim seemed relatively hygienic and normal. I sort of hoped that Elliott *would* hire him. He had an air about him—some light in his eyes, some curl of his mouth—that made me think he had a wicked sense of humor, and would be happy to help me play pranks on Elliott, or get beers after work and shoot the shit. I missed having co-workers I wasn't busy lusting after.

Jim led us into the building and down a long corridor lit with buzzing fluorescent lights and lined

114

with filing cabinets. The interior looked like it hadn't been updated since the 1960s: linoleum floors, white cinder block walls, and all the charm of a Soviet prison bloc. Every door we passed had a square of frosted glass set into it, and I wished I could peek inside at whatever mysterious experiments were taking place.

The corridor turned to the right, and Jim fished his keys out of his huge coat and stopped in front of a door with a sign on it that said: WARNING: GENIUS AT WORK.

I bit my tongue and, through a truly heroic effort, managed not to say anything.

Jim caught my look, though, and he grinned at me and said, "It's my labmate's. He thinks he's going to be the next Chomsky."

"I wasn't aware that Chomsky dabbled in ceramics," Elliott said.

Jim stared at him for a second, clearly nonplussed, and then laughed. "He's funny," he said to me. "Is he being funny?"

"I think he's *trying* to be funny," I said.

"I'll fire you," Elliott said, and I smirked up at him, because it was an empty threat and we both knew it.

Jim's lab was cluttered with—I didn't even know what. Machinery. Stacks of what looked like oversized coasters. I perched on a stool and tried not to touch anything. Elliott and Jim wandered around the lab and gesticulated at each other and used words I didn't understand. I still wasn't sure why

115

Elliott thought it was important for me to be here, but I didn't mind sitting and watching Elliott be businesslike and efficient, his brow furrowed as he explained something, his big hands tracing abstract shapes in midair.

I *liked* him.

Finally, after much longer than I would have thought possible, they stopped talking about ceramics and started talking about business. I perked up. Elliott was giving him the hard sell: salary, benefits, opportunities for glory.

"Yeah, I don't know," Jim said, running one hand through his hair and making it stick up even more than it already was. "My advisor's a little… I'm supposed to be finishing soon, and I don't think she'll be too happy if I like, decamp to New York and start working on something that is very clearly *not* my dissertation."

"Are you done with your research?" Elliott asked.

"Well, mostly," Jim said. "I mean, there's always more—but yeah, okay, I guess I'm pretty much done."

"I'm happy to be flexible with your schedule," Elliott said. "If you need to take a few hours a day to work on your dissertation, that can be arranged. And I won't need you to start for another month or two anyway."

What a persuasive, smooth-talking son of a bitch. Jim was going to crack: I could see it in his eyes. He was already halfway in love with Elliott, or maybe just with the silent promise Elliott made with his nice suit and his stylish hair. Everything about him said *I'm rich, and I'll make you rich, too*.

"Maybe if I send her weekly progress reports," Jim said, and Elliott smiled and tucked his hands in his pockets.

Case closed.

We left Jim in his lab, hyperventilating over the email he was drafting to his advisor, and walked back out into the cold. "You liked him, right?" Elliott asked me.

"Yeah," I said. "He seems like he'll be easy to work with."

Elliott nodded. "A little neurotic, but most scientists are. And the research he's doing is really promising. I think he'll be able to build the filter we need. And." He paused, and smiled, not looking at me, a little secret smile. "I just got an email from the gentlemen I met with last night. They want to invest in the company."

* * *

The good news buoyed us all the way home to New York. Elliott bought us a celebratory bottle of wine, and I drank more of it than I should have and ended up falling asleep. I woke with a start as we pulled into Penn Station, sitting up and wiping my mouth. I had a feeling I'd been drooling a little.

And, oh God, I had been sleeping with my head resting against Elliott's shoulder.

I was mortified, but he didn't say anything, and my embarrassment faded as we gathered our suitcases and went out into the train station. It was late afternoon, and we fought our way through the burgeoning rush hour crowds to the street.

It was snowing lightly. Elliott said, "I'll see you tomorrow. Don't set your alarm. We'll have a late start."

Bless the man. I'd never had a boss tell me to be deliberately late to work. It wasn't like we'd had a particularly strenuous trip to Boston, either. The train was just about the most relaxing way to travel. I said, "I'll be there at the crack of dawn, tapping my foot and wondering why you aren't there and ready to work."

He grinned at me and said, "Go home, Sadie."

I went home.

My apartment was dark and cold. I set down my bags in the quiet living room and turned on a lamp. Here I was: alone in my life.

Ugh. Self-pity was so unattractive.

I had a come-to-Jesus with myself while I cooked dinner. Nurturing my crush on Elliott had been fun, and I'd gotten a lot of emotional mileage out of it, but it was time to stop. It was no longer a harmless diversion. I had developed actual *feelings*, and I couldn't in good conscience let myself keep it up. Both because I had already met my lifetime quota of emotional pain, and because it was sort of creepy to obsess over someone without their knowledge or permission. That shit was okay in high school, but

118

Elliott and I were both adults, and I thought he would probably be pretty unnerved if he knew how much brainpower I had been devoting to thinking about his smile and his deliciously long fingers.

Maybe Regan and my mother were right. Maybe it was time for me to start dating again.

I had to get back on that horse eventually. And dating would help me redirect my emotional energy away from Elliott. The only way to deal with a crush was to mercilessly cut it off at the root, like ivy. And then hopefully it would wither and die, and I could stop feeling that giddy rollercoaster drop of my stomach every time Elliott glanced at me.

Okay. Decision made. I would put myself out there. I would smile at men in coffee shops.

And if someone asked me out, I would say yes.

I slept deeply and dreamlessly that night, as if my subconscious was soothed by my newfound resolve, and I woke at dawn ready to tackle the day's work. With two weeks left to go before the conference, Elliott and I were approaching my favorite part of any project: the last frantic rush of work, a blur of adrenaline and sleepless nights. Maybe I was a masochist, but something about panic brought out my best work, and I never felt more creative than when I was sweating bullets over a looming deadline.

I tried to give myself the leisurely morning Elliott had all but ordered, but I was full of new ideas for the website and wanted nothing more than to get to office and start working. And so as soon as I had finished my coffee, I got dressed and headed for the subway.

The office was empty when I arrived. I was a little surprised that I had beaten Elliott to work, but not unhappy. He needed to sleep more and worry less. I would make the website changes I had in mind and show them to him when he showed up. I turned on my computer and my desk lamp and got busy.

I was working on the Sponsors & Funding page, which was sadly devoid of any sponsors or funding. Elliott had written some pretty mediocre copy for me, and I worked on revising that, and then decided I might as well list the Boston investors. It wasn't official yet, of course, but Elliott said the money should come through within the next couple of weeks. It couldn't hurt to have them on the website. Having funding would give us an air of legitimacy that we badly needed.

The problem was, I had no idea what the investors' names were. Should I even *list* them by their names? Maybe they had a company.

I pushed my chair back and looked over at Elliott's desk. All of his paperwork was in hanging files in the bottom drawer. He didn't lock the drawer, and he didn't seem particularly protective of his papers. He had, on more than one occasion, handed over entire folders to me and told me to look through for whatever I needed. So I didn't think he would be upset if I looked for the names of the investors. They shouldn't be too hard to find. Elliott was meticulously organized, and labeled all of his folders with clear and precise descriptions—"2017 RECEIPTS FOR TAXES," "W.H.O. WATER STATISTICS."

So I went over and crouched in front of the drawer and flipped through the files. I felt a slight prickle of guilt, but I shook it off. As far as I knew, Elliott had nothing to hide. The folders were alphabetized, and I quickly found the one labeled "INVESTORS, POTENTIAL." It was fat with papers, and I pulled it out and tucked it beneath my arm.

The folder immediately before that one was labeled "INVESTORS, ACTUAL." Curious, I used two fingers to spread it open. There was a surprising number of papers inside—not many, but more than I expected, which was zero. Maybe Elliott had anticipated that the Boston men would agree to give him money and had preemptively switched their paperwork from one folder to the other.

I grabbed that folder, too, and went back to my desk to look through the paperwork. I started with "INVESTORS, ACTUAL." The top piece of paper was a print-out of an email. I scanned it quickly, looking for any mention of Boston.

But the email was dated November 14, and it didn't say anything about Boston at all.

It said something about funds being transferred.

Frowning, I went back to the beginning and read through the email more carefully. It was brief, and light on specifics, but it clearly said that red tape was delaying the promised funding, and that Elliott

121

would be kept abreast of any developments.

Why hadn't he told me about this? Boston was the first I had heard of *any* actual funding.

I went through the rest of the folder, one piece of paper at a time. There wasn't that much, maybe fifteen pages, and I didn't really understand what I was looking at. There was a company or organization called Uganda International Friendship, which seemed like a stupid name, and it seemed that they were funding Elliott, or attempting to fund him. And he hadn't said anything about it to me.

I ran a quick internet search on Uganda International Friendship and couldn't find anything relevant. Plenty of stuff about friendship missions and building schools, but nothing that seemed like it was the company in contact with Elliott. Not a single website. It was like the organization didn't even exist.

It was *weird*. That was all. And I didn't like that Elliott hadn't told me. But maybe he just didn't want to get my hopes up until he actually had the money in hand. That seemed like something he would do. It wasn't like I thought Elliott was doing anything underhanded or illegal. He wouldn't get involved in—God, money laundering or international smuggling or—I didn't even know. Tax shelters. Nazi gold. I was just a graphic designer; what did I know about any of this?

I put the papers back and turned my attention to "INVESTORS, POTENTIAL." Elliott had put the messages from the guys in Boston right on top, and they conveniently had the name of their organization in their email signatures. Easy. Problem solved. I updated the website and put both folders back in Elliott's desk, and did my best to put the weird mystery organization out of my mind.

Elliott finally rolled into the office around 10, holding a cup of coffee and looking like he had been awake for maybe half an hour. The dark circles beneath his eyes were a slightly paler shade of purple than usual, which I took as an encouraging sign.

"I thought I told you to sleep in," he said, taking off his coat and frowning at me.

"I got plenty of sleep," I said. "I'm full of beans. I want to get this website up and running."

He shook his head at me, slow and disappointed, like a parent who had just caught his toddler smearing paint all over the walls. "Workaholism," he said. "A potentially fatal disease."

I flipped him off, and he grinned.

I worked all day, intensely focused, and would have kept going into the evening if Elliott hadn't come over to my desk and said, "It's after five."

I looked up, feeling like I was surfacing from a dream. "What?"

"Go home," he said. "You can overwork yourself again on Monday. Have a good weekend."

"Right," I said, and rubbed my eyes. I was suddenly very tired. "Okay. You too."

It had started snowing that morning, just a light

dusting, but the flakes were coming down fast and heavy when I got outside. I sighed, dismayed. The evening commute would be a total shit-show, and I wanted to get home and put on my favorite pajamas, the really ugly flannel set with yellow ducks that Ben had bought for me years ago.

I didn't want to think about Ben.

A few blocks from the subway station, my phone rang. I fished it out of my bag and answered without looking at the screen. "Hello?"

"Yes, I'm calling for Sadie Bayliss," a woman's voice said.

"This is Sadie," I said. I pulled the phone away from my ear and glanced at the screen, but I didn't recognize the number.

"This is Tricia Evans with Airliner NY," she said. "You submitted an application recently, and I'd like you to come in for an interview."

"Oh," I said, and then, when her words sunk in, "*oh*. Yes, absolutely." Airliner NY was one of the top design agencies in the city. I had applied on a whim, never expecting to actually hear anything from them. A full-time job with Airliner was basically the Holy Grail. And I would have *benefits*.

I was getting ahead of myself. An interview didn't mean a job offer.

"I'm glad to hear it," she said. "How does Monday at 10 work for you?"

I would just have to tell Elliott I would be coming in late. "That would work great," I said.

"Terrific," Tricia said. "I have your email

124

address from the application, so I'll send you our address and directions. I'll see you on Monday morning."

We hung up, and I did a happy dance in the middle of the sidewalk until a passing man muttered, "Fucking tourists."

"I'm not a tourist," I snapped at him. He gave me a one-fingered salute and kept moving.

Lord, I loved New York.

CHAPTER 13

Elliott

I woke when my phone rang.

It was early, still: my apartment was filled with cold, gray light. I fumbled on my nightstand until my hand bumped into my phone, and I answered with my eyes barely cracked open. "Hello?"

"Elliott!" a voice said. I knew that voice. It was Carolina. "How are you?"

"Sleeping," I said.

"No!" she exclaimed. "You cannot be! You are three hours ahead."

"That's right," I said, and turned my head to look at the clock. "And it's only 7:00 here. On a Saturday morning. And I'm sleeping."

"You're awake now," she said, casually dismissive. "How have you been? We have not spoken in—"

"In less than a week," I said. "What do you think has happened to me in the last seven days? Do you think I've been kidnapped by smugglers? I haven't. You don't need to mount an expedition to

126

save me."

She laughed. "So grumpy! I *did* wake you."

"I don't know why *you're* awake," I said. "And drop the accent."

"Oh, fine," she said, her voice suddenly Jersey instead of Caracas. "Carter doesn't tell me to stop."

"Carter is a more patient man than I am," I said. "Hasn't anyone found your birth certificate yet? Don't they know you aren't actually from some exotic foreign locale?"

"Not yet," she said. "And you're not going to spill. I'm awake because we've been filming night scenes this month. It kind of sucks, but at least they have a lot of good food."

Carolina had moved out to Los Angeles a year ago to try her hand at acting, and had somehow landed a starring role in a show about a werewolf running for Congress, which had somehow become a smash hit. I thought the entire situation was ridiculous, but Carolina was happy, and I was happy for her. She and Carter and I grew up together, and even though I found her mystifying at times, she was still one of my dearest friends. "So the show is still going well?" I asked.

"That's why I called," she said. "We just got renewed for a second season! I'm going to negotiate a raise, and I think I might buy a house, so you and Carter need to fly out and help me pick something…"

She started talking about real estate agents and neighborhoods, and I closed my eyes and drifted—

not asleep, but heading there quickly.

"Elliott," Carolina said, startling me back to awareness. "You aren't listening."

"I'm listening," I lied. I needed to train this woman not to call me before 8.

"You aren't, but that's okay," she said. "I'll let it slide. What's this Carter tells me about a woman?"

I groaned. "There's no woman. Carter is blissfully in love and thinks everyone else should be, too. Whatever he told you is a lie."

"Carter doesn't lie," Carolina said. "He's too noble for that."

"He's an optimist," I said. "He's out of touch with reality. He also has an infant and is chronically sleep-deprived. I wouldn't listen to him."

"Hmpf," Carolina said. "Fine. But if anything happens, I expect to be the first to know! Don't make me find out second-hand from Carter!"

"Duly noted," I said. "I'm going back to sleep, now. Lovely talking with you." And then I hung up on her, tossed my phone back onto the nightstand, and pulled the covers over my head.

I needed new friends.

I managed to go back to sleep after that, and finally stumbled out of bed close to noon, gummy-eyed and fuzzy-headed. I felt absurd, but I also knew I needed the sleep. I had been working nonstop for weeks now, and a single lazy morning would do me more good than harm.

I checked my phone. Carolina had sent me a few rude text messages berating me for hanging up on her. I rolled my eyes and deleted them. I also had a message from Carter, asking if I wanted to get lunch. That one I replied to. *Of course. When and where?*

I went to take a shower, and when I got out, hair dripping down my back, Carter had responded. *12:30 at Paninoteca?*

Sounds good, I replied. I would have to get going: that was forty-five minutes from now, and Paninoteca was down in NoHo.

I arrived a few minutes late, and Carter was already seated near the windows at the front of the building, a pitcher of water on the table. "Sorry I'm late," I said, taking off my coat.

"I haven't been here long," he said. "And I didn't give you much notice."

"A man's got to eat," I said, and sat down. "I would have responded to your text sooner, but Carolina woke me up at the crack of dawn this morning, and I went back to sleep after and ended up passing out for about four hours."

Carter grinned. "Should I be hurt that she didn't call me?"

"Absolutely not," I said. "Maybe I should have a baby, too, and then she'll let me sleep in from time to time. Her show got renewed, apparently."

"That's terrific," Carter said. "God, she's hell on wheels, isn't she? What else did she want from you?"

"Help buying a house," I said. "I sort of fell back asleep at that point."

He laughed. "That's why I make you spend

time with me in person. It would be much harder for you to fall asleep in the middle of lunch."

"That sounds like a challenge," I said.

The waiter came to take our orders, and then Carter leaned toward me and said, "How are things going with the company?"

"Surprisingly good," I said. "I told you about the trip to Boston—"

He nodded.

"—well, those guys are interested in investing," I said. "Nothing's been finalized yet, so I'm not getting too excited, but it certainly seems promising."

"Congratulations," he said. "That's wonderful news. We should have some celebratory wine."

"Too early in the day for that," I said. "I haven't even been awake for two hours. And don't you have a wife to get home to?"

"She's at some baby yoga class," he said. "She told me to get out of the house and do something fun. I'm under strict orders."

"She thinks you work too much," I said. "I'm tempted to agree."

"No such thing," he said. "Anyway, I'm glad you've found some investors. It's a worthy cause."

"And now I'll actually be able to pay Sadie," I said, and rubbed a hand over my face. "Hiring her was a bad idea. I can't really afford it."

"You told me you had some start-up funding," Carter said, frowning at me.

"I do," I said. "My savings account. I've been paying her out of my own pocket, and the money won't last forever. These Boston guys are a good start, but they aren't offering me all that much funding. I need a larger commitment if I'm going to hire more employees and expand the company." He got a familiar gleam in his eyes, and I said, "Don't even think about it. I'm not taking your money."

"You're the most stubborn person I know," he said, "and I'm married to Regan, so I don't say that lightly."

"Sadie's worse," I said. "I can't believe you didn't warn me about her."

"The two of you deserve each other," he said. "The more I hear about your exploits, the more I'm convinced that I made an excellent decision in referring her to you."

"Stop matchmaking," I said. "You're worse than Carolina."

"The lady doth protest too much," he said, smirking.

"I'm going home," I threatened, but just then the waiter brought our sandwiches, and mine looked so good that it would be a shame to waste it.

CHAPTER 14

Sadie

On Monday morning, I woke up early and called Elliott to let him know I would be late to work. He didn't answer—maybe he'd taken my advice and was still at home—and so I left a message. I didn't try to sound sick or anything, and didn't make any excuses, just said I would be in late. I didn't intend to hide what I was doing.

I dressed up a little for the interview. Airliner didn't need a "look at me I'm quirky outfit"; they knew clothes had nothing to do with creativity. So I wore a pantsuit and a colorful blouse, and sensible heels. I wanted them to take me seriously.

I really wanted this job.

The office was in Soho, a light-filled loft on the top floor of a converted warehouse. The secretary, a perky white girl in her early twenties, smiled at me as I stepped out of the elevator, and said, "How can I help you?"

"I'm here for an interview with Tricia Evans," I said, returning her smile.

"You must be Sadie," she said, standing. "Right this way."

She led me toward the back of the building. I took full advantage of the opportunity to gawk. The workspace was open: no cubicles. People sat at long tables, clicking away at their top-of-the-line computers. In one corner, a sofa and several armchairs faced a white-board, and five or six people were having an animated discussion about the diagram a tall man was drawing. Leafy plants hung from the ceiling, trailing long tendrils down toward the floor.

And then I spotted it: not just a coffee maker, but a shiny espresso machine.

Oh God, I *really* wanted this job.

A row of offices lined one wall, each with a large window that looked out into the main room. The secretary led me to one and tapped on the doorframe. "Tricia? Your 10:00 is here."

I peeked in. Tricia was seated at her desk with stacks of papers arrayed around her. She smiled at me as she stood up and came over to the door. She shook my hand, her grip warm and firm, and said, "Sadie, thank you for coming. Thanks, Lulu."

"Sure thing," the secretary said, and left.

Really: *Lulu*? That sounded like a name for a child or a small dog, not an adult woman. But I kept my mouth shut and just said to Tricia, "Thanks for offering me the chance to interview."

"Yes, let's talk," Tricia said. She returned to her desk and shoved some papers aside to clear a small space. "Please, have a seat."

I sat, holding my bag in my lap. My heart beat rabbit-quick in my chest.

I was *nervous.* This job was everything I had ever wanted, and I didn't want to screw it up.

"I was really impressed with your portfolio," Tricia said. "Very fine work."

I glowed.

"Can you tell me a little bit about your design aesthetic?" she asked.

God bless Tricia. She had just tossed me the biggest softball of all time. I could talk about that for ten million years. "Well," I said, and drew in a deep breath.

Half an hour later, Tricia and I were laughing together like old friends. I knew, without her having to say anything, that I had aced the interview.

"We still have one other candidate to interview," Tricia said, standing. "But I'll be in touch. If I have any say in the matter, you'll be hearing from us very soon."

"Thanks," I said. My head was spinning. "Great. Thanks."

I gathered my things, and she walked me back to the elevator. "I think we'll put you at that desk by the window," she said, and winked at me.

Oh my God. I clutched my coat to my chest, too excited to speak.

We shook hands, and she said, "I'll call you soon. No later than tomorrow afternoon."

"Great," I squeaked, a frightened little mouse-squeak, too unaccustomed to good things happening to me that I didn't have any clue how to react.

Alone in the elevator, I curled my hands into fists, pressed my knuckles against my mouth, and let out a long, high-pitched noise, joy and terror bubbling inside me like the fizz in a soda bottle. Tricia *loved* me. She thought I was a *great designer*. She'd used the word "brilliant." I wanted to work there, in that light-filled office, with the espresso machine and the cheerfully bickering co-workers.

But I felt guilty about leaving Elliott.

Cart before the horse, Sadie. Airliner hadn't even offered me the job yet.

Elliott would be fine, anyway. I didn't owe him anything.

I couldn't worry about it now. I needed to book it to Midtown and hope Elliott wasn't too angry with me for skipping out on him. I couldn't imagine him yelling or anything, but I knew he was on a tight deadline, and every day counted. Maybe I would offer to do some work in the evening to make up for it.

The weekend's snowfall had turned into brown slush in the gutters and dirty, packed piles at every corner. By the time I reached Elliott's office, my boots were crusted with salt and my fingertips were frozen inside my mittens. But the inside of the building was warm and dry, and when I took the elevator up to the sixteenth floor, I was greeted with the sight of a rubber mat on the floor just inside the elevator, and a new floor lamp casting a wide yellow circle across the bare concrete.

Elliott, as always, was hunched over his desk. I wiped my feet against the mat and called out, "You've redecorated."

He looked up at me and smiled. "I decided it was time to stop tracking slush everywhere."

If I took this job at Airliner—if they offered it to me—Elliott wouldn't be my boss anymore.

And then, maybe…

Cart, horse.

I went to my desk and took off my coat and scarf. "I'm sorry I'm late," I said. "I hope you got my message."

"I did," he said.

That was evidently all he had to say about the matter. Talking with him could be pretty unnerving, because I was used to people who strung together more than three words at a time and gave me some hint as to what they were thinking. When Elliott felt like being inscrutable, he went all out. It put me on uneven footing. I wasn't sure of the right move. Should I apologize more? Leave it alone? Tell him I was a grown woman and could do whatever the hell I wanted?

I decided to just go directly to brutal honesty. "I had a job interview this morning," I said. "With a design agency. I think they're going to offer me the job."

An expression flickered across his face, too brief for me to identify. "Please let me know if they do," he said, and turned back to his computer.

Well, *okay*. Annoyed by his lack of a reaction, I booted up my laptop and got to work.

Irritation with Elliott's taciturn bullshit notwithstanding, I got so sucked into what I was doing that I worked straight through lunch and well into the afternoon without a break. I enjoyed branding work because there were so many different ways to go about creating a company's image, and the trick was to figure out how to do it in the most visually appealing and accessible way. It was like a puzzle: how to reach the right people and make them care about a product.

And then, mid-afternoon, my phone rang.

I snatched it up right away and walked away from my desk, heading into the dim recesses of the office. There wasn't anywhere really *private* unless I wanted to talk on the phone in the bathroom, but at least I could get more or less out of earshot before I answered.

I glanced behind me. Elliott was either ignoring me or pretending to.

I answered. "Sadie Bayliss."

"Sadie, this is Tricia Evans, with Airliner." I could hear the warmth in her voice: it was good news, then. "I've spoken with our partners, and we'd like to offer you the position."

The adrenaline rush was immediate and thrilling. I swayed on my feet a little, dizzied.

"That's terrific," I croaked out.

"I'll email you a written offer shortly," she said, "but I didn't want to keep you waiting. We can offer you 100 to start, and a competitive benefits package."

100? Did she mean 100 *thousand*? As in $100,000? That was $3,000 higher than what I made at my old job.

I was moving up in the world.

I opened my mouth to tell her yes, *yes*, oh God of course I will accept this wonderful, cushy job with a beautiful office and happy co-workers and benefits, but instead what came out was, "Wonderful. Thank you so much. I'll take a look at the offer and I'll be in touch."

Holy shit. Was I playing *hardball*?

"Of course, take your time," Tricia said. "We'd really like to make this work, Sadie."

I could have died and gone to heaven right then.

When I got off the phone, I went over to Elliott's desk and said, "They just offered me the job."

He spun his chair around to face me. "How much?"

"Not that it's any of your business," I said, "but $100,000. Plus benefits."

"I'll match it," he said immediately.

I frowned at him. "You can't afford that."

"The Boston investors," he said, which was a load of bullshit, because none of that was finalized yet. "I'd like to hire you on full-time."

My belly flipped. That was exactly what I wanted, if I was being honest with myself. I wanted to work with Elliott and help him make the company succeed. But the job security that Airliner offered was hard to turn down.

But the look he was giving me, clear and intense, with so much certainty behind it—

How could I say no to that look?

I sighed. "Let me think about it," I said.

* * *

I thought about it.

I thought about it all the way home on the subway, and all through my dinner preparations. I didn't cook as much as I used to, now that I was only making dinner for one, but recently I had decided that I needed to start making more of an effort and eating more vegetables. So I still cooked a lot of instant noodles for dinner, but now I added baby bok choy and carrots and pan-fried tofu and a hard-boiled egg, so at least it was more like an actual meal.

The fact of the matter was, I had drunk the Kool-Aid. I believed in what Elliott was doing. Yes, he was an idealist, but he was a *realistic* idealist. He understood that money made the world work. He was aiming high, but I thought he might actually be able to pull it off.

And I liked seeing him every day. If I went to work for Airliner, I probably wouldn't ever see him again.

I stopped mid-chop, knife posed over my cutting board, while the implications of that thought sunk in. Was I really considering passing up my dream job because of a *boy*?

Well. To be fair. He was no boy. He was most definitely a man.

But *still*.

"I'm going to do something really stupid," I said aloud, and decided that I needed to talk to Regan.

I texted her first, to make sure she wasn't in the middle of feeding the baby or something. *Can we talk?*

My phone rang a few minutes later, and when I picked up, Regan said, "Please say something to remind me that there's more in life than breastfeeding."

I grinned. "Feeling used, huh?"

"Caleb only loves me for my boobs," Regan said mournfully.

"Typical man," I said. "You need to get out of the house, girl. Tell Carter he's on baby duty tomorrow night. We'll go out for dinner."

"I can't leave the baby for that long," Regan said, sounding alarmed. Poor Regan. Sleep deprivation was really doing a number on her.

"You can and you should," I said. "You've still got a life. The kid's going to daycare when you start law school in the fall anyway, so he might as well start getting used to being without you. Carter can take care of him."

Regan sighed. "You're right. But I can't even leave him alone for fifteen minutes when he's sleeping. I have to go in there and check on him just to make sure he's okay. It's really sad, but—"

"I know, he's your slug creature and you love him," I said. "There's nothing wrong with loving a slug. But you need to get out of the house sometimes."

"Okay," Regan said. "You're right. We'll do dinner. But this isn't why you wanted to talk."

"No," I said. "Elliott offered me a job."

"That's great," Regan said. "I thought he couldn't afford to hire you on full-time."

"He's got some funding now," I said. "Or, he'll have it soon. That trip to Boston, you know. But, okay, I also had a job interview this morning with a big design agency, and they want to hire me. So I told Elliott, and he said he would match their offer. And I'm just—I don't know what to do."

"Well, which job do you want more?" Regan asked.

"I don't know," I wailed. "That's the problem. I can't decide. Airliner—the design agency—is basically my dream job, and Elliott works in a creepy office and refuses to turn on the overhead lights because he wants to save money—"

Regan laughed. "Does he really? That doesn't surprise me at all."

It occurred to me that I could pump Regan for information about Elliott. "What do you know about him?" I asked.

"Oh, I don't know," she said. "I don't know him too well. He was in Africa for a long time. I met him once right after Carter and I got engaged, when he was back for a visit, but then he left again."

I frowned. "Wait a second, I thought he was just in Uganda for the last year."

"No, he was in East Africa for like, five years. I don't really know the whole story. I think he's been abroad for years. Maybe a decade or more. He's an unusual guy."

"Sounds like it," I said. Not as much of an idealist as I had thought, then. Any wide-eyed naiveté was probably long gone after a decade overseas.

Or maybe he was one of those people who just stubbornly refused to give up on hope.

"Well, you know," Regan said. "You're working for him. He's really happy with you, by the way. He had lunch with Carter over the weekend and apparently he couldn't stop talking about how great you are and how you really understand his vision, or something."

"His vision?" I asked, pleased despite myself. "Is that really what he said?"

"Okay, not *exactly*, but I think that was more or less what he meant," she said. "Look, if you want the scoop on him, all I know is that Carter trusts him."

"Sound enough endorsement for me," I said. "Carter's a suspicious bastard. Okay. I know you can't make the decision for me. I guess the fact that I'm so conflicted sort of indicates what my decision is going to be."

"Even if it doesn't work out, this isn't the last job you'll ever have," Regan said. "So maybe do whatever will make you the happiest, at least for the time being."

"You're so wise," I said. "Is that something that happens automatically when you reproduce?"

She laughed. "I'm just talking. I haven't slept for more than four hours in a row in like, two months. I don't think you should listen to me at all until Caleb is at least a year old."

And that right there was why I was *never* having kids. I liked my sleep. "I'll keep it in mind," I said. "Thanks anyway. I'll text you about dinner tomorrow, okay? Don't punk out! Carter can watch that baby for a few hours. He knows what he's doing."

"Caleb stops crying as soon as Carter picks him up," Regan said. "It's incredible. He's the baby whisperer. I'll see you tomorrow."

We hung up, and I sighed heavily. It wasn't really Regan's job to tell me what to do, but I'd been hoping she'd make the decision for me anyway.

Well. I would just have to decide for myself, like a real grownup.

I did the dishes and thought about it. Really, I already knew what I wanted. Airliner was a dream, but my heart was with Elliott's work, and with Elliott. I was an idiot. It *mattered* to me, what he was doing. I wanted him to succeed. I wanted to help him succeed.

I blew out a long breath of air and looked up at the darkened window above my kitchen sink. My own face stared back at me, my braids and thin mouth reflected with the overhead light glowing behind my head. I had already survived the worst thing that could happen to me. Ben was dead, but I wasn't dead yet. I still wanted to live.

I would live, and be happy.

The next morning, I walked into the office feeling like a million bucks. I strode directly to Elliott's desk and paused there, waiting for him to acknowledge me.

He raised his eyebrows, but didn't look up from his computer. "Can I help you?"

"I accept your job offer," I said. "I'll work for you."

That got his attention. "What about the design agency?"

"I'm going to tell them thanks but no thanks," I said. "We're going to have to make some changes, of course," I said. "We need better lighting. And maybe a mini-fridge. I like snacks."

For a moment, he looked like he was going to argue, but then he just shook his head and said, "Sure. Whatever you want." He tipped his chair backward and gave me a speculative look. "Dare I ask what convinced you?"

"You conned me, you jerk," I said. "I care about clean water now. I'm all in. Congratulations."

"Okay," he said, and grinned. "If you're that devoted to the cause, you won't object to going to a fundraiser with me this weekend."

Shit. "I can't," I said. "I've got, uh. I have plans." Eating dinner on the couch in my pajamas, actually. But Elliott didn't need to know that.

"Right," he said. He smirked at me. "Plans. Since they're so vague and unspecific, you can probably reschedule."

"Do I have to?" I asked. Whined, really. Pathetic. I had never been to a fundraiser, but I had an idea that they were very stuffy and involved people wearing black tie attire eating tiny food. Not exactly my idea of a good time.

"Yes," he said. "Sorry. I'm exerting my authority as your boss. It's a silent auction for a variety of international aid organizations, and it will be a good opportunity for networking. And I absolutely detest networking, so I need you there to be charming to old men with deep pockets."

"I don't charm," I said, even though I was flattered that he thought I would be able to. "Also— okay. This sounds like the sort of event where everyone is white and they keep looking at me like maybe I got confused and wandered into the wrong building."

He gave me a startled look. "I don't think you need to worry about that," he said. "There will be lots of aid workers there, and former Peace Corps types, and diplomats. They tend to be a liberal and multi-ethnic group."

"I guess so," I said, even though I wasn't totally reassured by his assessment of the situation. "But I don't have anything to wear, so I can't go."

He grinned, and I realized too late that I had misstepped. "Oh, Sadie," he said. "Is that your only objection? I'll have a dress delivered to your house tomorrow morning."

"I'm not going to let you buy me a ball gown," I said. "That's ridiculous."

"Of course not," he said. "I'll borrow one. You're about the same size as one of my sisters. You're a little shorter, but you can wear heels. I'll raid her closet."

"I hope your sister has good taste," I said, "and if so, please let her pick. I don't trust a man to dress me."

"I'll have you know I have impeccable taste," he said. "All right. I'll make a deal with you: if you hate the dress I send over, you don't have to go to the auction. But if you like it even a little bit, you have to come."

"I have a feeling I'm going to regret this," I said, and he laughed at me and turned back to his laptop.

I sighed. I also had a feeling that Elliott would look entirely too appealing in a tuxedo.

CHAPTER 15

Elliott

Sadie didn't keep me waiting on Saturday evening. I texted her when I arrived at her apartment, and she appeared in the doorway mere moments later. She wore a black coat over her dress, but it ended at her knees, and below that her sapphire-blue gown flowed like liquid around her ankles. A narrow headband held her braids away from her face, and her long earrings brushed against the side of her neck as she carefully picked her way down the front steps.

She looked lovely.

I leaned against the car I had hired for the evening, arms folded, watching her come down the sidewalk toward me. "I guess you found the dress acceptable, then."

She rolled her eyes at me, and then, in an instant, tripped on the sidewalk and fell toward me, her eyes wide and frightened.

I caught her in my arms, the small solid weight of her, and held her until she got her footing again.

The scent of a crisp, citrus perfume rose from her skin. I was immediately aroused.

"Oh God, I'm sorry," she said, pulling away from me and raising one hand to touch her hair. "I wear heels all the time; you'd think I would actually know how to walk in them."

"No need to apologize," I said. I was intensely grateful for my long coat that covered the front of my trousers. "I know it's more difficult than it looks."

She raised an eyebrow at me. "You do?"

"Not from experience, of course," I said. "But I do have three sisters." I opened the door to the back seat of the car and gestured her inside. "After you."

"I feel so fancy," she said, when we were both settled and I had told the driver to head out. She smoothed her gown over her knees. "This nice dress, a hired car driving me around… It's like being a princess."

"Your hair looks different," I said inanely.

"Yeah, I did a French twist. I don't usually wear it like this. Do you like it?" She turned her head from side to side, holding one hand up behind her neck, posing extravagantly.

"I do like it," I said. Our eyes met. She looked down and away, her face unreadable.

Damn it.

It seemed that I was always overstepping my bounds with Sadie: saying the wrong thing, being too forward. Sometimes she seemed receptive, almost flirtatious, but then she would shut down unexpectedly. I was terrible at predicting when it

148

would happen, or why.

I never wanted to make her uncomfortable.

We rode in silence for a few minutes, and then she said, "So tell me what to expect at this fundraiser. I've never been to one. Is there going to be free food?"

I smiled, relieved that she had broken the awkward silence so that I didn't have to fumble around for something to say. "Sadie, there will be more free food than you can imagine," I said, and we spent the rest of the ride discussing social functions past and present and the various finger foods I had encountered over the years.

The fundraiser was taking place at a large converted industrial space in Chelsea. We arrived about half an hour after the event began, and well-dressed party-goers were milling around the sidewalk, laughing and talking. The building's large glass doors glowed with a warm yellow light, and lanterns shone from each window.

"Fancy," Sadie said.

"That's your word for the evening," I said, taking her hand to help her out of the car.

She smiled up at me. "I think it's an appropriate word, don't you?"

We went inside. The coat check was in a small room near the entrance to the building, and from the line stretching out into the hallway, it seemed they were understaffed. There was no helping it; I didn't want to carry my coat around all evening.

We got in line, and Sadie immediately occupied

herself with gawking at the decorations and the well-dressed revelers. I sometimes forgot that she'd had a very normal, middle-class upbringing and wasn't inoculated to blatant displays of wealth the way I was. The expression on her face was the same as it had been when we first walked into the hotel in Boston: wonder mixed with a bit of skepticism.

The wonder I could understand, although I had never felt it, and the skepticism endeared her to me, maybe more than it should have. She seemed to regard anything she considered *fancy* as being somewhat akin to a tiger: beautiful, deadly, and not at all practical as a part of everyday life. She enjoyed the zoo excursion, but was always happy to go home.

"Elliott? Elliott Sloane?"

The voice came from behind me. I turned, and smiled as I recognized Walter Verhaegen, an old friend of my mother's. I hadn't seen him in years, but he and my mother were friends from childhood, and he had always been kind to me.

We shook hands, and he said, "It's so good to see you. I heard rumors that you were back in New York, but I'm glad to have it confirmed with my own two eyes."

Sadie tapped me on the shoulder. "I'll take your coat," she said, and I gave her a grateful nod, handed over my coat, and stepped out of line.

Walter was just as I remembered him: friendly, engaging, and genuinely interested in what I was up to. He had the knack of asking just the right questions and setting a person at ease. It was a quality I admired and wished I could imitate, but conversation had never come that easily to me.

"Well, I won't keep you," he said at last, after he had somehow gotten me to tell him the entire story of my return to New York and attempt to start my own company. "There's that lovely lady of yours. Enjoy your evening."

He must have meant Sadie, and I turned to see her coming toward me, empty-handed, shoulders bare and burnished by the yellow light.

Watching her walk across the room was one of those moments that I knew I would remember until the day I died.

Kris had chosen a *good* dress.

Sadie stood beside me, smiling, glowing, and said, "Shall we?"

I held out my arm, and she slid her hand around the crook of my elbow. "Let's."

We went out into the large, open room where the auction was being held. The room was lined with tables, each one bearing goods up for bid: handicrafts, gift certificates, vacation packages. Each table doubled as an information booth for the aid organization that had provided the item being auctioned. Guests mingled with the aid workers staffing the event, and waiters circulated with trays of champagne and finger foods. Gauzy white fabric draped from the metal beams criss-crossing the ceiling. It had the effect of making the room seem smaller, cozier. Somewhere to make friends, and ideally agree to donate massive sums of money to an organization.

I paused in the doorway, a bit overwhelmed by the crowd.

"That's a lot of people," Sadie said.

"We'll have to linger on the outskirts," I said, "snatch whatever food comes our way, and hope nobody notices us." I tried to keep my voice light, as if I were joking, but the truth was, I would have been very happy to hide in a corner for a few hours and then sneak out unnoticed.

"No way," Sadie said. "You need to mingle, right? Let's get us a fat investment tonight. I'm going to make it happen."

I grinned, amused as always by her bravado. "That's why I brought you. I'll find you a nice old man to chat with and he'll have signed over his estate by the end of the evening."

"I like nice old men," she said. "As long as they aren't the creepy kind."

I drew in a breath. Once more unto the breach. With Sadie at my side, I waded into the sea of people. There was work to be done.

I made my way for a table on the other side of the room, one staffed by an old friend who had told me he would be here tonight. Along the way, I snagged a glass of champagne from a passing waiter and downed it in one gulp. I would need the fortification.

As I wove my way through the crowd, I scanned the room for Eric's distinctive red hair, and when I spotted it, I course-corrected toward his table.

When he saw me approaching, he broke into a wide grin and came around the side of the table to give me an appropriately manly hug and slap on the back.

"Jesus, Elliott, it's good to see you," he said, when we pulled apart. "It's been years."

"Hey, I told you to come visit me in Uganda, but you were too lazy," I said, and drew Sadie forward. "Sadie, this is Eric. We worked together in Kenya for a while."

"Charmed," Eric said, taking Sadie's hand in his own. I rolled my eyes. Eric loved women, and had slept his way through our NGO's entire roster of female volunteers and employees, even the ones who were married or two decades his senior. I waited for him to make a fawning comment about Sadie's appearance. Instead, he said, "I didn't know you'd gotten married, Elliott."

I nearly choked on my own tongue. Sadie looked up at me with wide eyes, and I smiled at her in a way that I hoped was reassuring rather than panicked. "Sadie is my employee, Eric."

He raised his eyebrows. "My mistake. Apologies. Does that mean I can ask her out for dinner?"

Sadie laughed. "Absolutely not. I don't go out for dinner with strange men."

"But we aren't strangers now," he said. "We've been introduced. So that makes it perfectly acceptable."

Sadie gave him a sly look, like she was actually *considering* it, and that was the last straw for me. I wasn't going to stand there while Eric blatantly hit on my—on Sadie. "Eric, great to see you again," I said, through clenched teeth. "We need to go do some networking, but maybe we can get a drink later, after you're done here." And after Sadie was safely on her way home.

Eric smirked at me like he knew exactly what I was thinking, but for once in his life he kept his mouth shut and simply said, "I'm looking forward to it. Sadie, a pleasure."

Greatly daring, I put my hand on Sadie's bare back, right between her shoulder-blades, and guided her away. Her skin was soft as silk, and blood-warm. The thought of Eric touching her, even *looking* at her, made a black rage churn inside my gut. I would never let it happen.

"He seemed nice," Sadie said, as we moved off into the crowd.

Nice. For fuck's sake.

My attraction to her was no revelation. I had been aware of my desire since our very first meeting. But slowly, over the last several weeks, we had become friends. I appreciated Sadie's shapely body, but I also admired her quick mind and off-beat sense of humor. It wasn't until Boston that I realized the full weight and meaning of my feelings for her. Sitting together on the bed in her hotel room, watching that awful television show, I was struck by how much I enjoyed her company. Without my awareness or permission, I had come to care for her.

It was a problem. No torrid fling would satisfy

me. I wanted the real thing: love, laughter, a life together. But she was my employee, and the power imbalance meant that if I propositioned her, I could never be sure she hadn't said yes simply out of fear of losing her job. Sexual exploitation was hardly the basis for a meaningful relationship. I never wanted to do anything that would make her uncomfortable.

But I still wanted her.

Behind me, Sadie asked, "Where are we going?"

I didn't have an answer.

Then, halfway across the room, I spotted one of the people I'd hoped to run into tonight: Gerald Hawthorne, wealthy philanthropist and notorious codger. He hated everyone, but I had a feeling that he might like Sadie—and if he liked her, he might be willing to give me some money. My plan was very simple: toss Sadie in Hawthorne's direction and hope they hit it off. Sadie would be displeased with me, I was sure, but I had survived worse things than a woman's wrath.

"We're going this way," I said, and steered her toward Hawthorne's distinctive white hair, thick and bushy as a lion's mane.

I knew Hawthorne primarily by reputation. He and my mother had traveled in similar circles, and I had been introduced to him a handful of times before I quit Harvard and left the country. I had no expectation that he would recognize or remember me, but as Sadie and I approached, he turned from the woman he was speaking with and boomed,

"You're Clara's boy, aren't you?"

"I'm afraid I am," I said, and we shook hands. His grip was firm enough to crush bone.

"What have you been up to, son?" he asked. "Last I heard you were still in East Africa somewhere." He glanced at the woman with him, and she touched his shoulder and slipped off into the crowd. Not a social encounter, then. We were talking business.

I drew Sadie forward, my fingertips on her back, steadying her at my side. "I'm recently returned," I said, "and I've started a company to develop a new water filter."

Hawthorne threw back his head and laughed. "So this is your lovely underling," he said, smiling at Sadie, "and you're setting her loose on me to charm me into giving you money."

"That's the idea," I said. "Will it work?"

"Elliott, you're terrible," Sadie said.

"Ah, I like her already," Hawthorne said. "Tell me your name, my dear. Sloane, that's enough of you, now."

Satisfied, I left them and went to forage for some hors d'ouevres.

I circulated, glad-handing as I went, and made a few bids on items I was sure I wouldn't win. I knew very few people in attendance, but the hapless aid workers manning each table were more than happy to give me the full spiel about their organizations, and I got sucked into an interesting conversation about international development as a

156

form of neocolonialism.

When the auction closed, and a tall woman stepped behind a podium to begin announcing the results, I realized I had no idea where Sadie was.

I had been keeping one eye on her as she spoke with Hawthorne. They were easy to track: his white head floating above the crowd, and her energetic hand movements tracing wide arcs between them. But at some point during my conversation I got so caught up in trying to frame the perfect argument that I forgot to monitor Sadie's movements; and by the time I remembered, and looked for her again, she was gone.

It wasn't cause for concern. Likely she had gone to the bathroom, or stepped outside for a breath of fresh air. There was no danger here, among all of these people, and at any rate she was a grown woman, and more than capable of taking care of herself.

To hell with it. I was worried anyway.

I waded through the crowded room, searching for Sadie, accidentally elbowing a few society matrons in the process. Behind me, the woman at the podium read off a name, and the gathered crowd broke into polite applause. I didn't see Sadie anywhere.

I went out into the foyer, where a few clusters of people were gathered, talking quietly. Still no Sadie. She wasn't in the coat room, or on the back patio. I loitered near the restroom for a few minutes, waiting to see if she emerged, but all I got for my efforts was a few strange looks from women going in and out.

Frustrated, and beginning to feel slightly panicked, I climbed the wide, curving spiral stairs to the second floor of the building.

Upstairs was deserted, white-walled, silent. Doorways opened off a long corridor, each one casting a square of light onto the floor. I moved toward the first entrance, my dress shoes clicking along the concrete floor, and then I stopped in the doorway when I saw who was inside the room.

Art lined the walls, framed photographs and black-and-white line drawings, and Sadie stood gazing at them, her back to me, her body a narrow column in her blue gown. It was a good color on her. I took a step forward, stopped, thought about it—but Sadie had turned at the sound of that single footstep, and it was too late for me to go back downstairs.

She offered me a smile. "Following me?"

It was too close to the truth. I didn't respond. I walked into the room and stood at her shoulder, gazing at what she was looking at: a photograph of a woman diving underwater, the sea dark blue around her and shattered by light.

"Nice picture," I said.

"I just read an article about freediving," she said. "If you dive deep enough, you don't have to keep kicking. Gravity takes over, and it just tugs you straight on down."

"Sounds terrifying," I said.

She shrugged. "It sounds kind of peaceful to

me."

"Sadie," I said, and she turned to look at me, her eyes wide and dark, and bright as the sun.

I could have turned away, in that moment. I should have. I should have returned to the auction and left Sadie to examine her pictures in peace.

I didn't.

I raised my hand and touched her cheek.

Her breath caught.

The familiar urge rose within me: to claim her, to make her mine. To show her, beyond a shadow of a doubt, that she belonged to me.

She looked up at me, her eyes wide and shining, her lips parted. She wanted me to kiss her. The desire was written on her face and in the way she trembled, ever so slightly, at my touch.

It was a terrible idea, and it would probably get me sued—but I had done worse and survived it. But I wanted her, and I was tired of waiting.

"Sadie," I said, and moved my free hand to her waist.

"'Scuse me, is there a bathroom up here?"

I jerked away from her like I had been burned. The man behind us, slumping in the doorway, glassy-eyed, clearly drunk, was no threat. But his interruption dumped metaphorical ice water on my ardor. Reality returned. Sadie was off limits. Kissing was out of the question.

"I'm sorry," she said, looking down, touching her cheek where my hand had been. She brushed past me, squeezed past the man still leaning against the doorframe, and disappeared toward the stairs.

CHAPTER 16

Sadie

I went to my favorite spinning class on Sunday afternoon. Afterward, when the guy who always smiled at me flashed his pearly whites, I smiled back.

It was just a smile, but it gave me a little thrill to be so forward. I had never paid much attention to him before—never *let* myself pay attention—but he was a good-looking guy, all dark curly hair and brown skin, and he had been devotedly trying to flirt with me for at least six months. It felt good to be interested.

He started making his way across the room toward me, and I wiped my sweaty face on my towel, hoping I looked at least somewhat presentable. Then I decided it was stupid to worry. He'd been looking at my sweaty clothes and wild, sweaty hair for months now, and it hadn't scared him off. If you weren't a disgusting mess after spinning, you weren't doing it right.

Then he was there, standing beside my bike, looking at me with one eyebrow raised, smiling. "I thought you would never give me the time of day."

I laughed, embarrassed and happy, and wiped my face again. "I guess I didn't miss my window, though," I said.

"For you," he said, "the window never closes." He extended his hand, and we shook. He had a firm grip, and his palm was just as sweaty as mine. "I'm Tavares."

"Sadie," I said. He hadn't let go of my hand.

"Sadie," he said, rolling my name around in his mouth. "Look, I'm going to be straight with you. I want to take you out. Let's go get something to eat."

"Right now?" I asked, laughing, a little overwhelmed.

"Right now," he agreed. "Spinning makes me hungry enough to eat an entire cow. There's a good burger place down the block. What do you think?"

I hesitated. I was thinking of Elliott, of his hand on my face, of his other hand touching my hip. I shoved those thoughts down deep, tamped them down where they couldn't bother me. Tavares was attractive, interested in me, and *not my boss*. Okay: game on. "I think a burger sounds really good right now."

We bundled into our coats and went down the street to the burger place. It was 5:00, too early for dinner in New York, and we were able to claim two prime seats at a long counter by the window, looking out on the pedestrians bustling around in the lowering dark.

Tavares talked more than he ate. I knew his

entire life story within about fifteen minutes. He was a marketing director at an ad agency in Dumbo, volunteered at a nearby community center, and called his mother every weekend. He was funny, engaging, and easy to talk to. We got into a heated debate about the relative merits of PhotoShop versus Lightroom.

It was like Jesus had sent him to earth to be the perfect boyfriend for me. Okay, Lord: I could take a hint.

But I felt like I was hanging out with my brother.

I tried to feel a spark. I really did. I even "accidentally" brushed our hands together. And still: nothing.

Elliott had ruined me for other men.

After, standing on the sidewalk outside the restaurant, he said, "I'd like to see you again."

I felt terrible. Who did I think I was, to turn down this kind and interesting man? But I had to do it. I couldn't leave him to languish in false hope. "Look, you're really great…"

He groaned and hung his head, shaking it slowly. "Right. Say no more. At least tell me that you think I'm great and you're just hung up on another man."

"I mean, you won't believe me now, but that's actually the problem," I said. "I wish I could date you. You *are* great. My mother would love you."

"Well, if you ever change your mind," he said, "or if the other guy ends up breaking your heart, I'll

163

be at spinning every Sunday."

I smiled at him, wishing that I felt something, wishing that life could be less complicated than it always, inevitably was. "I'll keep that in mind."

And then I walked home in the dark.

* * *

Monday marked the start of our final week before the conference. Elliott knew it too, because he was already in a frenzy of work by the time I arrived at the office, and he barely looked up to greet me when I set my things down on my desk—just glanced up and grunted before he went back to rifling through a stack of paperwork.

Fine. We could ignore each other. I still felt awkward about what had happened at the fundraiser on Saturday night, and I didn't want to talk to him either. I needed some time to lick my wounds: humiliation, anger, a little bit of wistful sorrow about Tavares. Fear that I was betraying Ben, guilt for my disloyalty, and also a hot, tense, claustrophobic feeling, like I was suffocating, like I was lying beside him in the coffin and unable to fight my way out.

He still haunted me. Little ghost, little lost love. That hollow place in my chest that would never be filled.

These were melancholy thoughts for a sunny Monday morning. I made a big pot of coffee and got to work.

When I took a break for lunch, Elliott approached my desk and said, "We'll need to work late tonight."

I paused in unwrapping my sandwich and looked up at him. "Why's that?"

He met my eyes, a quick hot glance like wildfire, and looked away again. "It's the website," he said. "I heard from the conference organizers today. They want a working website by tomorrow evening."

"But I'm still doing the—"

"I know," he said, stiff and distant as the North Pole. "It isn't your fault. I'll help you. I'll finish the coding. Let's finish it tonight, and then you can sleep in tomorrow morning."

"I guess so," I said. It was so strange to feel awkward around him again, as uncertain as I had been when I first started working for him. I didn't know what he was thinking, and I wanted to talk about Friday, to have him reassure me that everything was okay, but I didn't know how to ask him for that. "Okay. You're going to order pizza, right?"

He raised an eyebrow, and for the first time that day he actually seemed like himself. "Pizza," he repeated. "How… proletarian. Surely we can do better."

"Indian food," I said, and then, "Korean barbecue?"

"Now you're talking," he said.

After my initial rush of panic, I had to admit to

myself that the website really *was* almost ready, and that finishing it tonight was within the realm of possibility. I stayed hunched over my computer through the late afternoon, until the light faded so much that I had to get up and turn on the lamps. My spine cracked. I stretched my arms over my head, working the stiffness out of my body, and turned my head to see Elliott watching me.

I couldn't read his expression. He stood directly beneath one of the floor lamps, and his face was half-hidden in shadow. He looked mysterious and remote, like he was a stranger and not the man I had grown so fond of over the past month. I *was* fond of him. There was no point in denying it anymore. My failed date with Tavares had shown me that much.

"Are you hungry?" he asked. He took a step toward me, and the light shifted on his face. It still didn't tell me anything useful. His expression was mild, pleasant, meaningless.

I shook my head. "Soon, probably. Maybe another hour. I'll keep working. It was just getting too dark to see."

He nodded. "I'll order the food now. They always take a while." He paused, and I waited for him to continue, but after a long moment he turned away.

I worked. I was dimly aware of Elliott rustling around at his desk, and then, after some time, putting on his coat and leaving; and then, some time after that, I heard the elevator doors open, and the smell of Korean barbecue wafted toward me.

My mouth watered. I rolled my chair back from my desk, instantly starving. "Is that dinner?"

Elliott came around the low divider that blocked the elevator from my sight, a big paper bag in his arms, his cheeks red from the cold. "It's dinner," he said. He set the bag on his desk and began pulling out plastic containers of food. "And. A bottle of wine."

"Drinking at work?" I asked. "Human Resources won't be too happy about that."

"Oh, I've done far worse," he said, which was entirely too intriguing.

We sat at his desk and ate. I was too hungry to care about good manners, and I spent the first several minutes shoveling food into my mouth at a rapid clip without making any attempt at conversation. When the worst of my hunger was satisfied, I slowed, drank a few sips of the really quite good wine, and studied Elliott's profile as he worked on his ribs.

He was a bad idea, the worst I'd ever had, and I was still a mess over Ben. I needed to get my house in order before I invited anyone inside.

But I wanted him.

Impulsively, I said, "Can I ask you a question?"

He finished chewing, swallowed, and said, "Apparently you can."

I rolled my eyes. "It's just a figure of speech, Elliott."

He gave me a thin smile and poured some more wine into his coffee mug. "I know. Yes, you can ask me a question."

Well, I didn't really want to ask him after all that, but I was still curious, so I bit the bullet. "How did you end up in Uganda?"

He wiped his fingers on a napkin and leaned back in his chair. He gave me a long, narrow look, and I half-expected him to tell me to mind my own business, but he only said, "It's a long story."

"I'm not in a hurry," I said. "Indulge me."

He frowned. I knew I was pushing him, especially when things between us were still so raw and unsettled after the silent auction. But I wanted to know. I held his gaze, refusing to look away or admit defeat, and after a few moments he shrugged and said, "I dropped out of Harvard partway through my junior year."

I leaned closer, already entranced. I still knew so little about him. "You went to Harvard?"

His mouth twisted. "Of course. Only the best for my father's only son." His voice had a dry, hard edge to it that I didn't understand. He took another sip of wine. I thought maybe that was all he was going to say on the subject, but then he shrugged again, like he was making a decision, and said, "We traveled a lot when I was a kid. Mainly in Europe. I saw all the sights. I thought I knew everything there was to know about the world. But then I took an anthropology class on a whim, just to fill a requirement, and we read an essay by a man, a medical doctor, who opened a hospital in rural Haiti. He treated a lot of people with tuberculosis, and he talked about the barriers to treatment, how the medicine cost more than an entire extended family made in a month, how his patients would spend ten hours on a bus to get to the clinic, and most of them died anyway. I didn't know anyone still got tuberculosis. I thought it was something tragic young poets died of in the 1800s. I realized that I didn't know anything about the world at all."

"So you dropped out," I said, a little awed, at least in part by Elliott stringing that many sentences together in a row.

He nodded. "I backpacked for a while and gazed at my navel. I felt very sorry for myself for a long time. Then I decided that even though I had no actual skills, I was smart and could follow directions, and surely there was something I could do to make a difference. I started volunteering with various international aid organizations, and after a few years I got a job with MSF."

"What's MSF?" I asked.

"Médecins Sans Frontières," he said. I kept looking at him blankly, and he sighed and said, "Sorry. Doctors Without Borders."

"Wow," I said. "They won the Nobel Peace Prize, right?"

"Several years ago," he said, nodding, and then shrugged. "I was involved with clean water work for several years, and I spent a lot of time digging wells that caved in a year later. It seems to me there must be a better solution." He glanced at me from the corner of his eye. "I don't mean to bore you. I don't talk about this very much, so I don't have my one-minute summary perfected."

"I don't want a summary," I said fiercely. "I asked you because I'm interested. I think it's really cool that you've been so many different places, and that you're so determined to help people. I've never been anywhere, and I've never helped anyone, except maybe my downstairs neighbor who can't figure out how to use the internet."

"Hmm," he said. "You're helping me."

"That doesn't count," I said. "You're paying me."

He looked at me, and I looked back, studying his face in the dim lamplight. I felt like we were the only two people alive in the whole world, safe and warm in our cocoon, in the warm glow of the light, with the wine and food settling in my belly and making *me* glow. I didn't care about the conference or the website. I just wanted to be alone with Elliott.

"What's your family like?" I asked. If he'd answered one invasive question, maybe he would answer another.

"Rich," he said. "Complicated."

I smiled. "Isn't everyone's? I mean, not the rich part, obviously."

"Obviously," he said, dry as the desert.

"My family's pretty complicated," I said. Give a little to get a little. "My brother's gay, and my parents still haven't really accepted it. They're trying, and my dad's really making an effort, but my mom keeps acting like he'll grow out of it and settle down with a nice girl."

"That must be hard for him," Elliott said.

"I think he's used to it," I said. "They haven't stopped inviting him for Sunday dinner, so he's just waiting them out. Sooner or later they'll have to admit defeat."

"What does your brother do?" Elliott asked, so polite, so carefully interested, and I wondered who had taught him these social graces. I was sure he had been taught: he was too abrupt and taciturn to have an innate gift of small talk.

"He teaches high school math," I said. "In East Harlem. He's getting pretty fed up with the administration, though, so I'm not sure how much longer he'll last."

"I imagine that's a challenging job," Elliott said, smooth as the surface of a still pond, and I realized he was doing this on purpose: getting me to talk about my own family to avoid having to talk about his.

Very sneaky.

He finished his ribs and poured the rest of the wine into my coffee mug. "We need another bottle," he announced.

I would be on the floor if we finished another bottle, but maybe the alcohol would help ease the strange tension crackling between us. "Sure," I said. "I'll have a little more wine."

He went out again, bundled into his coat, and I made some final tweaks to the website's style sheet. The wine made me feel blurry, as if some great invisible hand was taking an eraser to my edges. We *would* finish tonight, somehow, miraculously, if Elliott finalized the coding as he said he would.

The elevator doors opened again, and Elliott came toward me, bearing wine.

"Great," I said, holding out my mug. "Let's do this."

We did it. I worked, took a quick break to eat a little more, worked again, drank another mug of wine, and finally, close to midnight, I cropped a few pixels from the last image file and was done.

I sat back and rubbed my eyes. Elliott was still typing. I was tired, but also full of unexpected energy, the adrenaline rush of finishing good work. I knew I wouldn't be able to sleep anytime soon.

I stood up and took my wine mug over to Elliott's desk. He typed for a few more seconds and then looked up at me, a question in his eyes that I didn't know the answer to.

"I'm finished," I said instead.

His smile was a slow burn. "Then we're done. I'll finish this coding. You should go home and sleep."

"I can't sleep," I said. "I'm too wired."

"Hmm," he said. He closed his laptop and gave me a searching look. "Then we'll just have to finish the wine."

He made it a ritual: arranging my chair beside his desk, pouring the wine into our mugs, toasting solemnly and drinking. "To our success," he said.

"May it be long-lasting and, uh, fertile," I said.

He laughed. "What an odd thing to say."

I couldn't think of a reply. We sat in silence, drinking our wine. Outside, a siren blared and faded into the distance.

"My father wants me to make something of myself," Elliott said.

I looked at him, too surprised to speak. Elliott, volunteering information about himself? What next: planetary invasion by tiny green men from Mars?

He wasn't done. "He cut me off. No money, no support. If I can't get this company off the ground—well. He thinks that I'll go crawling back, duly chastened, and take over the company. I'm afraid he'll be sadly disappointed."

"What would you do instead?" I asked, taking the risk, hoping my question wouldn't shatter this fragile intimacy.

"Go back to Africa," he said. "My old boss would be happy to give me a job."

"That's why you're doing this," I said, realizing. "You care about your father's approval. You want him to be proud of you."

He nodded tightly. "Yes."

He was ashamed, I saw. "There's nothing wrong with that. You shouldn't have to *earn* his approval. He should already be proud of you."

"He never will be," Elliott said. He took a sip of his wine. "It was a great source of tension between my parents. My mother thought he was too hard on me, but he said it was the only way to turn me into a man."

"What does your mother think about all of

this?" I asked.

"She doesn't," he said. "She's been dead for ten years."

"I'm sorry," I said. I could hear the pain in his voice. An old wound, but one that still ached.

"Ovarian cancer," he said. "By the time they found it, it was too late. I was in Laos. She told me not to come home, that there was plenty of time. There wasn't. I flew home for the funeral."

I nodded, hands curled around my mug. I knew all about funerals, and grief.

I drank my wine.

"My fiancé died," I heard myself say.

A mistake. The adrenaline rush was immediate. I flushed hot and heard a roaring in my ears. Elliott's startled glance compounded my sense that I had betrayed myself. After a year of sucking it up, of keeping quiet and forging ahead, all it took was a little wine and a few unguarded confessions for me to throw all caution to the wind.

"Oh, Sadie," Elliott murmured.

Why had I said it? I would cut off my own tongue if it kept me from blurting any more unpleasant revelations.

I sat frozen, hoping for the ground to swallow me.

Elliott's chair scraped across the floor. His hand touched my arm, just above the elbow, and then settled on my shoulder. "Sadie," he said again.

"It was cancer," I said, all in a rush, the words tumbling over each other as they spilled from my mouth. "Leukemia. He died a year ago. A little more than a year."

Elliott squeezed my shoulder, firm and reassuring. "This explains a lot about you."

"What's that supposed to mean?" I asked, more reflex than genuine offense, habitual belligerence that I couldn't shake.

"Exactly," he said, like I had given him any sort of answer. His hand moved from my shoulder to cup the back of my neck, his fingers sliding into my hair. "I'm glad you told me."

"I haven't told anyone," I said. Not said: choked it out. "I haven't talked about it at all."

He made a wordless noise, soothing.

I fought the pressure building behind my eyes. I wouldn't cry. I wouldn't.

I raised my head and looked at him. His expression, for once, was open and sincere. He wasn't trying to hide anything. And there was so much sympathy and kindness and *care* in his gaze that the tears I'd been fighting welled up and over.

"Oh, you sweet thing," he said. He spun my chair to face his, our knees brushing, and cupped my face in his hands. I bit my lip, feeling tears stream down my face, embarrassed and vulnerable, afraid to let him see me like this.

He leaned in and kissed me, gently, carefully.

He said my name.

I rested my face against his shoulder and wept.

CHAPTER 17

Elliott

"You're late."

I looked at Carter and sighed. "Only ten minutes. Traffic was terrible coming through Midtown. I'm sure Regan will forgive me."

"You brought flowers, so I'd bet on it," he said, clapping me on the shoulder, and stood aside to let me into the house.

Regan was in the kitchen, tossing a salad with the baby strapped to her chest in a tangle of fabric. She looked up as I entered the room, and smiled as she saw what I was carrying. "Elliott, you didn't have to," she said.

"Of course I did," I said, and bent to kiss her cheek. She took the flowers from me, exclaiming over their color and variety, and climbed onto a footstool to take a vase down from above the sink.

"What a charmer," Carter said. "You'll steal my wife away before I know it."

"Elliott wouldn't do that because he doesn't want to have to deal with the baby," Regan said, smiling at me as she filled the vase with water. "Don't worry. He's fast asleep, and I'll take him upstairs to bed before we eat."

"My relief can't be expressed in words," I said. I didn't *object* to the baby—I simply didn't want to hold it or interact with it—but Regan and Carter seemed amused by my ostensible revulsion, and I was happy to play along.

Regan went upstairs to deal with her spawn, and Carter handed me a beer and took dinner off the stove. "Regan's mother's recipe," he said. "Pork adobo. I hope you're hungry."

"Always," I said. Carter had developed a real knack for Filipino cuisine, and everything he cooked rivaled what I had eaten during the month I spent in the Philippines. Years ago, now, but the memories were still vivid enough to make my mouth water.

Carter transferred the adobo into a wide ceramic serving dish and took it into the dining room. I trailed after him, holding my beer bottle. I had been to dinner at Carter and Regan's often enough to know that any offers to help would be refused. Carter didn't like other people *doing things* in or around his kitchen. Even Regan's assistance was barely tolerated.

The doorbell rang, and I raised my eyebrows at Carter and took another sip of beer. "Special delivery?"

"Regan will get it," he said.

I heard Regan's footsteps coming down the stairs, and the door opening, and then a woman's voice, bright, cheerful, berating Regan in a casual, friendly way.

I knew that voice.

They came down the hallway, and I stood there, mute, clutching my beer bottle.

"So then he told me I should smile more, and I was like, what business of that is yours?" Sadie said, coming into the room carrying her coat and a bottle of wine. Regan came in with her, laughing, but Sadie had my full attention. Sadie was all I could see.

She wore her favorite red lipstick, and her braids hung loose, framing her face. She was dressed in jeans and a simple gray knit shirt that draped around her body, and she was beautiful. She was smiling at Regan, and then she turned her head and saw me, and the smile dropped off her face like she had just seen a ghost.

"Surprise," Regan said, looking a little guilty. "I thought it would be nice for all of us to have dinner together."

What could I say? I took another sip of beer.

Carter looked back and forth between Sadie and me, smirking, obviously adding two and two and coming up with four.

I hated everyone I knew.

"Sadie, good to see you," I said, to stave off anything awkward and irrevocable that Carter might be tempted to say.

"I didn't know you were coming for dinner tonight," she said, narrow-eyed. As if I had somehow arranged all of this to humiliate her.

I wasn't that conniving. Our friends were assholes. "Likewise," I said. "But the more the merrier."

Sadie scowled at me, so adorably suspicious that I longed to take her in my arms and kiss her until her frown melted away.

Carter clapped his hands together. "So, let's eat!"

Dinner got off to a slow start, with both Sadie and me picking at our food and making stilted, uncertain conversation, but Sadie was irrepressible, and after she finished her first glass of wine she seemed to make a conscious decision not to let me ruin her evening, and started regaling Regan and Carter with a story about her deranged landlord.

I ate in silence and watched her: her broad smile, the quick, darting movements of her hands. Somehow, this charismatic, bright-eyed creature was the same woman who had cried in my arms the night before. It was hard to reconcile the two. But that was Sadie in a nutshell: complex, changeable.

Not that we had talked about the crying. I had told her to take the day off, but instead of listening to me, she showed up at the office mid-morning, determinedly cheerful, acting like nothing had happened. And I was too cowardly or stupid to press the issue.

Maybe she didn't remember it. We'd had quite a bit of wine, after all.

Maybe she hoped *I* didn't remember it.

Sadie wrapped up her story about her landlord,

and launched into an anecdote about her father's ongoing battle against the barking dogs in his neighborhood. "So he went over there, past midnight, wearing nothing but his bathrobe and flip-flops, and he started banging on her door. She came downstairs, peeked through the curtains and saw him, and got real scared, and so she opened the door just a crack and *maced him*—"

"No!" Regan exclaimed, hand to her chest, laughing.

"—except it wasn't even mace, she had grabbed a can of compressed air, like, the stuff you use to clean your laptop—"

"On *purpose*?" Carter asked.

"No, she definitely wanted to mace him, but it was like, three in the morning, and I guess she wasn't awake enough to grab the right can," Sadie said. "So anyway, then my dad called the cops and tried to have her arrested. I think she's probably going to move soon."

"Your dad is so awesome," Regan said.

"Yeah, tell that to my mom," Sadie said. "She says she'll divorce him if he keeps terrorizing the neighbors."

"Your mom is also awesome," Regan said. "I still need to write her a thank-you note for coming over here the other day when Caleb was sick."

"Okay, enough about parents and sick babies, and absolutely enough about barking dogs," Carter said. "Just thinking about it is making me tense. Elliott, how is business going?"

"Well," I said, and stopped. I had spent all day doing my best to avoid thinking about what had happened, but Carter's words brought it rushing back, like water through a burst dam. But he had asked, and Sadie would have to know eventually. "You remember those investors I told you about—"

"From Boston," Carter said.

I nodded. "They backed out." I couldn't go on. The shame and disappointment were still too fresh.

Sadie's fork clattered to her plate. A look of horror spread across her face. "When did this happen?"

"This morning," I said. I'd gotten the email shortly after Sadie arrived at the office. She was busily ignoring me, and I got up from my desk and put on my coat and went out into the bitter wind blowing north along the avenue. I walked all the way to Central Park, my mind an empty shock of white heat, and stood overlooking the Pond, where a few ducks desultorily paddled around. All of my dreams crumbled around me.

Silence. I looked around the table at Sadie's expression of shock and dismay, Regan's sweet concern, Carter's angry frown. Sadie opened and closed her mouth a few times, and then said, "Did they say why?"

"Not in any meaningful terms," I said. "It was very polite. Not the right time, taking their investments in a different direction, best wishes to me in the future. I have no idea what happened."

"Corporate bullshit," Carter said. "Elliott, I'm

sorry."

"It's only a minor setback," I said, lying through my teeth. It was the end. If I didn't find an investor at the conference, I would be out of money. I would have to give up.

Regan turned to me and set one hand on my forearm. "Please let us give you some money. I need a venture capital project of my very own so that I can—Carter, why do I want to do it?"

"So you can diversify your portfolio," he said, smiling at her.

"That's right," she said. "Elliott, just say the word—"

"No," I said. "But thank you. We have the conference this weekend, and I have no doubt we'll be able to raise the capital we need." Another lie. Carter and Regan cared about me and wanted to help me, but my stupid pride wouldn't let me accept their aid.

Silence again. Regan and Carter had an intense, wordless conversation with their eyes. Sadie watched me with her fist pressed to her mouth. I couldn't read her expression. Disappointment, no doubt. Disappointment in me.

"I think we need dessert," Regan said, "and some more wine."

She got up and went into the dining room, and Carter leaned toward me and said, "Regan spoke for both of us. If you ever need help, just ask. I mean it, Elliott. I know you're a stubborn bastard, but there's more to life than keeping up appearances."

Sadie muttered something that sounded like *Fat chance.*

"I'll keep it in mind," I said. "Thank you." I sounded stiff and formal even to myself. It was a wonder Carter put up with me. But then, I had known him for most of his life, and I had dirt on him that he didn't want getting out.

Behind me, the baby monitor emitted a thin, high-pitched wail.

Carter chuckled and stood up. "Duty calls."

Then we were alone, Sadie and me, and she said, "Elliott, I'm so sorry."

I looked away. "Don't be. You should be upset with me, if anything."

"That's stupid," she said. She sipped her wine and looked at me over the rim of her glass. "What are we going to do?"

Her *we* reassured me more than it should have. In a way, I would have felt better if she abandoned me. Less guilty. "There's still the conference."

"Right," she said, and drew in a breath. "Okay. We should start—do you have a list of potential donors?"

The low-level headache I'd had all day throbbed behind my eyeballs. "Let's just have a nice dinner and not worry about it now, Sadie."

My voice came out sharper than I intended, and she frowned at me. My fingernails bit into my palm. I realized I had curled my hand into a fist.

I was an ass. "I'm sorry," I said.

"It's okay," she said. "You've had a hard day.

We won't talk about it. Let's just drink more."

As if on cue, Regan came back into the room, ice cream carton in one hand and a bottle of wine in the other. "Who's ready to party?"

"Not you," Sadie said.

"Where's Carter?" Regan asked.

"Upstairs," I said. "The baby was crying."

"Oh, he must be hungry," Regan said. "Let me go see. I put bowls on the counter in the kitchen—so please help yourselves. We're such bad hosts, aren't we? Abandoning you to fuss over our baby."

"Yeah, Elliott and I are really concerned about proper etiquette," Sadie said, rolling her eyes. "Go take care of the baby. I'm happy to be abandoned because it means I get to eat all the ice cream."

When Regan was gone, I stood and began clearing plates from the table. I needed a moment alone to clear my head, and doing the dishes was as good an excuse as any.

Alone in the kitchen, I set the stack of plates beside the sink and planted my elbows on the counter, leaning down to rest my forehead against my palms. I was tired: tired of wanting things I couldn't have, of trying and failing to win my father's approval, of working my ass off all the time and having nothing to show for it at the end of the day.

Behind me, the door opened.

I didn't look up. I knew it was Sadie, and I didn't want to deal with her right now. Couldn't. My whole heart yearned toward her, but I wasn't stupid enough to get involved with a woman who was very obviously still mourning her fiancé.

A lie. I was exactly that stupid.

"Are you okay?" she asked softly.

"Just a headache," I said.

She set her palm at the waistband of my pants, a small, warm touch through the fabric of my sweater. Every muscle in my body tensed at once with a combination of dread and desire. After another moment, I felt a pressure against my upper back, between my shoulder-blades. Her head, I realized. She was resting her face against my back.

"Sadie," I said, in absolute agony.

"You'll find an investor," she said. "I know it."

How could she possibly think about work when she was touching me like that? The last threads of my self-control frayed away into nothing, and I spun around and seized her and bent my head to claim her mouth with mine.

It was nothing like the gentle, comforting kiss we had shared the night before. Sadie was playing with fire, and I wanted her to know it in her bones. I wasn't a patient man, and the feeling of her body pressed against mine would have made a saint break every one one of his vows. She tasted like red wine and the spices of Carter's cooking. All of my concerns melted away. I thrust my tongue into her mouth, claiming her, and she made a soft noise in the back of her throat and wrapped her arms around my neck.

I had never imagined that she could be so

sweet, so yielding. I slid one hand down her back to cup her ass and draw her closer to me. My cock was stiff inside my pants just from kissing her, just from having her so near.

She broke away, and I kissed her neck, her ear. "Elliott," she said.

"Hmm?" I asked, not really listening.

"Elliott, stop," she said. "We need to—Elliott!" She put her hands on my chest and pushed me away, not hard, but it broke through my lust-induced haze, and I released her.

Had I just—

"They're coming downstairs," she said.

Oh. Was that all? I reached down to adjust myself, and saw her gaze follow the motion of my hand. She bit her lip and glanced away, and I grinned, triumphant.

I knew I wouldn't spend this night alone.

"Fuck," Sadie said, and raised her hands to her hair, patting her braids back into place. "Okay. What were we doing?"

"Dessert," I said. "Bowls."

"Right," she said. "Okay. We're eating ice cream. *Fuck*. Stop laughing at me, you asshole. Regan can *smell* guilt. She'll know exactly what we've been doing."

"This sounds like paranoia to me," I said, and she made a face and grabbed the stack of bowls from the counter.

We went back into the dining room. My erection had subsided enough that I didn't think it

186

would be immediately obvious what we had been up to in the kitchen, but Carter shot me a sidelong glance and a smirk that told me my cover was blown. He and Regan were meddling, matchmaking thorns in my side. This little dinner party was no accident, and I was sure they would chortle to themselves later over how well their plan had worked out.

Well. Let them be smug, then. I would be smug, too, nailing Sadie through the mattress.

"Ice cream?" Regan asked, innocent as anything.

Dessert was an exercise in torment. Sadie ate her ice cream like she was sucking off her spoon. It had to be deliberate. Nobody was that innocent or that oblivious.

Carter was saying something to me. I turned toward him, trying to look like I had been paying attention. "...next time, but I told her to expect the price to keep dropping."

I mentally rewound the conversation. Stocks. Carter was talking about investments. Right. I drew in a breath and tried to think of something marginally insightful to say.

Across the table from me, Sadie smirked and licked her spoon.

I had obviously entered some quantum space, a time dilation zone where dinner would drag on, interminably, until the eventual heat death of the universe.

I gritted my teeth and poured myself a glass of wine.

When the ice cream was gone, and the wine bottle was empty, Regan and Carter walked us both to the front door. "Let me call my driver," Carter said. "It's late."

"It's 9:00," Sadie said. "The subway isn't as terrible as you imagine."

"I'll walk Sadie to the subway station, since I believe we're both heading to 23rd Street," I said. "So you mother hens don't have to worry."

"Oh, we do fuss a lot, don't we?" Regan asked. "I guess we're so used to worrying about the baby that we've started worrying about *everyone*."

"Fortunately, Sadie and I are both potty-trained and even know how to feed ourselves," I said, smiling at Regan to show that I wasn't upset by her concern. "Thank you for a lovely evening."

Sadie embraced Regan and Carter in turn and zipped her coat up to her chin. Then she looked up at me and said, "Ready to go?"

The weather was milder than it had been in some time—a brief taste of spring before winter returned again, no doubt with a vengeance. Sadie and I walked in silence for several blocks. I glanced at her, and she was looking up at the sky, her head tipped back.

"Look at the moon," she said, pointing.

I stopped in the middle of the sidewalk and folded my arms across my chest. "Sadie," I said, "I don't give a shit about the moon."

She had walked ahead a few steps, but she turned at that and came back toward me, a question on her face.

I didn't give myself time to reconsider. I said the words. "Come home with me."

CHAPTER 18

Sadie

Elliott's apartment was in Midtown, not far from the office. We behaved ourselves on the sidewalk, and in the cab he insisted on hailing, and in the lobby of the building, but as soon as we were in the elevator, he pressed me against the wall panel and kissed me.

There was no room for thought, only sensation. With his hands resting on the wall above my head, his unbuttoned coat lapped around me, engulfing me in his scent of cologne and wool. His beard stubble prickled against my face, and his mouth was a warm, soft counterpoint. Not a gentle one, though: he was greedy, demanding, taking what he wanted, and I shivered and surrendered to him.

If I was going to make a terrible life decision, I might as well go all out.

The elevator doors opened with a ding.

I stumbled a step back, flushing. Elliott had a special talent for making me blush like a schoolgirl, and I was grateful—not for the first time—that he wouldn't be able to tell. If I was as pale as he was, I would really be in trouble.

An old woman waiting outside the elevator clucked her tongue and gave us a disapproving look as we emerged from the elevator, Elliott's hand enfolding mine. I expected him to ignore her and keep walking, but instead he flashed her a shit-eating grin and said, "How's your evening going, Mrs. Jefferson?"

"I know your father, young man," she said, like the archetypal Disapproving Old Lady, her face pinched with distaste as she looked me up and down.

"Kindly get in touch with him and report on my activities," Elliott said. "I'm sure he'll be delighted to hear what I'm up to." He started moving again, towing me down the hallway with him, and when we were almost-but-not-quite out of earshot, he muttered, "Meddling old bat."

I laughed, looking over my shoulder to see Mrs. Jefferson still standing there scowling. "Does she really know your father?"

"Highly unlikely," Elliott said, "given that she lives in this shit-heap of a building. My father doesn't associate with the peasantry." He stopped in front of a nondescript door and fished his keys from his pocket. "But let's not talk about her anymore." He unlocked the door and crowded behind me to nudge me inside, his chest pressed against my back.

His apartment was small, one open room with the bed shoved up against a window, but I didn't

191

have time for more than a quick glance before he hustled me inside and tumbled me down onto the mattress.

"Hey now, who says I'm that kind of girl?" I asked.

He just rolled his eyes and bent his head to kiss me.

After a moment, I raised my arms and wrapped them around his back.

It was absurd: the two of us still in our coats and shoes, making out on his messy bed like horny teenagers. I wanted to feel his skin against mine, but I also didn't want to stop kissing him long enough to strip off our clothes. I felt drunk on his kisses. He moved a hand to cup my jaw and hold me in place while he explored my mouth, and maybe I should have done something other than lie there like a limp rag, but I couldn't feel my toes and the rest of my body was tingling so much that it was hard to do anything but wallow in the sensation.

But I wanted *more*, and so I lifted my shaking hands and slid them beneath his coat. Better, but there were still too many layers of fabric between us. I tugged at his sweater, lifting up the hem, and beneath *that* he was wearing a t-shirt. I turned my head to the side, breaking our kiss, and said, "That's it. You need to take all of this off."

He laughed and rolled off me, which wasn't what I wanted. I made a protesting noise, and he kissed me again and said, "Let me at least get up to take off my coat."

"I *guess* that's acceptable," I said. God, my hair was a mess. All of me was a mess. I was so wet just from kissing that I was pretty sure I would have to throw away my underpants.

He sat up on the edge of the bed took off his coat and shoes. I hoped he would keep going, but instead he lay down again and pulled me toward him, unzipping my coat and pretending to peek inside. "How many layers are you wearing?"

"Not as many as you," I shot back. "It's cold out. It's January."

"Likewise," he said. "What was it you said? All of this needs to go."

I wasn't about to wriggle around on the bed trying to peel off my jeans. Too undignified. I got up and took off my own coat and shoes, and then hesitated. He was lying there looking at me, calm and a little amused, expectant, like there was no doubt in his mind that I was about to get naked and he fully intended to enjoy the show.

I wasn't sure how I felt about him lying back and watching me strip.

Good? Bad? Somewhere in between?

"Take off your shirt," he said.

His voice was soft, but there was a commanding edge to it that made me shiver. He sounded like a man who was accustomed to getting his way.

"Are you just going to watch me?" I asked.

"Yes," he said, and moved one hand to rest on his crotch, right on top of the bulge of his cock. Yeah,

I was looking.

I flushed again and glanced away, turned on despite myself. "If you want to watch porn, you can just watch some porn."

"You're better than porn," he said, actually unbuttoning his pants, because he was completely shameless. "Because you're real, and *here*, and you're going to make some incredible noises for me before the night is over."

"Oh, am I?" I asked. God, he was cocky. "What makes you so sure?"

He smirked at me. "It's simple. You won't be able to help yourself."

Who was this arrogant, aggressive man and what had he done with Elliott? But I wouldn't lie to myself: I liked it.

Before I could let myself over-think the situation and get all freaked out, I grabbed the hem of my shirt and pulled it over my head.

Elliott drew in a sharp breath.

I dropped my shirt on the floor and fought the urge to cover my breasts with my hands. At least I was wearing a sexy bra. My faded, sagging underpants were another story entirely. Sex had been the last thing on my mind when I got dressed for dinner. Maybe I could make up an excuse to go to the bathroom, and finishing getting naked in there.

"Keep going," Elliott said, and I thought he probably wouldn't want to hear any of my excuses.

With shaking hands, I unbuttoned my jeans.

My breath was coming fast and shallow. My

nipples were hard, sensitive points inside my bra. And something about the way Elliott was watching me—smug, predatory—made me want to fall to the floor and beg him to fuck me. I couldn't explain it. I was a rational, cynical, thoroughly modern woman. I didn't have any interest in that caveman stuff: club woman on head, drag back to cave, make babies. But Elliott short-circuited every one of my higher mental processes, and being with him like this, half-naked and three feet away from his bed, was more than my lizard brain could handle. I wanted him on top of me, and *now*.

I shoved my jeans down my thighs.

Elliott groaned, and slid his hand inside his unzipped fly. Watching him touch himself gave me an erotic thrill. Here I was, nobody special, and a rich, gorgeous man was so into me taking my clothes off that he couldn't keep his hands off his dick.

If nothing else, the guy knew how to make a lady feel good about herself.

"Sadie, you're killing me," he said, and I realized I was standing there like a fool, pants at my knees and my terrible underpants on full display. I hastily shoved them down, so eager to hide the faded floral print and fraying elastic from Elliott's view that I forgot about the unavoidable end result of taking off my panties: I was totally exposed.

Oh, God.

To be honest, it felt amazing.

"Now your bra," Elliott said, his hand moving, ever so slightly, inside his trousers.

After the underpants, the bra was nothing. I reached behind my back and unhooked the clasp, and drew the straps down my arms. I held one hand against my chest to keep the cups in place, half teasing, half nervous, until Elliott said, "Now, Sadie," and I let my hand fall away.

The way he looked at me—oh, Lord.

Like I was the only woman he'd ever seen.

I knew I wasn't bad-looking. I worked out a lot, and I had a decent body, small tits and flat ass notwithstanding. But the way Elliott's lips parted, and the slow flush that spread upward from the hollow of his throat—well, it was pretty flattering. If he was doing it on purpose, it was working.

"All right," he said. "As much as I enjoy watching you, I'm going to enjoy it much more when you get on this bed with me."

I felt like I should sass him a little, make him work for it, but I just could not be bothered. I wanted to feel his hands on me. Screw dignity. It was overrated.

I left my clothes in a heap on the floor and joined him on the bed.

"That's more like it," he said, sitting up from his lazy slouch, and then he seized me by the waist and rolled me onto my back.

And then he just sat there and looked down at me.

I met his gaze, feeling a little self-conscious and trying not to. His pupils were wide and dark, and he was flushed pink, his hair in disarray, the neckline of

196

his sweater crumpled. "Are you my Christmas present?" I asked.

That startled a laugh out of him. "Christmas was a month ago," he said.

"And Valentine's Day is coming up," I said. "Maybe Cupid sent you to me in advance. I must have been very, very good."

"Sadie," he murmured, leaning down, "I was actually hoping to hear that you've been very, very bad."

He kissed me, and all my weird nervousness, the jittery energy that kept sparking across my skin—it dropped away like a radio shutting off. With Elliott kissing me, there was no room for anything else. Our bodies knew how to fit together. Our mouths met, and his lips spoke a language I thought I had forgotten.

"Sadie," he groaned, trailing his mouth down my neck, his stubble scraping against my skin and making me squirm with delight. His hands came up to cover my breasts, squeezing roughly, his thumbs sliding across my nipples, and I felt my back arch off the bed. I was hungry. My skin was hungry for his. I wanted him.

His mouth moved lower, down to the thin-skinned hollow between my collarbones, down to the bony flat of my sternum, and then down lower to take one of my nipples between his teeth.

The noise I made was barely human.

He chuckled, and I felt it as a vibration, his chest quaking where it pressed against my thigh.

"Don't laugh at me," I gasped.

He pulled away enough to speak. "Not *at*," he said. "With? Nearby?" His breath gusted against my nipple, a cruel tease, and I took his head in my hands and guided him back to where I wanted him.

He was definitely laughing at me.

I didn't care. He was expert, casual, using his teeth enough to provide a delicious contrast to his wet tongue, but not enough to cause actual pain. He moved from one breast to the other, sucking and licking, and the heat between my legs grew and spread and made me squirm against him, desperate for some relief. When I couldn't wait anymore, I slid one hand between my thighs, ready to take matters into my own hands. So to speak.

Without moving away from my breast, Elliott seized my wrist in one hand and pinned it to the mattress.

"You are the worst person I know," I said.

He laughed at me again, the bastard. But he stopped sucking on my nipple and rolled to one side, trapping my pinned arm beneath his body, and trailed his free hand up the inside of my thigh.

I was afraid to blink, afraid to take a breath or do anything else that would cause him to stop.

But he stopped anyway, inches short of where I needed him, and said, "I take it there's something you want me to do."

I could have sobbed. I didn't understand how he was so cool and collected when I was made out of wildfire, ready to burn everything I touched to the ground. "Elliott," I said, frustrated, desperate.

"What's that?" he asked, all fake concern. "Do you want something?"

"Touch me," I wailed.

And he finally, finally did.

I expected him to tease me some more, but instead, he gave me exactly what I wanted: two fingers pressed inside of me, long and sure, and his thumb rolling carelessly over my clit, a little rough and exactly right. My hips shuddered upward, a helpless, automatic motion, and he clicked his tongue at me and said, "Now, now. Can't have you getting too excited."

"I thought that was the point," I said, voice ragged.

"Oh, there's going to be plenty of excitement," he said, "but not just yet." He moved his fingers, twisting them inside me, and I gasped and clutched at his sweater. "Hmm," he said. "On second thought."

"*Please*," I said, desperate for release, desperate for this ecstatic torture to come to an end.

"No, I think I'll make you wait a little longer," he said, and took his glorious fingers away and slid off the bed.

I made a pitiful whimper.

"Hush, I'm coming right back," he said, and tugged his sweater over his head.

Oh. This was interesting.

He wasn't slow or methodical about stripping. He yanked his clothes off like he couldn't wait to be naked, and I realized that he was probably just as eager as I was, just hiding it better. He wanted me to think he was totally in control, but his trembling hands and the eager, clumsy way he fumbled with his trousers gave him away.

And somehow that was even better than Elliott Sloane, Icy Sex God. I liked him real, overwhelmed, and *with me*. We were in this together. We were all in.

I ogled him as much as I could in the forty-five seconds it took him to get naked. Clothes didn't do him justice, I decided. He was hiding some serious muscles beneath those fancy suits he liked so much. His broad, freckled back rippled with each motion. Nice shoulders, nice arms. And—when he slid off his boxer-briefs—a surprisingly nice ass.

100% American grass-fed beef.

"What are you laughing at?" he asked me, naked, hands on his hips, cock hanging thick and heavy between his thighs.

"You don't want to know," I said, still ogling. "Not you. I would never laugh at that weapon of mass destruction you're armed with."

He smirked at me, obviously pleased. Men always liked it when you talked about how big their dicks were. Most of the time it was a polite exaggeration. Not with Elliott, though. That thing meant business. "Do you always talk this much during sex?"

"I talk this much during life," I said.

"I'll take it as a sign that I'm not working hard enough at distracting you," he said, and came back to bed.

After that there was no more hesitation, no more fooling around. He settled between my legs and kissed me deeply, his hands running across my body like I was known territory, a country he had already claimed. We worked together to roll a condom onto his cock, and then he seized a fistful of my hair and pulled my head back, tipping my chin up to force me to meet his eyes.

What I saw there undid me.

Longing, lust—everything that I felt, reflected back at me and magnified by my own desire. He was a dear friend, someone I respected and liked, and he was also a *man*. After tonight, I would never be able to ignore this rough, primal energy running just below the unruffled surface of his skin.

"This isn't your first time, is it?" he asked, a little mocking smile on his face.

He was a jerk, and I couldn't get enough. "Are you asking me if I'm a virgin? You think I was saving myself for marriage?"

"Some people do," he said. The green was almost gone from his eyes, crowded out by his blown pupils.

"Not me," I said. His cock was already nudging at my entrance. "I'm too impatient. I couldn't wait."

"I'm glad to hear that," he said, "because I don't think I could stand to be careful with you tonight." And that was all the warning I got before he drove home in one thrust.

I cried out and arched against him, overcome. It

felt so good and *right* to be filled by him, to have the weight of his body pressing me into the bed. He let go of my braids and dropped his head to rest his forehead against mine, releasing a long groan and twitching his hips against me.

"Christ, *Sadie*," he said.

We moved together in a timeless rhythm. Without words, without thought, our bodies knew exactly what to do. It was both easy and terrifyingly complicated: a simple pleasure, but weighted with meaning because of who I was with and the messy tangle of feelings I hadn't even begun to pick apart.

I hadn't lied to Elliott. I was no bashful virgin. I'd had years of good sex with Ben, warm, familiar, thoroughly satisfying sex, but it was never anything like this. Elliott was turning me inside out.

God. Ben had only been dead for a year, and here I was, already in another man's bed and having the time of my life.

Till death do us part, indeed.

I turned my face aside, afraid Elliott would see something in my expression that would make him stop. I didn't want him to stop. It was just—strange, being with someone new. Moving on with my life. Living.

Then he moved his hips again and I couldn't think anymore.

It didn't take very long. It couldn't, not with me so worked up from his teasing. Everything was heat and sweat and the feeling of the muscles of his back moving beneath my hands. I felt my legs tense in their familiar way, quivering with the strain of pleasure. He sat up on his knees and tugged my hips onto his lap, my ass resting against his thighs, and on his next thrust, something about the new angle made me moan so loudly that a dim, distant part of my brain worried that the neighbors might hear. He grinned, victorious, and drove in quick and deep, hitting that spot that made me feel like I was about to liquefy.

It was *so* good.

"I think you're about to come for me," he said, and I shook my head, not really denying it, but not wanting to give him the satisfaction of coming on command. But he just smirked at me and rolled his hips again, and my orgasm hit me out of nowhere.

The intensity of it bowled me over. I shuddered and wailed, nails digging into Elliott's back, and he didn't stop moving in me the whole time, not even when I begged him to, not until I was a limp puddle on the mattress.

Then he flipped me over and fucked me fast and hard until he came with a low groan.

CHAPTER 19

Elliott

I lay on top of Sadie until I caught my breath, and then I pulled away from her and staggered into the bathroom to clean up.

After I disposed of the condom, I stared at myself in the mirror while I washed my hands. I looked the same as I always did. There was no sign that I had become a predatory, morally bankrupt lecher who exploited vulnerable women.

Sadie wasn't my girlfriend. She wasn't even my no-strings-attached fuck-buddy. She was a beautiful, heartbroken woman who was still mourning her dead fiancé, and I had just taken advantage of her loneliness to get my rocks off.

Truly, not my finest hour.

It wasn't that I had forced her. I didn't have to worry about *that*, at least. She had been a visibly, vocally willing and eager participant. But I had taken advantage of the situation nonetheless, and maybe there was some subconscious part of her that felt she couldn't tell me no.

I exhaled and ran my wet hands through my hair, slicking the messy strands back into place. Cool and collected. Button it all down. No room for nerves. No time for anxiety. Pretend they're all naked. My old elocution teacher's advice ran through my head, the mantras he had drummed into me still useful after all these years.

I needed to apologize to Sadie, and tell her that it couldn't happen again.

I went back into the main room, bracing myself against the sight of a languid, post-coital Sadie and the unpleasant conversation that would ensue. But Sadie was sitting on the edge of the bed, fully dressed, leaning down to lace up her boots; and she looked up as the bathroom door opened, her face an expressionless mask, and said, "I should probably go."

I stopped dead, deflated like a popped balloon. How easily she took the wind out of my sails. I said, "Look, this was great, but—"

"It was a mistake," she said. "It was unprofessional. We work together, and I just think— this has the potential to get really messy, so. Let's just focus on getting ready for the conference."

All of which was more or less exactly what I'd been planning to say to her, but her words still pricked my ego. No man liked to hear himself described as *a mistake*. "Right," I said. "I agree. I'll see you tomorrow at work, then."

"Yeah," she said, and stood up, hoisting her purse onto her shoulder. "See you."

When she was gone, I stood at the window for a long time, staring out into the night. After a while, a light snow began to fall, tiny flakes drifting toward the street. I went to sleep, then, and didn't remember any of my dreams.

I woke at dawn and went to the office. It was Wednesday. The conference started in three days. We were ready—almost ready—so close to being ready that my to-do list had dwindled to a single page. We would be ready.

I had registered to give a short talk in one of the panel sessions, and I spent the morning writing an outline and assembling the slides for my presentation. I still had little fondness for public speaking, but I could do a passable job, and it was important for me to get my face out there. Recognition, visibility—all of those industry buzzwords. I would do whatever it took to get the company off the ground. Dance naked on stage. Sing, literally, for my supper.

And then I would just have to hope that an investor took pity on me.

I had tried to play it cool at Regan and Carter's the night before, but the Boston investors backing out had set me reeling. I couldn't understand what had made them change their minds, and I was afraid word would get around somehow and mark me as tarnished goods. Or my father would find out, and leave me a gloating message about how he'd known all along that I wouldn't be able to make it in the real world.

As if I hadn't spent the last decade confronting every harsh, messy, terrible, life-changing facet of human existence. In my father's world, none of that counted. Only money mattered.

I was sitting there brooding when Sadie arrived, and I quickly turned back to my computer and moved some text around to pretend that I was doing something useful.

She set her things down at her desk and gave me a look like she knew exactly what I was up to. "What's on the agenda for today?"

Everything as usual, then. Right. I could pretend it was a normal day at work, and that I hadn't sucked on her nipples last night while she writhed beneath me and moaned. I cleared my throat. "Have you finalized the paper goods?"

She nodded. "I did that last night. They're uploaded to the server."

"I'll send everything to the printer today, then," I said. She wore a blue dress that looked soft to the touch and hugged her curves in a way that was entirely too appealing. "What about the banners for the booth?"

"Still working on it," she said. "I'll finish those today."

"Great," I said. "We're getting there." I was proud of myself: an entire, coherent conversation about work and nothing else. No innuendo, no subtle undercurrents. It was foolish of me to be pleased, maybe. We were both adults. It wasn't like we would succumb to animal passion, strip off our clothes, and fuck on the office floor.

Come to think of it, that didn't sound like a bad idea.

We worked. I finished my slides, wrote my speech, and wandered around the office muttering to myself and periodically glancing at my cue cards. I made a second pot of coffee and drank a cup, then another. I looked out the window. I sent a few emails.

Sadie, intent on her computer, didn't look at me once.

The feeling I'd had the night before, staring at myself in the mirror while Sadie lay in my bed on the other side of the door—it was panic, and guilt. I didn't want her to think poorly of me. I didn't want to think poorly of *myself*; I didn't want to be the sort of man who used his power and position to take sexual advantage of women.

I was having second thoughts, now, watching Sadie ignore me.

Sex with her was only a mistake because of our circumstances. If she wasn't my employee—well, if she wasn't my employee, I would have asked her out to dinner weeks ago, and would be doing my absolute best to make sure she never looked at another man for the rest of her life. She was exactly my type: brash, confident, but with a quiet watchfulness that hinted there was more to her than met the eye.

And the sex was, quite frankly, exceptionally good.

Irrelevant. It didn't matter how much I liked Sadie or wanted to have sex with her again. Nothing had changed since last night. I was a grown man, not a horny adolescent, and I wouldn't let desire overrule rationality or common sense.

No matter how tempting it was.

With a sigh, I got up to pour myself another cup of coffee.

The day passed slowly. Truth be told, there wasn't much left to do before the conference. I ran through my speech a few times and then tried to act busy, when really I was just emailing Kris and reading the news. Finally, 5:00 rolled around and I decided that I could justify leaving. I gathered my things and put on my coat, and stood beside Sadie's desk until she finally deigned to look up from her work.

"I'm leaving," I said. "You should go home, too."

"Okay," she said. "I will, soon. I'm almost done with this."

"Okay," I said, and tried to think of something else to say, something meaningful but not inappropriate, that would convince her to get up and put on her coat and go home with me.

But even if I knew the right words, I couldn't say them. I wouldn't.

I went home, sans Sadie.

The next day, I kissed her again.

The day started innocently enough. We made polite conversation beside the coffee pot and then spent the morning working at our respective computers. She offered to go to the printer's after lunch to pick up the things I had sent over: business cards, pamphlets, prospectuses. I forced myself to get some work done while she was out, but when she came back an hour later, I looked up from my computer as the elevator doors opened and realized I wouldn't get anything else done that day. Or maybe even for the rest of my life.

She was beaming, luminous, carrying a large cardboard box full of papers. Her coat was open, and her hair was slightly mussed, a few braids falling out of her loose ponytail.

She was the most gorgeous creature I had ever seen, and I was fooling myself to think I could resist her.

"The stuff looks great," she called out, coming toward me with her box and her hair and her smiling face. "Let me show you."

I rolled my chair backwards to give her room, and she set the box on top of my desk. "They got the colors right?" I asked.

"Oh yeah," she said. "Even better than the proofs. I think they used nicer paper." She handed me a pamphlet, her eyebrows raised expectantly.

Not wanting to disappoint, I made a long, slow perusal of the glossy cover. The picture on the front was a small dark-skinned boy beaming as he clutched a glass of clean water—a tacky cliché, but Sadie had insisted it was important to play into investors' expectations. Beneath him was the company logo, and beneath that, the words "GIVE THE GIFT OF WATER" in a streamlined sans-serif font.

I opened the pamphlet. The colors were clean and crisp, and the paper was glossy but not *too* glossy. It looked great, sharp and professional, and better than I had hoped. "They did a nice job," I said. She was standing just slightly too close to me, and I could smell her perfume. It was intensely distracting.

"It gets better," she said, and gave me a business card. "Just look at that! Lord, I sure did a nice job designing that thing."

I laughed at her self-satisfied tone, but she wasn't wrong. She was still grinning, excitement oozing from every pore, and I was no saint. I was just a man, and not a very good one at that.

I stood up, and took her in my arms.

"Elliott," she said, eyes wide.

I kissed her.

She dropped the business cards she was holding, and they scattered across the floor. I had long since discarded my suit jacket over the back of my chair, and her hands clutched at my shirt, untucking a few inches of fabric from my trousers. I buried my hands in her braids, tipped her head backward, and took full advantage of my access to her soft, sweet mouth.

She made a hungry noise and pressed closer to me. Blanket permission, then, and I kissed her more deeply, imagining what I would do when I had her in my bed later, her soft skin beneath my hands, and the soft, slick heat between her thighs—

She shifted against me, twisting away.

She turned her face, breaking our kiss. "Elliott," she said, and this time she didn't sound so inviting.

I released her immediately and stepped back. "What's—"

"You know we can't do this," she said. She tugged her dress back in place and ran one hand over her hair.

I rubbed my face, reeling from arousal and confusion. "I don't see why not."

"You *know* why not," she said. "If we're going to work together, we need to have a professional relationship, and this," she gestured between us, "is not professional."

Elliott Sloane, my father's heir, agreed with her. He knew that screwing around with the help inevitably ended in misery, and that sexual harassment lawsuits were far more trouble than they were worth. But I didn't want to be that man—had spent years trying not to become him—and I said, "Maybe we should consider it."

"What, professionalism?" she asked.

I rolled my eyes. Sadie's most annoying trait was the way she deflected serious conversations with sarcasm or humor. It was clearly a defense mechanism, and I understood why she did it, but it irritated me anyway. "Not professionalism," I said. "Us. Kissing. Sex. What are you concerned about? That the other employees will find out, and think you're getting preferential treatment?"

She folded her arms and scowled at me, which I found far more appealing than I should have. "There's Jim."

"He doesn't count," I said, "seeing as how he's still in Boston. What are you so afraid of, Sadie? We get along well. We have killer, mind-blowing chemistry. Why can't we just give this a shot and see what happens?"

"I don't think it's a good idea. Because I'm not ready," she said, and raised her hands to cover her eyes. She took a deep breath and let it out, and then moved her hands to cup the sides of her face and looked at me. "I'm not ready for a relationship."

"Oh, Sadie," I murmured. It was the one reason I couldn't argue against—and didn't want to, even if I thought logic might change her mind. She deserved the time she needed to grieve and move on with her life.

"We can still have sex, though," she said. "And hang out. God, I sound like an undergrad, don't I? *Hang out*. Like we're going to head to the amusement park and kiss on the ferris wheel."

"Sadie," I said, "I have no idea what you're talking about."

"Yeah," she said. "Sorry. I just mean—the sex was really good, like, *really* good, and I'm—we can keep doing that. If you want to. Casually."

"Are you suggesting a no-strings-attached arrangement?" I asked, amused now. "I didn't think you were that sort of girl."

She dropped her hands to her hips and

frowned at me. "What's that supposed to mean? Why aren't women allowed to like sex? If a man likes sex, it's all well and good, but women are supposed to be frigid and — why are you smirking at me like that? Are you trying to make me angry on purpose? Oh my God, you *are*."

"I would never do such a thing," I said, even though she was 100% correct. The faces that she made when she was aggravated were entirely too delightful, and I couldn't resist teasing her to provoke a reaction.

"Fine," she said. "I take it all back. I'm never having sex with you again. You can just spend every lonely night dreaming of what you missed out on."

"Let's not be hasty," I said. Casual sex wasn't what I wanted from her, but it was better than nothing. I would just have to be very charming and persuasive and wait for her to realize that we were perfect for each other.

But for now, I was tired of talking and could think of far more rewarding ways to spend the afternoon.

I took a step toward her, and felt a rush of anticipation as her eyes widened.

Another step and she was in my arms.

"I didn't mean right *now*," she said, and I silenced her with a kiss.

As my lips touched hers, arousal slammed into me with all the force of an avalanche. I had intended to tease her for a while and leave her wet and begging, but the feeling of her body pressed against mine was too intensely erotic to resist. I slid one hand down her back to squeeze her ass, and used my grip to crush her closer against me. My erection rubbed against her hip, and I spent a brief but intense moment wishing I were the sort of man who carried a condom around in his wallet.

Minor problem. There were plenty of other things we could do.

The only obstacle was that Sadie was wearing far too many clothes.

Still kissing her deeply, I reached down to tug up the hem of her dress. The full skirt easily slipped up around her waist, but beneath that she was wearing every man's worst nightmare: those stockings with the elastic waist, weirdly tight and almost impossible to peel off. I groaned and broke the kiss. "You're going to have to help me out here."

Her eyelids fluttered open and she looked at me with her dark, endless eyes. "Help you with what?"

"Your tights," I said. "Unless you want me to rip them. Sexy, but you might be cold on your way home." Or her way to my apartment, to spend the night in my bed.

She leaned away from me, planting her palms on my chest to keep me at arm's length, and I clamped one arm around her waist so that she wouldn't topple backward. "We are *not* having sex in the office!"

I grinned, and bent to kiss her again, using my height to overcome her half-hearted attempt to hold me away. "Why not?"

"It's unprofessional," she said.

"Every single one of our interactions has been unprofessional since the day we met," I said, "when I couldn't keep myself from staring at your ass."

"You dog!" she exclaimed, and laughed. "Did you really?"

"I did," I said. "It was those pants you were wearing. And yes, I did feel like a creep, and no, I didn't stop. Now take off your tights."

We worked together to shove her tights down to her knees. That was far enough for my purposes, and I abandoned the effort. She stood there, hobbled, and said, "I feel ridiculous. Don't you want me to take these off?"

"Good enough," I said, and backed her up against my desk. She made a surprised noise when the backs of her legs hit the edge of the desk. I pushed on her shoulders, gentle pressure encouraging her to sit down, and she did, looking up at me with a question in her eyes that I couldn't wait to answer.

I kissed her, relishing the way she gasped and clung to my shirt, and then I slid one hand between her legs and tucked my fingers inside her little cotton panties, rubbing at the wet heat of her.

She moaned, her mouth slack against mine. I kissed her neck, her ear. I wanted more room, more access, but her tights prevented her from spreading her thighs, and I wouldn't stop now. Good enough. She was slick and swollen, eager for my touch, twitching slightly with each movement of my fingers. It was wonderful. I had never been with a woman who was so responsive, so uninhibited in her enjoyment of sex. Sadie knew what she wanted, and she was shameless in her pursuit of pleasure.

My cock ached. I needed to be inside of her, to move in her until we both exploded. In my next life, I would be the sort of man who kept a box of condoms in his desk. I would just have to wait, or go jerk off in the bathroom later, something I hadn't done since high school.

If I had known Sadie in high school—well, neither of us would have graduated, for one thing.

She shifted her hips, moving closer to the edge of the desk. I chuckled and gave her what she wanted: my fingers deep inside, and the heel of my hand grinding against her clit, firm pressure just where she needed it. She was so hot and wet that my fingers met no resistance as they sunk in. I moved my mouth to her ear and said, "Do you get this wet for all the boys, or should I be flattered?"

She moaned again, already past the point of words, and she sounded so eager and desperate that I immediately lost all interest in teasing her. I wanted to feel her come on my hand. I wanted to watch her face as she came undone.

I rocked my palm against her and crooked my fingers inside, pressing firmly, and kissed her neck just below her ear, which always made her squirm in the most delightful way. She was so sensitive, so *hungry*. I couldn't get enough.

"Elliott," she said, and gasped, and went to pieces against me.

CHAPTER 20

Sadie

I stayed late at work on Thursday evening to finish going over some paperwork. Elliott tried to convince me to go home with him, "just for dinner," but I knew that would turn into an all-night sex fest and probably a late start the next morning. We were two days out from the conference, and Elliott didn't seem nearly as concerned about it as I thought he should be. How like a man: as soon as sex was on the table, nothing else mattered. Typical.

I finished after a couple of hours and spent a few minutes tidying the office. I cleared off my desk, rinsed out the coffee pot, and then paused by Elliott's messy desk. Stacks of papers and file folders teetered precariously, and a half-empty coffee mug looked like it was in danger of spontaneously generating a new life-form. Elliott was untidy at the best of times, and with the conference looming he had descended into outright filth. Maybe it was a consequence of his upbringing. His family had probably had an entire army of housekeepers, and nobody to yell at him if he left his dirty socks on the floor.

Well, I wasn't his mother *or* his housekeeper, but that mug was gross. I took it into the bathroom to scrub it out in the sink. When I returned it to his desk, I glanced at the stack of folders, idly curious, and the one on top caught my eye: UIF FINANCIALS.

UIF. Uganda International Friendship, maybe?

I flipped my folder open without giving myself any time to think about what I was doing.

There it was, right on top: an email about an impending wire transfer, with so many zeros after the first number that my head spun. And all of this money going into Elliott's account came from a company that didn't seem to exist.

It was pretty strange.

I read through the rest of the file, one piece of paper at a time, but I didn't find anything that answered my questions. There was no smoking gun, no memo that said, "I'm stealing money from the Ugandan government and nobody can stop me, hugs and kisses, Elliott Sloane," but I was suspicious as hell. If it looks like a duck, and it walks like a duck…

I would ask Elliott about it. Tomorrow. And it would turn out to be completely innocent, and we'd laugh about it, and maybe he would chastise me a little for doubting him and going through his files, and I would pretend to be contrite. No big deal.

Elliott wasn't the sort of person who had sketchy dealings with fake corporations.

I needed him to not be that sort of person.

I went outside into the cold and the dark. I was starving—lunch had been a long time ago—and I just wanted to get home and sit on my couch with a bowl of cereal, the dinner of champions.

I was halfway to the subway station when my phone rang.

I fished it out of my bag and glanced at the screen before I answered. I didn't recognize the number. "Yes?"

"This is Eric Patterson," a man said. "Have I reached Sadie Bayliss?"

"This is Sadie," I said. I didn't think I knew anyone named Eric Patterson, but something about the name set a vague memory stirring at the back of my mind.

"Wonderful," he said. "I'm so glad I was able to get in touch with you. I'd like to offer you a job."

"Wait, hold on," I said. "*What*? I don't know who you are, and I don't know how you know who *I* am, and I definitely have no idea why you're trying to give me a job."

"You don't remember me?" he asked. "I'm hurt. We've met."

Had we? Eric, Eric—and then it came to me: he was Elliott's friend from the silent auction, the redhead.

I was instantly creeped out.

I was pretty sure Elliott hadn't told this Eric guy my last name, but somehow he had looked me up anyway, even gotten my *phone number*. But, okay—maybe he'd asked Elliott for my contact information, and Elliott had just forgotten to mention it to me. That was possible. Elliott had a lot on his mind. Maybe it was totally legitimate.

Somehow I didn't think that was the case.

"How did you get my number?" I asked. Might as well cut to the chase.

He laughed, like I had asked exactly the right question. "Clever girl," he said. My skin crawled. I wasn't a girl, and I certainly wasn't okay with him saying it in that voice. "I have my ways."

This guy had obviously watched *way* too many James Bond movies. "Look," I said, "it's late, and you're sort of creepy, so why don't you send me an email tomorrow with whatever weird proposition you have in mind? I'm sure you'll be able to find my email address."

He laughed again. "*Very* clever. You'll hear from me soon." And then he hung up.

Okay, file that under *surreal and unsettling*. Shaking my head, I tucked my phone back into my bag and decided to put the whole incident out of my mind. If Eric emailed me tomorrow, I would deal with it then. He was probably drunk, though, and would forget all about it by morning.

But on Friday morning, there was an email waiting for me, very innocent, subject "My weird proposition," sender Eric Patterson.

I sighed heavily and clicked on it.

"Everything okay?" Elliott asked.

"Spam," I said. "They want me to buy pills so I can have a firm erection."

He laughed, and went back to what he was doing. For being the son of a cutthroat business magnate, Elliott had a surprisingly unsuspicious nature.

I skimmed Eric's email. Exciting opportunity, new venture, ground floor, salary, benefits, yadda yadda. Nothing particularly interesting, although he *was* offering me a salary that was slightly higher than what Elliott was paying me. Not worth it to go work for a creep, though.

But there at the end, a single line: *You may have noticed something suspicious about Elliott's funding. I can tell you more.*

I swallowed. Clicked reply.

It was a long, agonizing thirty-eight minutes before Eric replied.

I'll be at the conference tomorrow. Let's talk.

And then, somehow, I had to work for the rest of the day.

Close to lunch, I gave up. It wasn't just Eric's email, either: I was done. I had done everything I could to prepare us for the conference, and there was nothing left to do. Sure, I could change a few words around, maybe quadruple-check that I'd packed everything for tomorrow, but it would just be busywork. There was no reason to stay at the office. And Elliott was always bugging me about working too hard, so maybe he would let me go home early. It was a sunny day, and fairly mild out according to the weather forecast. Maybe I could take a walk in the park and enjoy not being freezing cold for once.

I got up and went over to his desk. He glanced up at me, eyebrows raised, and I said, "I'm done."

"How should I interpret that statement?" he asked. "Done in what sense? Finished with life? Finished with working for me? Fully cooked, like a Thanksgiving turkey?"

I gave him a look that I hoped accurately conveyed my feelings about being compared to a fat bird.

He grinned. "Not a turkey, then."

"I mean I'm done *for today*," I said. "And so are you, obviously. Look. We're ready. There's nothing else to work on. I think we should both go home and relax."

"Sadie Bayliss playing hooky?" he asked. "I never thought I'd see the day. I agree with you, though. I'm just wasting time at this point." He tipped his chair back and gave me a speculative look. "I think we should get out of here."

"What do you mean *we*?" I asked, even though I knew exactly what he meant, and my heart was already beating faster in anticipation.

He smiled at me, slow and wicked, and my stomach flipped over. "*We*," he said again. "You and me. And a bed, ideally, and a full box of condoms—"

"Elliott!" I exclaimed, and slapped him lightly on the shoulder, my face heating. "We are *not* going to spend all afternoon rolling around in bed."

He tipped his head to one side, pretending to think about it. "Why not?"

"Well, because," I said, and swallowed. I

couldn't actually think of a good reason, and the idea of his hands on me was wiping every objection from my brain. "Because…"

"My place is closer," he said, and I turned back to my desk to get my coat.

* * *

We didn't, in the end, have sex *all* afternoon, but we gave it a good try. Elliott put me on my hands and knees on his bed, curled his big palms around my hips, and fucked me through three orgasms, each one more powerful than the last, until my arms gave out and I couldn't do anything but rest my face against the pillow and moan helplessly. Elliott manhandled me like we'd been doing this for years and he understood my body better than I did, and there was nothing I could do but come to pieces in his arms.

Afterward, we lay side by side on the mattress, panting, staring up at the ceiling. Elliott took one of my hands in his and held it against his chest, pressing my palm flat against his skin. His heart beat beneath my fingers, strong and steady, and I felt unexpected tears pricking at my eyes. I didn't want to believe that he was doing something sketchy with his company. Whatever I felt for him, whatever connection had grown between us, I believed that he was a good and earnest person.

I hoped that Eric wouldn't prove me wrong.

"What's wrong?" Elliott asked.

Get it together, Bayliss. "Just recovering," I said, turning on my side to face him. "You did a real number on me."

He rolled his head toward me and grinned.

A wicked spirit took hold of me then. "Am I the first black woman you've been with?" I asked. I didn't want to worry about Eric or the company any longer. Pulling Elliott's pigtails would cheer me up.

He raised his eyebrows. "No."

The man was impossible. I raised my own eyebrows and kept looking at him expectantly.

For once, it worked. He sighed and said, "I lived with a Kenyan woman for two years. I would have married her, but her family objected. I don't blame them."

"Hmm," I said. "So is it like a fetish kind of thing? You've got jungle fever?"

The look he gave me was utterly appalled. I wanted to burst out laughing, but I powered through, determined to play it straight and see how riled up I could get him. I wrinkled my nose and turned my head away slightly, looking at him from the corner of my eye like I was reconsidering his motives. To my utter delight, he turned pink, and said, "I do not have *jungle fever*. My God, Sadie."

"How do you know?" I asked, as earnestly as I could. "It's not something you can diagnose yourself. Maybe—"

"I'm sure," he said. Even his ears were turning pink. "I've had sex with enough white women that there is no doubt in my mind."

That was it for me. I rolled on my back and broke into hysterical laughter, waving my hands in the air above me like a helpless bug, too amused to speak.

"Were you—have you been screwing with me?" he asked, suspicious.

"Oh God," I choked out, a breathless squeal. "Oh my God."

"You *were*," he said. "Incredible. I'm fairly sure that violates the Geneva Convention."

I finally got myself under control and caught my breath. "The Geneva Convention doesn't apply to this situation. Don't be silly."

"I'm phoning The Hague tomorrow," he said. "Then you'll be sorry."

I turned toward him and rested one hand against his cheek. "My darling, you'll do no such thing."

"Ah, sweet condescension," he said. "Don't you know I have connections? I'm a *Sloane*. I'm a big deal. I could call my father up and—"

"I don't think you would," I said. "Even if you could. I don't think you would call him."

"Well," he said. He turned his head to look up at the ceiling, and sighed. "I suppose you're right."

Bad move. I didn't want him getting all depressed about his father, who sounded like a major jerk anyway. We were supposed to be relaxing and enjoying ourselves. "Sorry, I shouldn't have brought it up," I said. "Look, I'm going to take a shower, and then maybe we can order some food." I would have

227

been happy to stay in and cook, but Elliott's apartment was so small that he didn't even have a proper kitchen, just a mini-fridge and hotplate in one corner. I didn't know for sure why he was living in a shoebox, but I would have bet it had something to do with his father.

The shower had good water pressure, though, and so I was a happy camper. I scrubbed myself until my skin tingled, and used his conditioner on my hair. It smelled like almonds. The scent was so familiar to me now, but somehow it smelled even better on Elliott.

Thinking about it made me shiver. Food first, and then I was taking him back to bed.

Casual sex agreed with me, I decided. At least in this context. It wasn't like I was sleeping with some random stranger: I *knew* Elliott, and I felt safe with him. Well, less safe when he gave me that heavy-lidded look like he wanted to devour me whole. But mostly safe. It was nice to be able to relax and have a good time without worrying about whether I'd shaved my armpits well enough or if he would call me in the morning. I liked it. I liked doing this with him. I wanted to keep doing it.

I got out of the shower and went back into the main room, using Elliott's towel to gently squeeze the water out of my braids. "I used your soap," I said. "Sorry."

He rolled toward me and gave me a stern look. "That soap cost me a lot of money," he said. "It's handmade by French virgins out of the milk of sheep born under the light of the full moon."

I laughed at him. "Oh, stop. You bought it at the bodega. It's Irish Spring."

He shrugged, totally unashamed. "Busted. You said you wanted food?"

"I'm starving," I said. "Sex makes me hungry. Can we order something? What's good around here? Maybe we should go out, so we don't just spend the entire day inside your tiny apartment."

"I like my tiny apartment," he said. "It's cheap. I like saving money."

"Are all rich people as stingy as you are?" I asked. "You're the cheapest billionaire I know."

"I'm not a billionaire," he said.

"You basically are," I said. "You would be if you went to work for your father."

"Exactly," he said, and pressed his lips together. "Let's just order some food."

Okay. I could take a hint. I sat on the edge of the bed and said, "What do you want?"

He scooted closer to me and pushed his face against my hip. "There's a place down the street that does good sandwiches. And they deliver."

"Okay," I said, and tentatively stroked his hair. "I could do a grilled cheese with tomato soup. You think they have that on the menu?"

"Worth a shot," he said.

I looked up the sandwich place on my phone and called in an order, one hand buried in his hair. "Half an hour," I said, after I hung up.

"Great," he said. "I'm hungry." He kissed my

hip. "Do you want me to oil your hair?"

I glanced down at him, a little surprised. "Really?"

"Sure," he said. "It's still wet, right? I've got some olive oil. I'll give you a scalp massage."

"Only an idiot would say no to an offer like that," I said.

I sat on the floor, leaning back against the bed, while Elliott sat on the mattress behind me and rubbed olive oil into my roots. It felt incredible. Nobody had done this for me since I was still a kid and my mother sat me down once a week to oil my hair. Elliott scratched gently at my scalp and I felt my eyelids sinking closed. If I were a cat, I would have purred.

"Did you do this for your Kenyan girlfriend?" I asked.

"Haiba," he said. "Yes."

"Are you still in touch with her?" I asked.

"Some," he said. "Sometimes. We email a little. Her husband doesn't approve of her contacting me, but she's never cared too much about what men think."

"A woman after my own heart," I said. "Tell her thank you from me. She did all the hard work. It's nice that you're pre-trained. My fiancé was white, and he didn't know about any of this stuff. One time he told me that my hair looked like a Brillo pad."

"That wasn't very nice of him," Elliott said, so carefully neutral that I knew he was diplomatically withholding judgment.

"He didn't always think before he spoke," I said. "But the good parts made up for it. You know how it is. Nobody's perfect."

"Didn't you accuse me of having a fetish?" he asked. "It sounds like you have some sort of fetish for white men."

I laughed. "I don't! I even promised myself I was done fooling around with white boys. So you should count yourself lucky."

"I have to wonder why you would decide something like that," he said.

I shrugged. I didn't want to get into it, not now. "It's a long story."

"Right," he said. "It usually is." He took his hands out of my braids and bent down to kiss my neck. "How does your hair feel now? Moisturized?"

"For some reason, that question strikes me as being really creepy," I said.

"Moisturized," he said, and kissed my cheek. "Moist. Mmm. Get back up here."

"You're gross," I said, laughing, but I went, and then we didn't say anything for a while until the doorbell rang and Elliott had to put on some pants to go get our sandwiches.

CHAPTER 21

Elliott

I did my best to convince Sadie to stay the night, but she insisted she needed to go have dinner with her parents and then sleep in her own bed, "Without you groping me all night."

"I'm not a sleep-groper," I said. "I prefer to fondle women when they're awake."

"Yeah, that's what you say now," she said, "but I know I'm going to wake up at 3am with you humping my ass. I need my beauty sleep if I'm going to charm a bunch of investors tomorrow."

She wouldn't budge, so I admitted defeat and walked her to the elevator.

"Get plenty of sleep," she said, and pushed up on her tiptoes to kiss me. "We're going to kick ass tomorrow."

"If you say so," I said, taking the opportunity to squeeze her ass.

She swatted at me, winked, and said, "I'll see you tomorrow."

Alone in my apartment, I fired up my laptop

and sorted through my email. International development mailing list digest, cheap plane tickets to Dar, update from Kris about her latest dating antics—and an email from my mother's law firm.

Shit. Kris had told me to call them… weeks ago, now, when we met for dinner, the last time I had seen her in person. It had completely slipped my mind. I opened the email and read through it quickly. I didn't recognize the name of the lawyer who had sent the email, but Kris had told me it was some new guy. He gave me his phone number and asked me to call at my convenience.

I glanced at the clock on my computer. It was only 4:30, and any lawyer worth his salt would still be in the office for another couple of hours.

I pulled out my phone.

He answered on the second ring. "Sekeley Lightner, this is Mark Amery."

"Mark, this is Elliott Sloane," I said. "I just received your email. I have to apologize for not getting in touch sooner. My sister told me that you wanted to speak with me, but I'm in the process of launching a new company, and it completely slipped my mind."

"I understand," he said. "Thank you for calling. Ordinarily I would do this in person, but we need to get the paperwork signed and filed soon, or the trust is going to default to—"

"Wait," I said. "I'm sorry. *Trust*?"

Mark was silent for a few moments. Then he said, "I think you had better come by the office."

I took a cab downtown. A mistake: it was rush hour, and traffic crawled maddeningly along. I stared out the window and tried to prepare myself for whatever the lawyer was about to tell me. If my mother had set up a trust that I didn't know about, that *Kris* didn't know about, and that Mark assumed I *did* know about—well, knowing my family, I expected drama, secret letters, hidden bank accounts, and a variety of intricate arrangements to keep my father in the dark.

Sekeley Lightner had its offices in a nondescript high-rise in the Financial District. Stepping out of the elevator, I experienced an immediate, crushing wave of painful reminiscence. After my mother's death, and my belated return to New York, I had spent long, bitter hours in these offices, sorting out the details of my mother's estate. She had made me executor, and I would rather have died myself than turned the duty over to my father. More than a decade ago, but change came slowly to old New York law firms, and all of the fixtures were the same, the furnishings, the wallpaper.

The receptionist—young, blond—smiled at me from behind her wide desk and said, "Can I help you?"

She was different, at least. Not someone I recognized. "I'm Elliott Sloane," I said, "and I'm here to see Mark Amery."

"Of course," she said, perky, painfully young, and got up from the desk to lead me to Mark's office.

Mark was younger than I expected, my age or

even slightly younger. There was a time when all lawyers were impossibly old men, grey-haired and dignified, but I was older now, and starting to understand what my mother meant when she complained about her "boy dentist." Soon I would be middle-aged and crotchety, and the world would be full of fresh-faced, adolescent doctors and lawyers, fetuses walking around in lab coats.

"I hope I'm not ruining your Friday night," I said, after we shook hands and made our introductions.

"Not at all," he said. "I'm low man on the totem pole, so I'll be here until at least 10. The partners tell me that suffering builds character."

A lawyer with a sense of humor. Wonders would never cease. I took the seat he gestured to, and he sat as well and pulled out a thick manila folder.

"I won't waste time dancing around the issue," he said. "Before she died, your mother established a trust, with you and your sisters as beneficiaries. The age of inheritance is set to when you turn thirty-five, which—"

"—is next month," I said. "Right. That's why you've been trying to get in touch with me."

"Exactly," Mark said. "Mr. Sloane, I'm not sure how much your mother told you about this trust—"

"Nothing," I said. "I had no idea it existed until I spoke with you on the phone earlier today."

He nodded, and opened the folder. He took a piece of paper from the top of the stack, glanced at it, and handed it to me.

I took it from him and glanced down at the page. The numbers made no sense to me at first, but my brain parsed them, mercilessly, and I looked up at Mark with the distinct sensation of having had the rug pulled out from under my feet. "This is millions of dollars," I said, struggling to understand.

"Yes," he said. "Two hundred million."

"This isn't possible," I said. "My mother never worked a day in her life. How could she possibly—"

"It's her own inheritance," he said. "She never touched it. She married your father before she came into her own trust, and she decided to bequeath it to her children. She was a Vanderbilt, you know."

"I know," I said. My hands had started shaking. Two hundred million dollars, my God—

"It's to be divided evenly among her surviving children," he said. "Held in trust until each attains the age of thirty-five. Your sisters will receive their own portions on their thirty-fifth birthdays."

I exhaled and looked down at the paper again. The numbers didn't change. "I'm sorry," I said. "I'm having some difficulty grasping the situation."

"Understandable," Mark said. "I'm sure it's a lot to take in. If you aren't ready to sign the paperwork this evening, we can certainly do it sometime next week instead."

"There's no need," I said, numb, dumbfounded. "I'm ready now."

I walked home afterward, four miles in the winter dusk. I wasn't wearing the right shoes for it, and my feet ached by the time I got back to my apartment, but I needed the time and the cold breeze to clear my mind. Fifty million dollars in less than a month, and I would be free, free of my father forever, free to do whatever I wanted and create the changes I longed to see in the world.

And I hadn't earned it, had done nothing to deserve it, and my father would never see it as a meaningful commentary on my worth as a human being.

I needed to call my sisters. Cassie would be furious. Julie would camp out at my doorstep until I gave her some money. Both of them would run to my father with the news as soon as they found out. Maybe I should call him first, which would at least deny him the pleasure of thinking he had caught me sneaking around.

I could imagine that conversation already. He would tell me that my mother's weak female sensibilities had prompted her to establish the trust, that she knew I would never make anything of myself and wanted to provide for her pitiful, helpless offspring. A mother's coddling, oppressive love. A son's failure.

And what could I say in response to his accusations? What reply could I make that wasn't a pathetic excuse?

Everything he would say to me would be true.

CHAPTER 22

Sadie

I woke up on Saturday feeling like a little kid on Christmas morning. The conference started today, and it would go *great*. It had to. We had worked so hard, and if we weren't able to secure an investor, I knew it would break Elliott's heart. It would break mine. We were doing good work. We *deserved* funding.

Too bad the universe didn't give a shit about justice.

The conference was being held in the Javits Center, in Hell's Kitchen. I took the subway into Manhattan and bought myself a shitty cup of coffee in the labyrinthine bowels of Penn Station, and then fought up to the street through the crowds of tourists and commuters. The weather was overcast and drizzling, and the sidewalk outside the station bristled with umbrellas. I should have taken a cab.

The crowds cleared out a few blocks west of Penn Station, though, and I quickly made my way to the convention center. It was still early, not even 8:00,

238

and the conference wasn't set to start until 9, but the broad plaza in front of the center was already swarming with people. I hadn't realized until that moment how much of a big deal this conference really was. I knew that it was important, and that Elliott was taking it very seriously, but seeing the size of the center and the number of people bustling around really drove home the fact that this was happening, now, today, and all of our hopes were on the line.

I went inside and checked in at the registration desk. The woman I spoke with gave me a name tag, a cheap canvas totebag filled with all sorts of crap that I didn't bother sorting through, and a map. Elliott would be in the vendor room, setting up. I located it on the map and headed that way.

Elliott had arranged for all of our promotional materials to be delivered to the center, but we still needed to get everything set up and organized. The vendor room was a massive, high-ceiling exhibition hall, cold as a mausoleum and buzzing with activity. Even half-full—the conference wasn't all that large— it was still impressive. I wandered through the endless aisles of tables and posters and banners, feeling a little overwhelmed, until I finally spotted Elliott's blond head above the crowd. Thank God he was so tall.

His face lit up as he saw me approaching, and my stomach flipped over in response to the honest, uncomplicated pleasure I saw there. He was so happy to see me, and I hadn't even done anything. I was just walking toward him. I wasn't even wearing a particularly nice dress.

"This is it," he said, as I came within earshot. "The big day."

I smiled at him, charmed by his enthusiasm. He was usually so stoic that it was nice to see him excited about something for a change. "It'll go great," I said.

"Sure," he said. "I just have to survive giving this talk."

He was speaking in a session that afternoon. "What time is it?" I asked.

"Oh no," he said. "You don't get to watch. You have to stay here and man the booth."

"I think I can leave for fifteen minutes," I said. "You just don't want me to watch your talk."

"I plead the Fifth," he said, and then, very blatantly changing the subject, "Help me set up this banner."

I rolled my eyes and helped him.

By 9:00, our booth was plastered with posters, and our table was covered with neatly organized stacks of pamphlets and business cards. We had spent entirely too long wrestling with the banner stand, but it was up, finally, and as glossy and eye-catching and well-designed as anyone could have hoped. There was a box beneath the table filled with water bottles and snacks.

We were ready.

"Just leave it to me," I told Elliott, as we stood there surveying our work. "I'm going to sweet-talk some nice old man into leaving us his entire estate."

To my surprise, he leaned down and hugged me: very chaste, his hands on my mid-back and no lower, and then he kissed my cheek and said, "Sadie, I couldn't have done this without you."

I patted his back, feeling awkward but touched. I was just a graphic designer, and anyone competent could have done the same work for him; but it was sweet of him to say. "It'll go great," I said. "You don't have to worry."

He released me and stepped back, running one hand over his hair like he was a little embarrassed. "I'll worry no matter what," he said, "but thanks for the vote of confidence."

And then the first conference attendees wandered into the vendor room.

We spent the next couple of hours talking to people. Or, well, mostly Elliott talked. I handed out pamphlets and answered basic questions for the people who were just wandering through, and beside me, Elliott lectured the true believers, the ones who had come to our booth because they were interested in his work. It was a marvel. I had seen flashes of his charisma, but now he was so earnest and charming and impassioned that it was like he had been body-snatched. The people listening to him nodded thoughtfully and flipped through the pamphlets and asked pointed questions. Business cards were exchanged. Hands were shaken.

During a brief lull when there wasn't anybody at our booth, Elliott turned to me and slumped his shoulders, miming exhaustion.

"You're doing great," I said. "I didn't even think you knew that many words."

He grinned at me, unruffled. "My father made me take speech lessons for years," he said. "I was a very timid child. Shy. I still can't make small talk worth a damn, but I'm very good at performing like a trained monkey."

"Your father sounds horrible," I said passionately. "I hope I meet him so I can tell him what an enormous jerk he is."

He took a sip from his water bottle and raised his eyebrows at me. "I'll arrange a meeting."

Shortly before 11, the room emptied out like someone had pulled the stopper from a drain. I looked at Elliott, confused, and he said, "Plenary session at 11. It's one of the conference's headline speakers, so everyone wants to go."

"Don't you want to go?" I asked. "You should. I can hold down the fort here."

"I—actually, yes," he said. "I'd like to go. Thanks. It's just an hour. I'll bring you some lunch."

"No pickles," I said.

Even with the plenary session, there were still enough people milling around the vendor room that I kept very busy. I talked to an older white lady wearing an actual mink stole and, ludicrously, opera gloves. She paused by the booth and looked down her nose at me, and I braced myself for whatever thinly veiled racist bullshit was about to come out of her mouth, but she only said, "You don't look like your name is Elliott Sloane."

"You've got me there," I said, "but I'm happy to talk to you about the company, if you have questions. We're doing some very exciting work with ceramic water filters."

"Very well," she said, so regal that she was basically a parody of herself—surely they didn't let people like this wander out of the Upper East Side without a chaperone. "I would be delighted to listen to your sales pitch."

What a condescending hag. I plastered a fake smile on my face and launched into an explanation of the company's mission. But despite her pinched look and haughty attitude, the woman listened intently and asked surprisingly insightful questions, and I found myself relaxing and even enjoying our conversation.

We talked for half an hour, and when at last she glanced at her watch and announced that she needed to go, she gave me an appraising look and said, "Kindly give me one of those business cards. I'll need to speak with my husband before making any decisions, but I'm sure he'll agree with me that your company is a worthy investment."

"I hope he will," I said, giddy beyond words and trying to hide it. I scribbled my phone number on the back of a business card and handed it to her. "That's Mr. Sloane's contact information, and if you'd like to talk with me again, I put my cell number on there too."

"A pleasure," she said, and sailed off.

I shook my head to myself, bemused. Rich people were *so* strange. Lord, and so was my life. Before I met Elliott, I never in a million years would have envisioned spending half an hour chatting casually with a blue-blood heiress.

When Elliott returned, bearing two boxed lunches, I said, "I think I landed us an investor."

He raised his eyebrows. "Already?"

"I told you I was going to do it," I said, a little annoyed that he wasn't more excited. "She said she's going to talk to her husband and get in touch."

"Well, let's not celebrate until we get a firm commitment," he said, "but that's great. I knew bringing you to this conference was a good idea."

"Bringing me a sandwich was also a good idea," I said, stupidly pleased by his faint praise. Was I really that desperate for his approval? Let's be real: yes.

While Elliott was in the plenary session, I had looked up the time of his talk. It was at 3:00, and as the afternoon wore on, I watched him become progressively more nervous and withdrawn. By an hour out, he had stopped interacting with the people who came by the booth, and was sitting bent over his notes and looking pale and a little clammy. Finally, I said, "You're making people nervous sitting there like grim death. Go take a walk or something. I've got this."

"Okay," he said, and rubbed his face with both hands. "You're right."

"You're going to be fine," I said. "Lots of

people are afraid of public speaking. It's totally normal."

He cracked a weak grin. "What makes you think I'm nervous?"

"My keen observational skills," I said. "Just go."

The afternoon was quieter than the morning had been. Most people were in talks, and when only a handful stopped to speak with me in the hour before Elliott's session, I didn't feel so guilty about abandoning the booth. I set out some more pamphlets, made an impromptu sign that read "BACK IN 20," and made my way to the room where Elliott was scheduled to speak.

I slipped into the back of the room just as the previous speaker left the stage. A short, balding man stood up from a table on the stage and said, "Our next talk is by Elliott Sloane of One Drop, LLC, titled 'Differential advantages of mediums for water filtration.'"

What a terrible title. Boring. He should have asked me for advice. Men always thought they could handle everything themselves. Elliott mounted the stage to a polite but unenthusiastic smattering of applause. It didn't seem to bother him, though. He looked crisp and confident in his suit. He adjusted the microphone to point upward, paused, made a skeptical face, and tilted it a little higher. The audience laughed. "Good afternoon, everyone," he said, warm and amused, inviting the audience to share the humor of the situation. "Today I'd like to speak with you about a common problem in clean water interventions…"

The man on stage was a totally different creature from the nervous wreck I'd sent out for a walk. He was funny and relaxed, using his slides to bolster his point but not relying on them to convey his message for him, gesturing for emphasis, moving confidently around the podium. I tried to be an objective observer, to watch him the way I would watch a stranger, and I thought it was clear to everyone in the audience that he cared very deeply about subject. Here was a man who wanted to transform the world. Elliott's fire was no secret to me, and now it was on display for everyone in the room. I knew that he would find investors after this.

I was so proud of him that I felt like I might burst.

When his talk ended, the session chair asked if there were any questions, and so many hands went up that I saw Elliott blink and jerk his chin slightly in surprise.

I stayed for the questions—thoughtful, probing—and then slipped out of the room. Elliott would probably stay until the end of the session, and I needed to get back to the booth. I could congratulate him later.

He didn't return until past 6:00. I was sitting at the booth, bored, waiting for someone to come talk to me. "Sorry," he said, taking the chair beside me. "A couple of people wanted to talk to me after the session ended. I didn't meant to abandon you here for so long."

"No problem," I said. "I watched your talk."

He groaned and covered his face with one hand. "How bad was it?"

"Elliott, are you kidding me?" I asked. "It was incredible. You did a wonderful job. I don't know how, because you were so messed up beforehand that I really thought you were going to throw up or something—"

"I did," he said, and grinned. "In the bathroom, right before my session started. Glamorous, huh?"

"Well, you pulled it off," I said. "I never would have known."

"I'm just glad it's over," he said. "Christ. I hate giving talks."

"Let's go celebrate," I said impulsively. "We can go out for dinner. Nobody's going to come to the booth this late. They can just take a pamphlet and come back tomorrow."

He laughed. "Okay. You've convinced me."

We walked a few blocks east to have our pick of the restaurants along 9th Avenue. "Nothing fancy," Elliott told me as we walked. "I want a burger. A huge, juicy burger. With onion rings."

"You got it," I said. "Whatever you want. You're the boss."

We looked at a few menus and settled on the place that had, according to Elliott, the most promising burger. It was still pretty early for dinner, and we snagged a secluded table in the back. Our waiter came by, and Elliott ordered a bottle of wine.

"Really?" I asked. "Wine and a burger?"

"The finest of dining," he said. "My ancestors came over on the Mayflower, which means I can do whatever I want and nobody can judge me."

I rolled my eyes. "Is that how it works? I must have missed that memo."

We made light, pleasant conversation while we ate. The wine was pretty good, and Elliott was in a buoyant mood, riding high on the success of his speech. He ordered a second bottle of wine, and then dessert for us to share, a ridiculous brownie sundae drenched in chocolate syrup and whipped cream.

"There's no way we're going to be able to eat all of this," I said, laughing.

"The effort is the reward," he said. "We'll make a good go of it."

I dug my spoon in and glanced up to see him watching me, a small smile on his face. "What?" I asked, suspicious.

"Nothing," he said. "Today went well. I'm happy."

"Okay," I said, and narrowed my eyes at him. "Is this a date? Are we on a date right now?"

"It can be a date if you want it to be," he said.

"No," I said. I took my spoon out of the sundae and pointed it at him. "We aren't doing this."

He held up both of his hands in a placating gesture. "Okay, it's not a date. We're just two people eating dinner together. Platonically."

"Okay," I said, even though I didn't really believe him. Part of me wanted him to insist. I wanted it to be a date. I wanted to date him. I wanted him to be my boyfriend. I wanted to hold hands with him in public, and come home to him every evening and tell him about my day.

And I couldn't. I couldn't.

We only got halfway through the sundae before I admitted defeat. With a groan, I leaned back against my chair and folded my hands over my belly. "I regret eating that."

"But it's so delicious," he said. He took another bite and then set his spoon down on the tablecloth. "Sadie, there's something I need to tell you."

That didn't sound promising. "Okay."

He sighed deeply. "I met with my mother's attorney yesterday."

I waited, but he didn't say anything else, which meant I would have to drag it out of him one sentence at a time. He did this whenever he felt uncomfortable or wasn't sure how to phrase something, and it drove me crazy. I wished he would just spit it out. "Her attorney," I said.

He nodded. "He told me—well. Apparently my mother left me some money."

"Okay," I said, trying to figure out why he was telling me this. "And you didn't know about it?"

"No," he said. "Not until yesterday. It was being held in trust until I turned thirty-five, and my birthday is next month." He grimaced and took a sip of wine. "It's actually… it turns out that it's quite a bit of money."

"How much money," I said slowly.

"Fifty million," he said.

It took a moment for that number to sink in. "Fifty—wow. Okay. But that's great, right? Now you don't have to worry about finding an investor! You can bring Jim down here and get started on the prototype—"

"I'm not accepting it," he said.

I stared at him. I couldn't think of a single thing to say.

"I'll give part of it to my sisters," he said. "And the rest of it I'm going to donate to charity."

I could not *believe* what I was hearing. "Elliott, that is by far the stupidest thing I've heard in at least a year. Are you on drugs? This is exactly what you need to get the company off the ground. Why would you turn down the money?"

His lips compressed into a stubborn line. I'd pushed him too far. "I want to make my own way in the world," he said, "instead of relying on my mother's generosity."

"This is about your father, isn't it?" I asked. "You're turning down the money to spite him. My God."

"That's not true," he said, but I could tell from his expression that it was.

"This is ridiculous," I said. "You're a grown man. Why do you still care what your father thinks of you? Are you really so desperate for his approval that you're going to throw away your chance to change people's lives for the better?"

"That's not what I'm doing," he said stiffly.

"You really ought to put this behind you," I said. "Just, I mean. Just tell him to get lost. Tell him you don't care what he thinks. You need to get over your daddy issues."

"Well, you know what, Sadie," he snapped, "we all have our cross to bear. You're still mourning your dead boyfriend. Why don't you get over *that*?"

I flinched. That was a low blow, and it *hurt*. But at the same time, I couldn't deny that I deserved it. It was no worse than any of the things I had just said to him.

But Elliott's scowl instantly crumpled into regret. "I'm sorry," he said. "That was cruel of me. I didn't mean it."

"No, you did," I said. "And I meant what I said. And we're both right. So where does that leave us?"

He sighed heavily. "I don't know, Sadie."

The waiter, with impeccable timing, appeared beside our table. "Is there anything else I can get for you?"

CHAPTER 23

Sadie

We ended the night on reasonably good terms. Elliott walked me to Penn Station and kissed me on the sidewalk before he continued on to Herald Square. It was a polite kiss, though, dry and close-mouthed, not at all the sort of passionate embrace I had come to expect from him. He was still angry about what I had said. Well, fine: I was angry, too.

"I'll see you in the morning," he said. "Sleep well."

"You too," I said, and turned and went down into the station, leaving him behind.

I didn't sleep well. I tossed and turned all night, wondering how I could change, how I could make *him* change. How we could both make peace with our stubborn, prideful hearts.

The other reason I couldn't sleep was that I had told Eric I would meet with him tomorrow, and I was terrified about what he might say to me. What he might tell me about Elliott. I wasn't sure I wanted to know.

I finally fell into a fitful sleep and dreamed that I was walking through an enormous, empty house, opening the door to every room and peering inside, searching for someone, but there was nothing in any of the rooms but dust.

I woke before my alarm went off, feeling tired but also weirdly energetic. It was a sunny morning, and bitterly cold. I stopped in a bodega a couple of blocks from the conference center and bought two cups of coffee: one for me, one for Elliott. A peace offering. We had both said unkind things. Tempers had frayed. We had been under a lot of pressure for a long time; it was understandable. We could put it behind us.

I felt magnanimous. Forgiving.

I thought I had gotten an early start, but Elliott was already at our booth in the vendor room, sitting at the table with his laptop open in front of him, scowling at the screen.

There were two cups of coffee on the table beside him.

I started laughing, and he looked up, eyebrows raised in inquiry. "I got coffee," I said, holding out my hands, each one wrapped around a cardboard coffee cup.

A slow, rueful smile spread across his face. "So did I," he said. "O. Henry would be proud."

"Nice reference," I said. "I didn't cut off all my hair, though. Buying coffee doesn't have the same sacrificial irony to it."

"Well," he said, and shrugged. "I could

probably use two cups of coffee this morning."

So could I, but I didn't want to admit that I'd slept so poorly. "So what's the plan for today?"

He shrugged again. "More networking, more talks. There's a session this afternoon that I'd like to attend, so I'll leave you to man the booth. I may have dinner tonight with a few potential investors."

"Really? You didn't tell me you had anyone sniffing around," I said.

"Oh, am I supposed to tell you everything now?" he asked, smirking at me. "A man needs to have a few secrets. No, these are people who spoke with me yesterday after my talk. It's likely that nothing will come of it."

"Such a pessimist," I said. "Something could come of it. Just be your charming self and they'll cough up a billion dollars."

"Sound advice," he said, with that tilt to his mouth that meant he was making fun of me.

I didn't care. It felt good to banter with him just like always. I hadn't ruined everything last night, then. We could still be friends.

Things got off to a slower start than they had on Saturday. By 10:00, only a few people had trickled past our booth. "Everyone was out drinking last night," Elliott told me, when I asked him what was going on. "Aid workers love to party, especially when they can claim it's 'networking' and justify their hangovers as part of the cost of doing business."

"Sounds like my kind of people," I said.

"Where are the investors, though?"

"They were probably out drinking, too," Elliott said. "Or else they're sleeping in. Rich people don't believe in waking up early on Sunday mornings."

"So why are you here, then?" I asked.

He grinned at me. "I'm the particular subspecies of rich person known as a 'businessman.' Found in tropical environments, we shun daylight and prefer to lay our eggs in pools of stagnant water."

I rolled my eyes and went back to reading design blogs on my phone.

A little while later, Eric showed up.

I didn't see him coming. I wasn't paying any attention; I had moved on to the international development blogs I'd added to my daily regimen, and was totally engrossed in a post by a guy arguing that digging new wells made people feel good about themselves but didn't accomplish much in the long run. I took vague note of someone approaching our booth, and then I heard Elliott exclaim, "Eric! I didn't expect to see you here."

My heart dropped into my shoes, and I glanced up, hoping I didn't look as guilty as I felt. Eric was shaking Elliott's hand and slapping his shoulder, making a pretty good show of Gosh Old Chum Fancy Meeting You Here, Quite Delightful, and then he cut his eyes at me for a single instant and winked.

Lord, what a creep. I never should have gotten involved with him. I should have hung up on him when he called me.

But I hadn't, and now I was too curious to let it go.

I put my phone away and stood up, trying to look polite and disinterested. "Sadie, you remember Eric," Elliott said, one hand on my lower back, drawing me forward.

"Of course," I said, offering my hand to shake.

"I'm glad to hear I left an impression on the lady," Eric said, and bent to kiss my knuckles.

Ridiculous. I made a face at Elliott, who brought one hand up to conceal his smile.

"Elliott, you don't mind loaning her to me for an hour or so, do you?" Eric asked, still holding onto my hand. "I'm sure you've been keeping her here at the booth, doing your boring dirty work for you—"

"Yes, the dirty work that she's getting *paid to do*," Elliott said.

"—and she should have a chance to walk around and experience all that the conference has to offer," Eric finished, flashing a winning smile. His teeth were too white and too even. It didn't look natural.

"Right, the exciting benefits of hearing other people pitch their companies to her," Elliott said. "Thrilling. But sure, you can take her if she's willing to be taken."

I gritted my teeth. Eric had outmaneuvered me. We had agreed to meet later that day, during the conference's designated lunch hour, but for whatever reason he had decided to change the plan without notifying me. I suspected that he just wanted to make me uncomfortable. Why did Elliott like this guy?

"Wonderful," Eric said, all teeth and slick charm. "We won't be long. I'll have her back before you miss her."

I really, really did not like the way he kept talking about me like I was an object, or a wayward pet. "You can show me all the sights," I said, smiling, hating him. I prayed that Elliott would object and tell Eric I needed to stay, but he just shrugged and turned to speak with a woman who was approaching the booth, and it was clear there was no hope for me. I would just have to deal with this situation I had gotten myself into.

Eric and I left the vendor room and went up to the convention center's main concourse, a huge and echoing space of glass and light. A few people meandered around, but we were more or less alone. He led me to a bench near the wall of windows and sat down, looking up at me expectantly.

I had brought this on myself. I sat.

"I'm looking forward to working with you, Sadie," Eric said, which was essentially the conversational equivalent of trying to stick it in without any foreplay.

"Hold up," I said. "I never said I would work for you."

"Well, it's a foregone conclusion, isn't it?" he asked. "Especially after I tell you what I've learned about Elliott's start-up."

God, he was *enjoying* this. He was drawing it out and trying to make me squirm. Well, I wouldn't squirm; I wouldn't give him the pleasure. "Feel free to share that with me whenever you're ready," I said.

He chuckled. "All right. You may have noticed something unusual about one of his investors."

"Unusual in what way?" I asked. I wasn't going to give him anything.

"*Very* clever," he said. "I know you noticed something, or you wouldn't have responded to my email. But that's fine. I'll let you play dumb. He's getting money from Uganda International Friendship, which doesn't exist. It's a shell corporation. Now, you may ask yourself: who would need to illicitly funnel money out of Uganda? I can't say for sure, but there are plenty of unsavory types who would like to have a few million stashed in an account overseas, just to be safe. You never know when you'll need to flee the country on short notice."

The implications made my skin crawl. Was Elliott really in cahoots with *war criminals*? I found it hard to believe, but Eric didn't look like he was lying, and it matched up with everything I'd found out on my own. "Why are you telling me this?" I asked.

"Because I want you to come work for me, of course," he said. "And I don't see you jumping ship unless you can't imagine staying."

As if I would ever work for a back-stabbing two-faced creeper like him. "I thought Elliott was your friend."

He shrugged. "He is. But business is business. You have to make some enemies on your way to the top."

"Right," I said, and stood up. "I need to talk to Elliott."

"Of course," he said. "Take as much time as you need. And feel free to tell him where you got your information."

I would, even though I knew it would hurt him. I didn't want him to keep being friends with someone like Eric.

I didn't do it right away. I waited until the conference ended that evening, and we were packing up the booth. Elliott had secured an investor—signed, sealed, delivered; not a ton of money, but a good start—and I actually caught him *whistling* as he put away our remaining business cards. I hated to rain on his parade, but I couldn't wait any longer to ask him about what Eric had told me. The knowledge was a hard, heavy knot in my chest, and I just wanted to get it over with, whatever *it* might be, whatever angry or sorrowful conversation we were about to have.

I started packing pamphlets into a box so I didn't have to look at him. "Eric told me something today."

"Oh yeah?" he asked, distracted, cheerful. "What's that?"

"He said—he told me…" I closed my eyes. Spit it out, Bayliss. "He said you're getting funding from an organization called Uganda International Friendship, but it's not—he told me it's a shell corporation."

I glanced up him, afraid to see his reaction. He

hadn't paused in moving business cards, but his mouth had compressed into a thin, unhappy line.

"Elliott," I said, terrified that it was true, and that he wasn't the man I had thought him to be.

"We aren't going to talk about this here," he said, and I nodded, grateful for any reprieve.

We finished packing up the booth in silence. Elliott had arranged for everything to be picked up later that evening and delivered back to the office, and so when the final lid was on the final box, he turned and walked off without saying anything to me or checking to see if I followed.

I scurried after him. It didn't make sense: he was potentially conspiring with evil people and doing very illegal things, and yet I felt incredibly guilty. "Elliott, wait," I said.

He didn't answer. He strode ahead, not looking back.

I followed him, hoping he would turn, hoping he would say something to acknowledge me, even one word. He didn't. We went upstairs, past where I had sat with Eric earlier that day—guilty, *so* guilty— and down a wide hallway into the windowless depths of the building. Elliott stopped in front of a large door and pushed it open, and gestured for me to go inside.

It was one of the meeting rooms, empty now except for the stage and the chairs lined up before it. I turned to face Elliott as he closed the door, and then he said, "Tell me exactly what Eric said to you."

"Not too much more than I already told you," I

said. "He said you're getting money from an organization that doesn't actually exist, and he implied that you're, um. That you've been funneling money out of the country for, like. I don't know. Joseph Kony. Warlords. Terrible people."

"Right," Elliott said, very stiff and distant, formal, like he was a million miles away.

"It isn't true, right?" I asked him. "You wouldn't—that's not something you would do."

"I can't believe you're asking me that question," he said.

"Well, I don't know what to think!" I exclaimed. "Was Eric just telling me a bunch of lies? Are you getting money from Uganda International Friendship or not?"

"I am," he said.

"You're impossible," I said. "Was he lying or not? Are you working for warlords? Why are you getting money from a shell corporation? Just please tell me," I said, begging now, desperate for him to reassure me that he was still the good man I knew him to be.

"I don't see why I should waste time defending myself," he said, "when you and Eric have already played judge and jury. Why did he tell you all of this? What's in it for him?"

"He wants to hire me," I said, defeated. "He's starting his own company."

"Of course," Elliott said, with a bitter twist to his mouth. "Very sensible of him."

"Elliott, don't be like this," I pleaded. "I'm sure

there's a reasonable explanation. If you would just tell me—"

"And then what?" he asked. "You'll believe me, and all suspicion will be wiped from your mind? You don't trust me. If you can think this about me, that I would deliberately—that I would *steal money*, or whatever it was Eric decided to accuse me of—"

He was angry: voice raised, nostrils flaring. I took a step back, without really meaning to. His face crumpled. "Sadie…"

"I don't know what to think," I said quietly. "We seem to be getting mad at each other a lot, lately."

He sighed, and rubbed his hands over his face. "Fuck. Sadie…"

"Maybe you're doing something fishy," I said. "I don't really know. Maybe it's totally innocent. Maybe you got tricked. I don't know. I'm not going to work for Eric, though, that's for sure. And you shouldn't trust him. He is *not* your friend."

"I'm getting that impression," Elliott said.

"And past that, I don't know," I said, and swallowed, and then said, for once, exactly what was in my heart. "I'm afraid. You scare me. Maybe I was ready to believe Eric because it was the easy out. Working with you has been—you make me want to be a better person. I had stopped caring about anything except my own suffering, and you showed me a way toward living in the world again. And the way you touch me, like I'm—like I *mean* something to you… It scares me."

He took a step toward me, closing the distance between us.

I backed up again, feeling like a skittish horse. If he put his hands on me now, I would crumble to pieces. "Anyway, I don't think I can work with you anymore."

He stopped, hands hanging loose by his side, green eyes dark in the dim light. "You're quitting?"

"It's too hard for me," I said. "Working with you, and feeling—feeling—"

I couldn't say it. I wasn't even sure what I felt. It was too grand and formless for words.

"I'm bewildered by this entire conversation," he said, rubbing his hands across his face again. "Let's accept that we're both stubborn and irrational people. I'll write a strongly-worded email to Eric and tell my father to go fuck himself, and you'll agree to be my girlfriend. We'll bring Jim down from Boston and make a successful prototype that will net us several million dollars in investments. Water-borne diseases will become a thing of the past. Stay with me."

I couldn't. It was choking me. I shook my head, telling him no, telling myself to stop hoping for things I was unable to let myself have. He wanted me to *be his girlfriend*, like we were kids in the throes of puppy love. "Elliott, it won't ever work. We have absolutely nothing in common. I'm a middle-class black girl from Queens, and you're the son of a billionaire."

He frowned at me. "Do you think that matters?

263

The last woman I loved was born in a hut with a dirt floor, and she didn't learn to read until she was ten. And you're worried that—what, that you won't know which fork to use during formal dinners at the family compound? We don't have a compound. My father likes to eat at Burger King."

I laughed, and then was mortified when it turned into a sob. I covered my mouth with one hand and turned away from him. I couldn't bear to look at the desperate hope scrawled across his face. "I need to go," I said.

"Sadie," he said, his voice catching.

"I'm sorry," I said. "I really need to go."

And I left.

CHAPTER 24

Elliott

On Monday morning, I woke before dawn and watched as the first pale light hit my grimy, east-facing windows. I could rent a better apartment, now, with my mother's money; but I had grown fond of my dismal shoebox. It was easy to keep clean, and it was close to work. I didn't really know what else I was supposed to look for in an apartment.

Comfort, maybe. A sense of home.

Those were things that New York couldn't offer me.

I walked to work through quiet, empty streets. A few taxis rolled past, and a man came out of a coffee shop and heaved a trash bag into a dumpster. Maybe there were parts of the city that never slept, but Midtown wasn't one of them.

In the lobby, the security guard nodded to me from his post.

I still didn't know his name.

The office was dark and silent. I turned on a few lamps, and sat down at my desk to read through my email. Nothing interesting. A mass email from the organizer of the conference, thanking everyone for attending. A quick note from an old friend who was now working against human trafficking in Cambodia, asking me if I had seen a particular article.

Nothing from Eric, or from Sadie.

I didn't know what I was expecting.

I worked for a few hours, sending follow-up emails to people I had spoken with at the conference and skimming through my news reader, until it was past the time that Sadie usually showed up for work. I waited a while longer, thinking that maybe she had slept in, maybe… But soon it was clear that she wasn't coming, and I gave in to the inevitable and made myself a second pot of coffee.

The righteous indignation I'd felt the night before had ebbed. I was sad, now, and a bit bewildered. I still wasn't sure of Eric's motive, or exactly what he had told Sadie, or how he found out about UIF in the first place. But my interaction with Sadie, after, was now, in hindsight, painfully clear. She had wanted nothing more than for me to reassure her, and I—all wounded pride—had been too busy blustering to set her mind at ease. A mistake. I should have unbent, and told her the truth.

It wasn't too late for that.

I gathered the documents quickly: the initial emails, the signed contract. I wrote a note to her, explaining everything. I packaged it all up and took it down the street to a courier service. The bearded hipster at the front desk told me it would be delivered that afternoon. And then I would just have to wait.

I went back to the office and stared at my computer for a while. There was no point. I wasn't getting anything done. I had some funding, now; I should email Jim and make arrangements for him to come down from Boston, find him a place to stay and some lab space for his experiments. I should contact Mark at Sekeley Lightner. It all seemed insurmountable. Without Sadie, I was adrift.

There was one thing I could do, though. One monumental task I could square away for good.

I put on my coat, and went to pay a visit to my father.

His lair was downtown, at the top of a huge skyscraper in the heart of the Financial District. I hadn't been to the office in years, not since I spent a few months in New York before I left for Southeast Asia and then the job with MSF. Security had been tightened, it seemed: where before I could stroll into the lobby and take the elevator directly to Sloane Worldwide's offices, I was now stopped by a burly man perched at the main desk, who said, "How can I direct you today, sir?"

Cerberus at the gates, I thought, amused. He didn't care if I got lost: he was there to turn away the unwashed masses. "I'm here to see Rupert Sloane," I said. "I'm his son."

If I had expected him to be impressed, I would have been sorely disappointed. He picked up the phone at his elbow, spoke into it briefly, and then said, "Someone will be down to escort you."

I slouched against his desk and waited. Men and women in business suits flashed security badges and passed by uncontested. Others paused and asked for directions, and the guard pointed them to the elevators or told them which floor to go to. Nobody else was forced to wait. A special privilege for those who wished to beard the lion in his den.

After about ten minutes—my father wanted me impatient and annoyed—a woman emerged from the nearest elevator, and I recognized my father's venerable battleship of a personal assistant, Henrietta, who was eighty if she was a day and had been working for my father since the Johnson administration.

"Henrietta," I said, straightening up. "What a delight."

She pursed her mouth and said, "Mr. Sloane will see you now."

Of course. No time for chit-chat. I followed her into the same elevator she had exited from. She swiped her security card and punched the single button on the control panel. A private elevator, then, with direct access to my father. That was new. I was surprised he didn't intend to make me go through the servants' entrance.

The elevator rose smoothly upward. We rode in silence, Henrietta staring straight ahead, oozing disapproval. She was loyal as a dog, and anyone who got on my father's bad side became the immediate target of Henrietta's wrath. I suspected brainwashing, but couldn't prove it.

The elevator stopped, the doors slid open, and we emerged into the waiting area outside my father's office.

Henrietta went straight for her desk and pushed the button to activate the intercom. "Sir, your son is here."

The intercom crackled. "Send him in," my father's voice said.

I went in. My father's office was a cavernous space, dimly lit, with his enormous, antique desk backed against the far wall. It was a long walk across the carpet, and the effect was that of a displeased king awaiting some wayward knight. I could easily imagine hapless underlings quaking in terror as they made the approach.

Long practice had inoculated me against my father's intimidation techniques. I strolled toward his desk, hands casually shoved in my pockets—a habit he hated; he said it was sloppy and unprofessional—and said, "Kind of you to make room for me in your busy schedule."

"Elliott," he said. He didn't stand to greet me. "You know I expect you to call Henrietta twenty-four hours ahead of time if you want to see me."

Talking to him was like entering a time warp. I was sixteen again: sullen, resentful, and tongue-tied. "It's important," I said.

"Oh, I'm sure," he said, and rolled his eyes. "Vastly more important than the conference call you just interrupted."

I worked my jaw. Words piled up in my mouth, unspoken.

"Cat got your tongue?" he sneered. "Spit it out."

I breathed in. I exhaled. There was a time when I *hated* my father, when every interaction with him set a terrible fire burning in my gut. I fought that fire now. He was a petty tyrant, a bitter man who found no joy in life except through making money. I wouldn't end up like him.

I wouldn't hate him any longer, I decided. I would try to understand him. I would be kind. I would feel pity for him instead of rage.

"I'm here to tell you that I'm done," I said. "I won't ever work for you. I won't take over the company. I'll go to your funeral, but I'm finished with being your son."

He smiled. He thought I was playing the game with him. "I've cut you off," he said. "You won't last six months."

"I know you have," I said. "I've lasted this long. Go ahead and disinherit me for good. You can do it tonight."

He gave me a narrow look. "Play your card, Elliott."

This was my father's life: machinations, strategy. Everyone was out to get something. "I spoke to mom's lawyers recently," I said. "Turns out she left me a pretty sizable trust fund."

He started laughing. "Of course. So that's your

ticket out, is it? Still clinging to mommy's apron strings. You'll never be a man, Elliott. You're still just a nervous little boy."

I considered all of my possible responses. I could argue with him, insult him, try to convince him that he was wrong. None of it would work. He would never be proud of me, no matter what I did. There was no point.

And so I turned my back on him and walked out of his office.

"Elliott," I heard him say behind me, but I didn't stop.

Henrietta, in grim silence, escorted me back to the lobby. I walked out of the building into the weak January sunlight, trying to decide how I felt. Angry? Humiliated?

I felt nothing. I was free.

Three decades of trying to please my father, and I was done. I didn't care anymore.

In a month, I would have fifty million dollars, and I could do anything I wanted.

I took a cab home. Speeding along FDR Drive, my phone rang.

It was Sadie.

"I got your note," she said.

"And?" I asked.

She was silent for a few moments. "I'm sorry for doubting you," she said at last. "But I need some time."

It wasn't *I'm going to work for Eric*. It wasn't *don't ever contact me again*. Time I could work with. I could give her that. "As much as you need," I said. "But I hope it won't be too long."

Another pause. "I'm scared," she said.

I closed my eyes. Brave, fragile Sadie. I could hear in her voice how hard it had been for her to admit her fear. "There's nothing to be scared of," I said.

She sighed. "I guess not." I listened to her breathe, in and out, a quiet presence at the other end of the line. "Look, I'll call you in a few days, okay? I'm just… I need some time."

"Okay," I said. "Whatever you need."

After we hung up, I told the cab driver to turn around, and texted Kristin that I was coming over. Sadie needed time, and I needed an evening spent drinking wine with Kris and listening to her talk about what she termed "boy problems."

CHAPTER 25

Sadie

I was still in my pajamas when Elliott's package arrived well past noon, and I had to go downstairs and talk to the bike messenger with my hair wrapped in a scarf like somebody's grandma. The guy didn't bat an eye, though, and I reminded myself that this was New York: half the people I knew worked from home, and the other half had weird hours that meant they were home in the middle of the day. Like I was. Nothing unusual.

After I had signed for the package, and taken it back upstairs to my apartment, I set it on the coffee table and looked at it. It was completely ordinary in every way: fat, rectangular, that funny orange-brown color like all shipping envelopes. My address was written on the back in Elliott's firm hand.

Well. It probably wouldn't bite me.

I opened it up and slid the papers out. On the top of the stack was a handwritten note. I looked at it, at the black ink scrawled across the page, and I closed my eyes. I wasn't sure I wanted to read what he had to say.

I had to. I had to be a grown-up and read it.
I took a deep breath.

Dear Sadie,

Uganda International Friendship is a shell corporation for a Ugandan NGO. They received funding from the World Health Organization, with the stipulation that the money can't be spent outside of the country. But they're interested in my work with water filter technology, and they offered to help fund me while I develop a prototype. UIF was created to funnel the money in question out of the country without raising any red flags. The Ugandan government might be displeased, but there's nothing truly illicit going on.

I've attached some relevant documents. Please know that I wasn't deliberately concealing information from you. I simply thought the entire situation was a non-issue, and not something you would find particularly interesting. Eric has a real talent for putting a dark spin on just about any scenario.

I hope you'll come back and work for me again. We're great together. And yes, I do mean that as an innuendo. I want to wake up beside you every day for the rest of my life.

With all my heart,

Elliott

I dropped the letter on the coffee table and sank down onto the sofa, bending forward and pressing my forehead against my knees. I didn't need to read the documents he'd sent. Everything he said made sense—more sense than what Eric had told me. And I knew that Elliott was a good man.

I read the papers anyway. I was curious, and he'd sent them to me, so why not? Everything was exactly as he said. The Ugandan woman he'd been corresponding with was apologetic about all of it in an "oh isn't this silly" sort of way. The problem was the Ugandan government: they received money from the WHO, and then doled it out to various charity organizations, and they didn't want the money leaving the country. I could understand the reasoning, although it seemed a little short-sighted to me.

So Elliott wasn't a liar, or a thief. I didn't have to stop associating with him. I could keep my job. I could keep making out with him. We didn't have to stop.

I should have felt relieved, but instead I just felt a sad muddle of worry and confusion churning in my gut. I didn't know what I wanted, but I knew I had to figure it out pretty soon.

I called him and told him I needed some time.

I could tell he wasn't thrilled, and I felt bad, but I was undergoing a sea change, and that wouldn't happen overnight. I needed a few days to get my head straight.

After I got off the phone with Elliott, I went to take a shower. It looked pretty nice outside, sunny and not too cold, and I didn't want to waste the entire day sitting on my couch like some pathetic basement-dwelling shut-in. My heart ached. I needed advice, and a metaphorical shoulder to cry on.

I called Regan.

"I would *love* to get out of the house," she said. "Can you come here? We can go to the park. I haven't been outside in two days."

"Oh, Regan," I said, and sighed. She really needed to get back to work. "Of course I'll come to you. I just need to do my makeup, so I'll leave in like ten minutes, okay? Put that baby in a stroller. I'm going to bring you some vodka in a water bottle."

"I'm not supposed to drink while I'm breastfeeding," she said.

"I think you can have a little bit," I said. "I'll call my mom on the way over. She'll know."

"She's an oncologist," Regan said.

"She's still a *doctor*," I said. "Don't argue with me. I'll come prepared."

"Okay," Regan said, laughing a little.

I took the subway to 23rd Street and walked the few blocks to Regan's house. She was sitting on the front steps waiting for me, the stroller parked on the sidewalk at her feet. She stood up and waved when she saw me coming.

"I hope you haven't been out here long," I said, giving her a hug.

"Not long," she said. "It's nice to get some fresh air."

I bent to peer into the stroller. The baby stared at me and tried to shove its fist in its mouth. Okay. Nothing exciting going on there.

We walked to the small park a few blocks away and sat on a bench beneath the leafless trees. Children ran and shouted, chased by harried mothers—or, since this was Chelsea, nannies.

"Elliott wants a relationship," I said, because I didn't believe in beating around the bush.

Regan smiled. "I know," she said. "He called Carter last week and they had one of those conversations where men try to talk about their feelings but they're really bad at it."

"And then Carter told you all about it," I said.

"Of course," Regan said.

"Oh, good," I said. "So my personal life is already common knowledge."

"That makes it easier for you," Regan said. "You don't have to explain it to me."

I snorted. "Okay, so tell me what I should do."

"You like him," Regan said. "I know you do, because I saw how you were when you both came over for dinner. He's a good guy. I think it's a good idea for you to start dating again. So that's all. That's what I think. I don't know what you should do, though. What do you want to do?"

"I don't know," I said. "I was hoping you would tell me."

"It's hard making decisions, isn't it?" Regan

asked. "I know that probably sounds like I'm making fun of you, but I'm not. I don't mean decisions like what to eat for dinner. The big stuff, though. It's really hard. I always thought that grown-ups had all the answers, and that someday I would be an adult and know everything, and I wouldn't ever be scared or uncertain. But that's not how it goes."

"Yeah," I said. "Isn't that the truth. We're all just making it up as we go."

"Yeah," she said, and sighed deeply, and said, "I think I'm a bad mother." And then she started crying.

"Regan, honey," I said, horrified. I wrapped my arms around her, and she sobbed against my shoulder. I wasn't sure what to do. I experienced a brief moment of resentment that Regan had hijacked my complaining about Elliott, but I quickly pushed that aside. If Regan was weeping openly in public, something terrible was going on, and she needed my support.

"I'm sorry," she said, "I'm sorry," and kept crying.

A passing woman stared at us. I stared back, daring her to say something, and she moved on by.

Lord. We were making a scene. "Honey, come on," I said. "What's wrong? How can you say you're a bad mother? You know that isn't true."

She pulled away and wiped her eyes with the back of her hand. "I don't love him enough," she said, sniffling. "I should be—I'm supposed to be happy just being with him, and changing his diapers, and—and—but I'm so bored. I'm trapped in the house all day, and Elliott works all the time, and I *hate* it. Sometimes I feel like having a baby was a huge mistake."

"Oh, *Regan*," I said again. I'd known she was going a little stir-crazy, but I hadn't thought it was this bad. Guilt sat heavy in my belly. I should have noticed that something was wrong.

"I know," she wailed. "I'm a terrible mother. If I loved him more, if I—if I could just—"

"Stop," I said sternly, before she could start crying again. "You love that kid more than anything. You're *not* a bad mother. You're just having a hard time right now. I would be going crazy, too. It's not like newborns are all that interesting. Your life has changed completely. It makes sense that you need some time to adjust."

"It's supposed to be easy," she said. "It's supposed to be easier than this."

"A lot of people have trouble," I said. "Regan. You know I'm right. This is so normal."

Her lower lip wobbled, but she nodded, finally.

"We'll help you," I said. "Me and Carter. Okay? You aren't alone. You can put that kid in daycare a couple of days a week and work on taking care of yourself. Okay?"

"Okay," she said, her voice thin and shaky.

"Let's call Carter," I said.

"He's at work," she said. "We shouldn't bother him."

"He would skin me alive if I didn't bother him

for this," I said. "I'm going to call him."

Regan looked like she intended to keep protesting, but just then the baby let out a thin cry, and Regan immediately bent to lift it from the stroller, cooing and kissing its little face. Her love and devotion were so clear that I couldn't imagine why she thought she was a bad mother. Hormones, probably. Babies did strange things to a body.

I didn't get home until after dark. By the time Regan and I walked back to the house, Carter was waiting in the entryway, practically vibrating with concern. Regan started crying again, and then the baby started crying, and for a moment I thought *Carter* might cry; so I took myself and the baby back to the kitchen, but the baby in its little seat on the countertop, and made some sandwiches. When people started crying, it was time for food.

Sandwiches finished, I discovered that I could get the baby to smile by making weird faces, and the little dude was sort of cute, really, in a toothless, bug-eyed sort of way. I did that for a while, until the kitchen door opened and Carter came in. He looked very tired.

"You made sandwiches," he said.

"Yeah," I said, and offered him the plate. "I figured you guys could use it."

"Thanks," he said. He took one of the sandwiches and looked at it. "Regan's mom is going to come out to stay with us for a while."

"I'm really glad," I said. "That's great. That's what she needs." I patted him on the shoulder, feeling awkward. "You're both going to be okay."

"I think so," he said, and gave me a weary smile. "Thank you, Sadie. Your friendship means a lot to both of us."

I went out into the living room, where Regan was sitting on the sofa, hunched over, looking very small. I sat down beside her and hugged her tightly. "I'm going to get out of your hair," I said. "I love you, kid. Call me tomorrow and let me know how you're doing."

"I will," she said, and I kissed her on the cheek and left.

Walking to the subway, I thought about what had happened that day: about Regan's charmed, imperfect life, and the unshakeable love between her and Carter. About hope, and second chances, and starting over. About forgiveness.

Everyone had their own grief. Nobody's life was without pain. The only thing to do was hold tight to someone you loved and refuse to let go.

It was time for me to put my old sorrows to rest.

When I got home, I turned on all of the lights in my apartment and looked around with fresh eyes. It was a mess. I hadn't ever dealt with Ben's things, not really, and they were strewn all over the apartment in drifts of clutter and dust. How had I been living like this? Well: I hadn't been living, really. Just getting by.

I turned on some music, poured myself a glass of wine, and got to work going through the stacks of papers piled on my kitchen pass-through. Old receipts, bills I had long since paid, random takeout menus. And then, crumpled, stained with coffee, the to-do list I had written the night I got fired from my old job.

Find interesting work.

Go on a date.

I grinned, reading down the list. I'd done a lot of the things I listed. But now it was time for a new list.

I fished a pen out of my junk drawer and scribbled on the list to make sure the pen still worked. Good enough. I thought for a minute, and then wrote:

Hang out with Regan more.

Learn to like babies.

Take a trip somewhere exotic.

Finally learn how to drive.

That was a pretty ambitious list. Why not go all out?

Win the lottery. At least a million dollars.

Buy a huge loft in Soho.

Fall in crazy stupid love.

I started in the hall closet. It was still full of Ben's clothes: his winter coat, his boots. I sorted through everything, folded it, and packed it in trash bags to take to the Salvation Army. The bedroom closet was worse. Harder. They were just clothes, I kept telling myself, fighting the tears stinging my eyes. Ben's favorite sweater. The t-shirt that still smelled faintly of his deodorant. Just clothes. Ben wouldn't want me to keep anything for sentimental reasons; he would say there were people who needed it, who could get a good job if they went to an interview wearing his one suit.

I had loved him. I would miss him every day for the rest of my life. But it was time to move on.

I broke down, then, standing in front of the open closet, holding Ben's t-shirt in my arms. I cried with heartsore grief for what I had lost, and with immeasurable gratitude for what we had shared.

And then I dried my eyes, and got back to work.

I didn't sleep that night. I stayed up until dawn, alternately laughing and crying as I went through Ben's things — kitchen utensils, boxes of old photographs, love notes I wrote to him when we first started dating that he had stashed in a shoebox. Even my handwriting looked young: loopy, dramatic. I had loved him.

Most of it went in the trash. Some things I kept, packed away in a plastic box I slid beneath the bed. I didn't want to forget Ben, or pretend our relationship never happened., but it was time for me to stop living in the past. I was ready for whatever would happen next.

Finally, a little after 8:00, I was done. I gave the kitchen floor a quick mop and realized there was nothing left to do. Ben's things were either thrown out, packed away, or ready for donation. The clutter on the kitchen counter and coffee table had been put away. The apartment was cleaner than it had been in months. And I was exhausted. I checked my email, drank a few cups of coffee, and then decided that I absolutely wasn't going to get anything useful accomplished and I might as well go back to bed.

I could call Elliott later. Maybe tomorrow.

In the end, it took me close to a week. I just wasn't sure what I wanted to say to him. I had to think of the right words. So I putzed around the house, went to a lot of spinning classes, and threw a dinner party for the first time in a year. I applied for some jobs—with NGOs, because Elliott had ruined me. I took Regan shopping and made her buy a dress that she insisted she was still too fat to wear.

I was a coward. That was all. At least I could admit it to myself.

On Saturday afternoon, a letter arrived in the mail. I recognized Elliott's handwriting and tore the envelope open with shaking hands. I wasn't sure what I would find inside. But it was just a check—my paycheck, mailed to my home address because Elliott had never gotten the payroll system set up. There was no note inside.

I rubbed my face. I really needed to call him.

Okay. Fine. I could put on my big girl pants.

I dialed the phone.

He answered, sounding a little out of breath. "Sadie," he said.

"Hi, Elliott," I said, and swallowed. I still wasn't sure what to say.

"How are you?" he asked.

"Good," I said. "I—I'm good." And then I had

to laugh, because we were making idiotic small talk like we barely knew each other. "I'm sorry I didn't call you sooner. I was—I've been processing, I guess. Working through some things."

"I figured," he said. "Where are you? Are you at home?"

"Yeah," I said.

"I'm at home, too," he said. "Do you want to come over? I'd like to see you. Or I can come there—"

"I'll come to you," I said. "I wanted to stop by and see Regan, anyway."

"That's good," he said. "Carter told me she's having a hard time."

"Yeah," I said, "but I think she'll be okay."

"That's good," he said again, and then cleared his throat. He was *nervous*. I thought it was very sweet. "Just text me when you leave their place."

"I'll see you soon," I said, and then I put on my coat and went out into the rest of my life.

CHAPTER 26

Elliott

With Sadie coming over soon, I sprang into
action. My apartment was, to say the least, not clean.
I had let tidiness fall by the wayside over the past
several days, as I finalized things with my new
investor and made arrangements to bring Jim down
from Boston. My armchair was buried underneath
stacks of discarded clothing, and the toilet had a
suspicious ring below the rim of the bowl. I could all
too easily imagine Sadie's face when she saw the
squalor I was living in.

By the time I heard a knock on the door, the
apartment was as clean as a hotel room—one of the
benefits of living in a small space. I had even
changed the sheets on the bed, just in case. You never
knew.

I drew in a breath, and went to let Sadie in.

She stood in the doorway, wrapped in her coat,
and looked up at me with eyes dark as a winter sea.
Seeing her again was a punch directly to the solar
plexus.

"Hi, Elliott," she said.

"Sadie," I said, and stood aside to let her come inside.

"I'm sorry it took me so long to get here," she said, unbuttoning her coat. "I stopped to check on Regan, and I ended up staying longer than I intended to."

"How is she doing?" I asked. Carter had mentioned postpartum depression, which as I understood it could run the gamut from periodic crying to hospitalization. I was fond of Regan; even crying was more than I would wish on her, and the thought of anything worse was incredibly alarming.

"She's okay," Sadie said. "Doing better. Her mom's here now, and Carter's working from home more. I think it'll help when the baby is a little older and doesn't need to eat, like, every two hours. Right now she feels like she can't go anywhere or do anything that doesn't involve her boobs."

"Hmm," I said, trying to decide if it would be crass to make a joke. It probably would be. "Do you think she would appreciate a visit? I was thinking about going to see her, but I don't want to intrude."

"I think she would love to see you," Sadie said. She draped her coat over the back of my now-bare armchair—success—and unwrapped her scarf. She was wearing a skirt and knee-high boots, and I liked the thought that she had dressed up for me.

"I'll go visit her tomorrow, then," I said. "Sadie, it's good to see you."

"Yeah," she said, ducking her head and

glancing up at me, unexpectedly shy. I wanted to take her in my arms and never let her go. "I'm sort of—I had a weird week."

"I know the feeling," I said.

"Yeah," she said again, and then looked away from me and folded her arms across her chest. She turned her back to me and walked toward the window, pausing for a moment and gazing down at the street. She was delaying the inevitable, but I was content to wait while she worked through whatever mental process was a necessary pre-requisite for her to actually talk to me.

But then she turned her attention to the top of my dresser and the collection of framed photographs there, and I winced. If she found—

And of course she did, unerringly. "Oh my God," she said, bending down to peer at the picture in question.

I rubbed one hand over my face. I should have tossed that one out years ago.

"Is this you?" she asked.

"Yes," I said.

"Oh my *God*," she said again. "And this is Carter?"

"Yes," I said. "And our friend Carolina."

"You have *dreadlocks*," she said.

I sighed. "Yes."

She started laughing, and looked at me with sparkling eyes. "You know, the first time I talked to Carter about working for you, he described you as a hippie," she said. "I never really understood what he was talking about, but now I totally get it."

"He's never gotten over that… unfortunate stage of my life," I said. "It was years ago. I promise I have more sense now."

"It was a good look for you," she said. "I bet you smoked a lot of weed and like, participated in drum circles."

"I've done a drum circle or two in my time," I said. "But you didn't come over here to make fun of me for my former lifestyle decisions."

"No," she said. "I didn't. It's a nice side benefit, though." She shrugged one shoulder. "I read your note."

"I know you did," I said. "We talked about it." My patience ran out. I had no desire to make small talk all afternoon while she nosed around my apartment. "Sadie, I want you to come back and work for me. I want you in my life, in every way that counts. I want you in my bed every night and at my side every day. You've made me wait long enough."

"I know," she said, nodding, and drew in a deep breath. "I'm ready."

I raised my eyebrows. "For?"

"You," she said. "Us." She drew in another breath. "My apartment was still full of my fiancé's stuff. I never cleaned it out after he died. So that's what I've been doing. I finally went through his things and dealt with all of it. So I guess I'm ready to move on, now."

"Oh, Sadie," I said, my heart aching and glad. I took a step toward her, and she came into my arms and clung to me. I stroked my hand over her hair, careful not to disturb her braids. "I went to go see my father."

"Oh yeah?" she asked, her breath warm against my chest through the fabric of my t-shirt. "And?"

"I told him to go fuck himself," I said. "In more or less exactly those words."

She laughed. "I don't believe you."

"I was a bit more tactful than that," I admitted. "But only slightly."

"So you're going to accept your mom's money," she said.

"Yes," I said. "You were right. I was only refusing it to spite my father. Fuck him. I don't care what he thinks."

"I think you still care a little," she said.

"You're right," I said. "But I'll get over it."

"I'm really glad," she said. "Now you can build the epic ceramic water filter of your dreams."

I grinned. Her hair smelled like lavender. I squeezed my arms around her waist, holding her closer. "You're going to help me, of course."

"Of course," she said. "I want a raise, though."

"Demanding woman," I murmured. I slid my hands a little lower. "We're going to have make-up sex now, right?" We had more talking to do, but it could wait until later. I had spent a long, lonely week with nothing but my right hand to keep me company.

"You men are all alike," she said, but she twined her arms around my neck and lifted her face toward mine to receive my kiss.

It had been too long. I'd forgotten how good she felt in my arms, and the first taste of her mouth set wild lust roaring through my veins. She was mine, now, at last. Taking things slow was off the table.

I claimed her mouth, one arm around her waist and the other at the back of her neck, holding her in place, forcing her to accept my hungry kisses. She gave a soft, breathy moan and relaxed against me, giving me tacit permission to do whatever I wanted. She was perfect for me: eager, experienced, happy to submit.

My cock ached. I pressed my hips against her, giving her undeniable proof of my desire. She laughed against my mouth, and I pulled back and said, "Is something funny?"

"No," she said, smiling up at me. "I would never laugh at your, uh. Endowment."

"I should hope not," I said. "You'll make me self-conscious."

"Mm, you have absolutely nothing to be ashamed of," she said. "Trust me."

"Flattery," I said, pleased despite myself, and kissed her again.

I undressed her one piece of clothing at a time, standing there in the middle of the floor with the pale afternoon sunlight streaming through the windows. Sadie let me turn her this way and that as I disrobed her, docile, raising her arms at a single word, smiling at me. I sucked hot kisses along her neck while I unbuttoned her blouse, and then bent to trail my mouth along the newly exposed territory. Her skin was warm and smooth, dark and gleaming, and I intended to put my mouth on every inch of it.

I unfastened the final button and dropped her blouse onto the floor. She gave me a baleful look, which I ignored. I didn't care if her shirt got wrinkled. I would buy her a new one.

Her bare skin prickled. "Are you cold?" I asked.

"No," she said, and raised her arms to fold them protectively across her chest. "Maybe a little."

"I'll get you in bed soon enough," I said, with one hand at her shoulder, urging her to turn her back to me. She went without resistance. I unhooked her bra and slid my hands back up her shoulder-blades, then down the front of her body until I was cupping her breasts with both hands. Her nipples hardened at my touch, and she tipped her head back against my shoulder with a sigh.

"That feels good," I said against her ear, both asking and instructing.

"Yeah," she said. "It feels really…" She trailed off without finishing her sentence.

I took her meaning, though. I rubbed my palms against her nipples, very lightly, teasing, until she arched her back, lifting her breasts into my hands, mutely asking for more.

I took my hands away and dropped them to the waistband of her skirt.

"Elliott," she said, audibly frustrated.

I grinned with fierce delight. I was glad she couldn't see my face. I wanted her to beg me for it. I wanted her so wet and throbbing and eager that she begged for my cock.

I unzipped her skirt and slid it down over her hips. She was wearing tights again, the bane of my existence, and I tucked my fingers in the elasticized band at her waist and tried to decide how irritated she would be if I ripped the damn things from her body.

"Don't even think about it," she said.

I sighed. How did women always do that? "You're no fun."

"These were expensive," she said. She unzipped and tugged off her boots, and then expertly shimmied the tights down her legs, giving me a nice view of her ass in the process. She was wearing a little lacy thong that I wanted to peel off with my teeth.

I slid one hand across the bare skin at the top of her thigh, right at the crease where her ass and thigh met. It was my favorite place on a woman's body.

"Handsy," Sadie said.

"You don't know the half of it," I said, and roughly pulled her back against me, pinning her against my chest. My free hand roamed her body: her round tits, her soft belly, the gentle slope of her hip. I reached down and cupped the cloth-covered heat between her legs, and she gasped and twitched against me.

"Do you like that?" I asked. She didn't respond,

and I stroked her through her panties, running my fingers along her slit until the fabric grew damp. Still she said nothing, and I craned my neck to glance at her face.

She was biting down on her lower lip, eyes closed, face a mask of pained ecstasy.

Perfect.

I slipped my hand inside her underpants and touched her directly, my fingers moving over her swollen flesh. She did make a noise then, a high-pitched, bitten-off squeak of a sound, and I buried my smile against the side of her neck. She was perfect. Even when she drove me crazy, she was still perfect.

"These need to go," I said, and was surprised by how rough my voice sounded. "I don't want a single scrap of clothing on you."

"But you're still wearing all of *your* clothes," she said, turning her head to look at me over her shoulder. "It isn't fair."

"None of this is about fairness, little girl," I said, and slapped her ass hard enough to make a loud, satisfying *crack*.

She yelped and jumped away from me, then gave me a look of such extravagant woundedness that I couldn't take her seriously. "Do you have a spanking fetish or something?"

"Let's find out," I said, and took a step toward her.

I stripped off her thong and pushed her down onto the edge of the bed, gently but firmly, and she gazed up at me with eager heat in her eyes. She talked a good game, but I knew she loved it when I shoved her around a little.

"Lie down," I said.

"What are you going to do?" she asked.

"I didn't say you could ask questions," I said. "Lie down on the bed."

She did it, frowning, gorgeous, and I sank to my knees and knelt before her on the carpet.

"Elliott," she said.

I spread her legs apart, my hands on her thighs to hold her open, and bent my head to taste her.

She cried out and arched her hips off the bed, but I was ready for her and held her down. She was slick beneath my tongue, wet and heated, and she tasted good enough to make my head spin.

"Oh God, Elliott," she said, and buried her hands in my hair.

I settled in for a long, slow exploration. Her hips twitched with every movement of my tongue and teeth, and I couldn't get enough of her soft noises or the way she lightly scratched at my scalp with her fingernails. I licked her with the broad flat of my tongue, and then fluttered the tip against her most sensitive spot. I curled my hands around her thighs, tracking each minute quiver of her muscles. My cock throbbed between my legs, and I wanted nothing more than to bury myself in her willing body, but I was determined to make her come first. There was a time and a place for selfishness, but make-up sex wasn't it.

That didn't mean I had infinite patience, though. I wanted to get Sadie off hard and fast, and then commence with the delightful business of fucking her into the mattress.

She would be happy to lie there all day and let me work her over with my mouth. It was time to pull out the big guns.

I tucked one hand between her legs and rubbed at her slick entrance. She let out a long, contented sigh and spread her legs apart a little further. It was all the invitation I needed. I sank one finger inside of her, and when she squirmed against me and moaned, I added a second.

"Oh my God," she said, slurring her words together.

I smiled, and sucked hard on her clit.

Sadie was no match for me or the fingers I curled relentlessly inside of her. In very short order she was moaning and tossing her head from side to side, pinching her nipples and rolling her hips against me. I sat back and stroked her clit with my free hand. "You're going to come for me now, aren't you?"

"I. I'm. I don't," she said, panting, incoherent.

I couldn't get enough. I would never have enough of her, not if we both lived for a hundred years. I set my mouth to her again, using my tongue to rub firmly against her, and she arched off the bed like a drawn bow, tense, shaking, and came.

I held my mouth in place and let her work herself through it. She clenched around my fingers, three times, four, and then fell back to the mattress, boneless.

"Wonderful," I murmured, and kissed her thigh.

"Come up," she said, grasping at me, her hands in my hair and on my face. "I want—come here. I need you inside of me."

"I will never argue against that," I said, and went to the nightstand to fumble around for a condom.

I was still fully dressed, somehow. Removing my clothes would have taken too much time. I unbuttoned my pants and shoved them down to mid-thigh, and rolled the condom onto my aching erection.

Sadie, propped up on her elbows, laughed at me. "You look ridiculous."

"I'm glad you approve," I said. "You won't laugh when I'm fucking you."

She raised an eyebrow at me. "Is that a promise or a threat?"

"Darling, that's a guarantee," I said, and lay down on the mattress with her, the full length of my body pressed against hers. She tangled her limbs with mine, a jumble of arms and legs and her warm, smooth skin, and I kissed her and rolled on top of her and guided my cock into her hot, tight body.

There was no finesse to our coupling. I had thought about this a lot in the past week, eased myself into sleep most nights with my hand around my dick and my head full of Sadie, but no fantasy could compare to the mind-blowing reality of feeling her stretched out beneath me. I moved quickly and carelessly, and she wrapped her legs around the backs of my thighs and moved with me, our bodies striving together, both of us greedy for our shared pleasure.

"You'll be the death of me," I gasped, and she laughed and scratched her nails against the back of my neck.

I couldn't last any longer. I buried my face against her neck and shuddered through my orgasm.

Later, after we cleaned up and I finally took off the rest of my clothes, we lay down in bed together, facing each other, close enough to share breath.

"Stay the night," I said, running one hand along her hip. "Stay here and sleep with me." I liked the idea of sleeping curled against her all night, listening to her breathe in the dark.

"I don't have a change of clothes," she said.

I rolled my eyes. "Really, Sadie? You've never done the walk of shame before? I find that hard to believe."

She laughed, and inched closer to me. "Okay, you make a good point. I'll stay. What will we do tomorrow?"

"Well, it's Sunday," I said, pulling her close and tucking her against my chest. "We'll sleep in. Maybe go for brunch."

"And what about the day after?" she asked.

"I'll go to the office," I said. "And you'll come with me, I hope. There's a lot of work to be done."

"What about the day after that?" she asked.

"I don't know," I said. "Go to work again. Find a woman who asks me fewer questions."

"Never," she said. "You're stuck with me now."

"It's not too late for me to trade you in for a newer, less curious model," I said, and bent to kiss her cheek.

"Nope, sorry," she said. "It's too late."

I felt a foolish grin spread across my face. "That's it for me, then. Is that what you're saying? I'll never get to prowl the streets again, or cajole young, nubile women in my bed…"

"Nope," Sadie said. "Wait, are you saying I'm not nubile enough for you?"

"I would never say that," I said. "You're perfect in every way."

"You're damn right I am," she said. "Wait, really? There's no way you really think that about me."

"I sort of do," I said, "but I'm sure it will pass in time."

"I hope it never does," she said, smiling, and I rolled her onto her back and kissed her and never wanted to stop.

EPILOGUE: ONE YEAR LATER
Sadie

"Ladies and gentlemen, we will be landing at Entebbe in approximately thirty minutes. Local time is 12:45 P.M., and the temperature is 27 degrees Celsius, 81 Fahrenheit. Thank you for flying with us, and we hope you enjoy your stay."

The announcement cut off, and I turned to Elliott, who was finally waking up. "They said we're landing in half an hour," I said.

He rubbed his eyes. "I heard."

"I can see the lake," I said. "And Mount Kilimanjaro!"

He leaned across me and peered out the window. "Wrong mountain," he said. "That's Mount Elgon." He frowned. "At least I think so. We're coming from the northeast, right? I'm disoriented."

"That's because you've been asleep since we left Dubai," I said. "You missed everything. I saw the desert, and the Red Sea…"

He kissed my cheek. "You forget that I've seen these things before," he said.

"I know," I said, a little embarrassed. I was like a little kid on Christmas Eve. "Sorry I'm so excited."

"Never apologize for that," he said. "It's wonderful. I love that I can watch you have these experiences for the first time."

"You're sweet," I said. "What a charmer. Do you say things like that to all the girls?"

"Of course I do," he said. "And the other women in my life appreciate it very much."

"Your sisters don't count," I said.

"I'm not talking about my sisters," he said. "You don't know what I do in my spare time. All those nights I work late, alone at the office…"

I rolled my eyes, trying to hide my amusement. I didn't want to encourage him. "You're right. You're a real ladies man."

"Just one lady, now," he said, and I smiled at him then, because I couldn't help it.

"So what's the itinerary for the rest of the day?" I asked. It was time to change the subject before he started detailing the appearances and personalities of his imaginary girlfriends.

He smirked at me like he knew exactly what I was doing. I gave him a bland look, playing it straight, and he caved and pulled a folder out of his seat pocket. We had gone on trips together before, weekend getaways in the tri-state area, but this was my first experience with Business Travel Elliott, and I was simultaneously terrified and awed by his intense preparation.

He took a sheet of paper from the folder—an

301

actual printed itinerary, because he was deranged. "We won't do too much today," he said, reading. "I figured you would be tired after the flight. We'll stop by the embassy, check into our hotel, and then have a meeting with the local MSF head of mission before dinner."

"What about tomorrow?" I asked.

"Recovery from jet lag," he said. "We'll stay in Kampala. We can sightsee, if you'd like, or just stay at the hotel and sleep. And the next day we'll drive north."

"Sounds good," I said. I turned my head to look out the window again. The plane had turned slightly to the left, and Lake Victoria was in full view, glinting in the sunlight.

We would be in Uganda for the next two weeks, distributing water filters and coordinating with local organizations. I had a shiny new passport and I was so nervous and excited that I felt like I might puke. We had spent the night in Dubai, and that alone had been an incredible, once-in-a-lifetime experience, the sort of thing I would recount at parties for years to come. Two weeks in Uganda was more than my tiny brain could process. Elliott had promised me that we wouldn't spend the entire time working, and I had pored through every travel book I could get my hands on. I wanted to see an elephant.

The past year had been good to us. Jim created the ceramic water filter of Elliott's wildest dreams: cheap, effective, and easy to manufacture. Investment money had poured in, dozens of NGOs all over the world were interested in the technology, and Elliott had recently been contacted about potential commercial applications.

The company was thriving, and I was happier than I had ever been. My relationship with Elliott was so warm and rich and satisfying that I had on more than one occasion cried actual tears of gratitude. Elliott thought sex made me emotional, but I just used that as a convenient excuse for my unexpected waterworks. He was kind, dryly funny, and more passionate than anyone else I knew: passionate about life, and about making the world a better place. He had made *me* better. I was a better person because of him.

I slid my hand into his where it rested on the seat between us. "Thank you," I said.

He gave me a questioning look. "For what?"

"For everything," I said. "This trip. The last year. Being yourself."

"You're welcome," he said, still looking a little confused.

I didn't feel like explaining. I knew what I meant. I leaned up and kissed him on the cheek, and his expression cleared as he smiled at me.

"I love you," he said.

"You're sweet," I said, brimming over with joy. "I love you, too."

I held his hand as we descended toward the ground.

Author's note

While I fudged many things about Elliott's work and about international development in general (if you work in the field, please forgive me), access to clean water is a real and serious problem. According to the World Health Organization, 1.6 million people die each year from diarrheal diseases that result from inadequate access to sanitation and safe drinking water.

I'll be donating a portion of the proceeds from this book to Médecins Sans Frontières (Doctors Without Borders).

Acknowledgments

Many thanks to D, for helping me come up with the title, and to Debbie, for the truly excellent photomanipulation work.

I am grateful to Mr. Linder, as always, for everything. I would not have finished this book without his unwavering encouragement and support.

And thank you to all of my readers.